Black Pearl | Gibran Tariq

BLACK PEARL

Copyright©2012 by Gibran Tariq

All rights reserved. No part of this book may be reproduced or used by any means, Graphic, electronic or mechanical, including photocopy, recording, or any retrieval System without the written permission of the author/publisher, except in cases of Brief quotations embodied in critical reviews and articles.

This is a work of fiction. All characters, incidents and dialogue are either the product of the author's Imagination or used fictitiously.

ACKNOWLEDGMENTS

I salute the SoulFire Team, Nathan, Alex, and Krista who have been so very instrumental in the launch of the company, and for providing the expertise required to move the company forward.

I extends big props to the soldier-comrades who are still inside. First and foremost among these is Pee-Wee Malker, (who is due to get out soon.) Oh yeah, a major salute to Big Red,(Harold Roberts) and PJ Laney from DC. I met PJ waaaay back in 77 way up in the fed joint in Wisconsin. I extend my greeting to my homie, Rusty Bolder.

Chapter 1

Pearl was black.

Actually, it wasn't quite that simple since Princess Washington was not blue-black like the African model Alex Wek, nor was her name Pearl. These distinct factors, more than anything else, provided her with a guilty pleasure that almost freed her from the stress of her very complex life which she so badly wanted to alter.

So here she was, at twenty-one, a Brandy look-alike (only with bigger titties and ass) galloping into urban history as a "Goody-Two-Shoes". This frustrated Pearl because her deepest, darkest secret was to dirty up her halo, and to wallow in sin. Yet she knew nothing of how to peddle herself as a bitch.

"Girl, you suffering from a terminal case of silliness with your Brandy-looking ass. Evidently, you don't know the untold story."

Pearl stared at her church-going, but more (much more) worldly friend, LaNisa Johnson. "What untold story?"

"The real story."

That puzzled Pearl who glared at LaNisa quizzically. "How do you know it's real if it's untold?"

"Because it's true, that's why."

"Well, I love the truth...so tell me."

"Okay." LaNisa smacked her lips loudly. "According to those in the know, there are more freaks in the church than in the strip clubs."

Pearl jumped back.

"Honey, ain't no lightning gonna strike you, so calm your Brandy-looking ass down."

"You talking like that, I don't see why not."

"You wanna know why?"

"Why?"

"Because freaks in the church keep in on the DL."

"I-I don't believe you."

LaNisa played with her manicured nails. "Hmmph, what you believe or don't believe is on you, but let me put it like this. Every profession has its, shall we say, secret institutions."

Pearl rolled her eyes. "You sure you don't mean sacred institutions. You know how you get things mixed up."

It was now LaNisa's time to roll her eyes. "Girl, I do know the difference between sacred and secret, and if I had meant to say sacred, that is what would have come out of my mouth." LaNisa put her hands on her hips. "Big Mama didn't make no mistake. Now, run and tell that."

Pearl wanted to groan. LaNisa, her big-legged, red-boned friend, was so melodramatic, but Pearl, for some reasons, felt inclined to believe LaNisa this time.

"Okay." Pearl's voice cracked with embarrassment. "How do you know about you know what?"

LaNisa chuckled. "Now, I hope you not thinking that I just got lucky." She sipped her Diet soda like it was no big deal. "So," she asked, "do you think that I know because I'm lucky or that I know. You know....really know?"

"Oh my God, LaNisa?!" Pearl shrieked. "I-I can't say for sure."

"Go 'head, take a guess. You my girl."

Pearl didn't say anything.

LaNisa smiled slyly. "Girl, I can almost hear you thinking, but it's almost time for us to get back to work so perhaps you need to think this over. Maybe you really don't want to know about church."

"All of a sudden, I'm beginning to get the feeling that you need to fall down on your knees and pray."

"That's funny. A certain reverend told me the same thing, only he didn't see me having much time to pray while I was on my knees."

"That's-----"

"What, scandalous?"

Pearl felt flushed. "But when we were young, we both said we would wait until we were married."

"Oh, my plans didn't change. I did."

"Durn, girl, why you didn't tell me you were doing the nasty?"

"Pearl, get real. You think I wanted you lil' goody-two-shoes ass praying for me, trying to get me to quit." LaNisa stood up. "Girl, if you would've messed around and got me cut off from the dick, then me and you would have had us a major problem."

"Wow, you even talk hip."

"I am woman," LaNisa purred. "All woman." She smiled at Pearl. "You got all that female stuff and don't know how to operate any of it. Shame of you for wasting one of the greatest commodities on the planet."

Pearl anxiously waited for LaNisa out in the parking lot. The work day was done and the two friends had chatted over the phone, agreeing to meet for a quick meal before heading to their respective apartments.

LaNisa approached, talking to a short, dark-skinned girl who Pearl knew worked on the seventh floor in accounting.

"Pearl, this is Angie," LaNisa said by way of introduction. "Angie, Pearl." After the brief introduction (which was more of an appraisal) LaNIsa put her hand on Pearl's shoulders. "Angie goes to chuuch."

From the moment, LaNisa uttered the word chuuch, sounding like Snoop Dog, Pearl instantly knew that Angie was a DL church freak.

"You will love chuuch," Angie gushed.

"But I attend church." Pearl's diction was flawless.

"And that is precisely why," LaNisa frowned, "you have never had a truly religious experience."

LaNisa and Angie high-fived each other, enjoying the joke.

"I just happen to have a lot of respect for the church." Pearl suddenly felt defensive. "And I will apologize in my prayers for the two of you if you have somehow mistaken it for a night club. It's God's House, not the Gold Club."

"Bitch, stop it," LaNisa groaned. "You wasn't talking that shit on the phone."

"Well, that was before you put my business all out in the streets." Pearl glanced at Angie. "It was private."

"But in chuuch, we delight in helping underprivileged sistas like you," Angie remarked sincerely.

"Hmmph, I bet you do."

"We find strength in numbers."

"Why," Pearl snapped, "you think there won't be enough room in hell for all of us if there's enough of us?"

"Hell," LaNisa cracked, "that sounds like a plan to me. We could start a group, Jezebels Anonymous, and our motto would be: Do your thang. Ain't enough room in hell for all of us!"

"I'm so glad you have it all thought out," Pearl commented irritably, "but personally, I want to go to heaven."

"An orgasm is heavenly," Angie chimed happily.

"That strikes me as so masculine, something a brotha would say. All of them promise to ride us to heaven on their dicks." Pearl shuddered.

"Look at her. Look at her." LaNisa laughed. "Chile can't even use the word dick in a sentence and not have a hot flash."

Pearl pouted. "Goodbye, LaNisa. I'll be in touch. Angie, it was a pleasure to meet you. May I suggest that the two of you try not to corrupt each other too much?"

"No."

"Can't say I didn't try."

"Pearl--------" LaNisa began.

"Yes."

"I know your tired ass, so work on something else other than becoming a den mother 'cause the last thing I need is for somebody trying to babysit my pussy."

"Yeah," Angie added. "Just be happy for us."

Bitches going straight to hell, Pearl thought as she drove out of the parking lot.

Chapter 2

Pearl managed to get in trouble with herself just as soon as she got home. Instinctively, she understood that if she had desired music, she should have put on some Vickie Winans, some Mary Mary, or some Yolanda Adams, but instead she popped that "Oops" song by Tweet into the CD player.

Unfazed by the suggestive autoeroticism of the lyrics, Pearl found herself bouncing around, studying her thoughtful profile in the full length bedroom mirror.

Moving to the beat, Pearl reminded herself that as a church girl, she should be openly contemptuous of the song, rejecting it for it lyrical worthlessness, but what she discovered instead was that she was subconsciously following Tweet's instructions.

Oops, there went her shirt!

Staring at her breasts as she unclasped the bra, Pearl knew it was time for her to rebuff her lewd intentions and actions, but she couldn't fight against the intense euphoria she was experiencing. She was high on herself. At least that was a good enough explanation for herself, and at that moment she didn't give a damn about anyone else.

"Oh my goodness," Pearl gasped. This was her favorite part of the song. "Oh my goodness!" she gasped again. Before now, she didn't even know she had a favorite part of that song. In fact, she didn't even recall where she had gotten the CD, but none of that mattered now because all that was on her mind was getting out of her clothes as soon as she could. At the moment, she was not particularly attracted to anything that came between her fingers and her flesh. She wanted to touch herself. Badly.

Handling her beasts cautiously, Pearl could feel her insides grabbing back, and for the first time an orgasm was something she could sense, so almost daring herself to do it, she rubbed herself high on the inside of her thigh, and without warning her breathing fell further and further behind the loud thumping of her heart. She broke out in a cold sweat.

This was no sexual prank! It felt too damn good and her pussy, which she had forever regarded as a furry, wrought-iron gate, now expressed itself as a portal to paradise while sensations she couldn't decipher invited her inside.

Coming of age in front of her bedroom mirror, Pearl smelled the fragrance of her vagina for the first time. It was a sweet, musky nectar that overpowered her, overwhelming her senses, making her want to experiment with herself just that much more. And she did.

Initially, she merely touched herself. Then she went further, wanting more, boldly taking on an even bigger role in finding her own pleasure, and by gently applying pressure to the tip of her distended clitoris, she instantly savored the intimate drama of having a personal moment with herself. She squeezed. She screamed. Her body shook.

Quickly, she pulled her hand back but utterly convinced herself that she had to do it again. She fought against the impulse to be sexually greedy so she took a deep breath and counted to ten. Then she had a second private engagement with herself, but this time her touch was more nuanced, her untrained fingers spreading warmth and joy throughout the entire front entrance of her pussy.

Pearl growled like a lion.

Staring at her contorted face in the mirror, she wondered if this was how Brandy looked when she was doing it, but when her facial expression changed again, she noticed, that like a ballerina, she was perched on the tips of her toes, and that her fingers were jabbing in and out of her sucking pussy like meat-filled pistons.

"Oh Jesus!" she cried aloud, whooping wildly at the wet intoxication of an orgasm. Her first.

Her body lovingly cared for, Pearl recognized that getting a nut was a lot like taking a sedative, and she found that she was absolutely relaxed with only a faint trace of guilt.

Sitting up in her room listening to Brandy sing "Sitting Up In My Room", she wondered what to do now. She had no clue because where did you go when you had already gone too far?

Playing with herself had been a risky, complex adventure and she, though still sexually numb, had been quite fascinated by the choreography of her fingers, but it had shocked her that she had known how to use them! She found it remarkable that a full-fledged virgin would understand the delicate intricacy of a pussy she had not familiarized herself with beyond the clinical experience of personal hygiene. How could she have known to be so alert to the magical possibilities of self-stimulation? She had no answer for that.

Abruptly, Pearl felt she had better renew her faith to ward off any more idle thoughts of her wicked behavior so she grabbed her electronic King James Bible. She retrieved a passage from Psalms to serve as her devotional, but when instant inspiration didn't come, she got worried. Suddenly, she wanted to listen to Oops again!

Two minutes later, she phoned her cousin Joy.

"I got a question for you." Pearl paused. "It's about size."

"What about it?"

"How do you know what size is right for you?"

"Unless I'm missing something, I take it that you mean dick size. Am I right or wrong?"

"You're not missing anything, so can I get my answer and go on about my business."

"That's simple, cuz. A gang-bang."

"What?!"

"Yeah, you let four or five nigga run a train on you."

"That's the craziest---"

"Hold on, cuz. You asked, so hear me out. You owe me that much."

"Okay," Pearl relented, "go on."

"You see, there's some technical aspects to a gang-bang

that a bitch must absolutely get right if she expects any kind of success. Anyway, you get these five niggas and let them fuck you in sequence."

"In sequence?"

"That's right. You let the one with the littlest dick go first. Then you move up the scale, increasing the size. Believe me, cuz, you'll know when you hit your dosage-----"

Pearl quickly hung up. She didn't know if she was hot and bothered or bothered and hot. All she knew was that she was sweating and that she already felt flushed.

Damn! She was going to hell!

Chapter 3

Ennis Wallace wished he had someone to talk to, someone he could confide in, but who the hell would understand. He smiled. The genie was out of the bottle. He shook his head as he rolled down the street in his black Audi. Hell yeah, the genie was out of the bottle.

Basically he was neither surprised nor shocked. The girl----whoever she was----with her Brandy-looking ass----was fine, and despite all the bullshit about how he would never get down with a church bitch, he was attracted. Imagine that! Ennis knew he was a pretty boy, but he had never had to go up against Jesus before, so he wasn't sure if he was ready for that kind of stiff competition.

Just the same, he felt that if he paid attention to all the small details that he had a better than average chance of getting the girl. Plus his reputation would be on the line, and dating back to when he was nine years old, he had fucked an impressive array of bitches. He always got the girl.

In high school, he had experimented with bitches like most of his friends had experimented with drugs. His strategy had been to savor the full cornucopia of black femininity until he had discovered his own personal flava. With the impartial dedication of a rocket scientist, he had started with a high-yellow sista, and had methodically worked his way down the color spectrum until he had ended up in the arms of a girl darker than blue. And then he had started all over again....and again....and again.

Though no other man in his family had done it quite like that, Ennis had wanted a hedge against marriage. He didn't want any surprises, didn't want his name given to a bitch who didn't deserve it, only to have it thrown back at him in divorce court, so all along his sexcapades, he had compiled notes and had jotted down observations.

Sometimes his data squared with the conventional wisdom of the brothas on the block. Sometimes, it didn't. Ennis had to conclude, though, that not all red women were hot-tempered or that all dark sistas were not evil. He had also personally discovered that fat girls could fuck real good too, and that all skinny bitches didn't have big pussies. Everything he did find that even remotely resembled a class pattern, he held it against them, using it as a mirror to reflect their flaws and short-comings.

Finally, after years of experimentation and study with his sexual science, he was fairly comfortable in the belief that that 5-star Brandy-looking bitch would be his flava if he could get her out of church and into his bed.

But who was she?

It was already three o'clock in the afternoon when Ennis showed up at his partner's condo.

"Yo, V-Man, whatcha cooking for Labor Day?"

Vernon Gerald studied his road dawg crazily. "Same as it ever was, got pipe to lay. Just 'cause it's Labor Day don't stop a real playa from putting in work."

Ennis made a face. "I don't believe the holiday calls for that kind of labor."

"Why not?" V-Man retorted mildly. "Put a bitch in labor on Labor Day."

Ennis changed the subject. "What Terrell say? Is some nigga in the choir pushing up on homegirl?"

V-Man shook his head. "That ain't your problem, dawg."

"If she ain't got no man, then I ain't got no problem, period." Ennis snatched his car keys off the counter. "I'm gone, chump....I mean champ."

Popping the tops on two beers, V-Man set them on the bamboo place mats. "I wouldn't get missing so fast if I were you. There's more." V-Man spoke calmly. "Want me to hold you lil' hand when I tell your trick ass?"

"What up?"

"Terrell thinks your girl is gay."

"Nigga, stop playing."

"Word, dawg. Homegirl might be funny."

"Bitch ain't no dyke."

"C'mon, Ennis, don't start fooling yourself. You don't even know enough about her to know what the fuck she is."

"She church, so I know she must love Jesus. That says a lot about her ass."

"You got that, fool, but that don't mean she still don't like pussy. She ain't got no man."

"Hoo-motherfucking-ray for me. Only thing her being by her lonesome means is that she sincerely believes in the Good Book or she simply saving herself for me, a real-life goddamn hero."

"A hero?"

"Yeah, but one who got a scrub for a sidekick." Ennis shook his head. "Niggas is something. Why we don't never put forth the best construction on shit when we hear it? Too damn much like doing right, that's the fuck why."

"What's your point, Ennis the Menace?"

"Why, when you heard my peeps didn't have a man, you automatically jumped to the motherfucking conclusion that she suck pussy? Did it ever cross your lil dirty mind that the motherfucking reason she ain't got no man is because she's a virgin? Did you consider that?"

V-Man shook his head.

"And why the fuck not?"

"Ain't no virgins in the hood."

Ennis exhaled deeply. "Nigga, you must be stuck on stupid."

"I am, am I?"

"Damn right."

"Then tell me the reason why a motherfucka can find an angel in the hood faster than he can find a virgin."

Ennis was silent.

"Case closed," V-Man replied. "Now, fire up a blunt."

It was midnight. Tuesday.

"You don't look square enough, that's what it is," V-Man finally concluded. "Your gear got thug written all over it, and this is a nigga rich neighborhood."

"First, you didn't want to come, and now I can't keep your ass quiet."

"I'm talking 'cause I'm scared. The police call what we doing stalking." V-Man scowled at his friend. "Tell me one more time why we here?"

"To prove a point to your Mr. Know-It-All-ass."

"Which is?"

"Nigga, you remember Sunday when I was at your crib and you went there with that bullshit about which was easier to find in the hood, an angel or a virgin. Well, this is why. The honey, as you can damn well see, don't live in the goddamn hood, so that's why a nigga won't find a virgin there."

"Goddamn, dawg!," V-Man yelped, "That's the point you trying to make. I don't believe this shit. Your got our black asses way out here on front street, all because you want to prove your Brandy-looking ass secret lover a virgin."

"She a virgin."

"Okay, okay, bitch a virgin. Naw, on second thought, homegirl a saint. Now, can we go?"

Ennis wrapped his arm around V-Man's shoulders. "It don't work like that, dawg. You owe me."

"You got it. I'll buy the beer."

Ennis shook his head. "Nice try."

"What you----?"

"Go knock on the door and invite yourself in."

"And then what?"

Ennis' mind raced. "Ask questions. Find out where her head is at. I need you to see what the deal is so that when I make my move, I won't look like a fool."

V-Man laughed. "You bullshitting, right? This the same shit I used to do for you in high school, put in a good word for you with the chickenheads you were interested in."

"And you used to be so good at it back in the days. I just wanna see if you still got your game." Ennis smiled in the dark. "Do it just like you used to do it when we were in school. You know, tell her that you got a friend---"

"Man, that shit played out. Plus, we damn near twenty-five years old, and that ho ain't no chickadee in 8th grade."

"C'mon, V-Man, one more for the road. Get this one for me, dawg," Ennis pleaded, "and I'll get the rest of 'em myself."

"Shit, nigga," V-Man cracked, "if I get your ass hooked up with this honey, dawg, you getting married." V-Man popped a mint in his mouth. "Anything else?"

"Yeah, what we gonna tell the police?'

"The po----?'

"Yeah, here they come."

"Oh shit!"

After Pearl watched the police chase the two men out of the neighborhood, she felt sad. Maybe they would have liked to have seen her dance. She pretended they were watching.

Sashaying naughtily, she shivered in pure delight as the satin robe shimmied slowly down the length of her 5'7" body, caressing her silky smooth skin as it fell to the plush carpet.

She stepped out of her panties, flung off her bra. Feeling ultra sexy, Pearl danced, letting the eyes of her imaginary playmates warm her nude body to the roasting point as thin beads of perspiration quickly coated her skin, making her flesh glow, oozing heat.

Pearl danced.

In church, she merely swayed, rocking from side to side, her bodily movements tightly controlled by the texture of the hymn. But Oops brought out the devil in her, giving her the sexual authority to free her body, to let the rhythm of the streets, the rhythm of the night, connect her with her inner ho.

Pearl danced.

Temporarily obsessed with the imaginary eyes upon the sheer nakedness of her body, she swung her wide hips wildly. Then she watched in the mirror in stunned amazement at the power in the physical motion of her ass cheeks as they gyrated like two huge, black planets, going round and round, up and down.

Pearl danced.

Pinching the nipples of her ripe, overstuffed breasts, it gave her such a thrill when she made her titties jiggle with so much force they looked as if they were ready to somersault off her chest.

Pearl stopped dancing.

It was time now to play with her pussy so she stood in front of the mirror and ran her fingers through the pubic hairs, jump-starting the fire inside. Spreading her legs farther apart, she pushed her pelvic area out, exposing the moistened slit between her thighs. Her pussy bloomed like a flower.

Pearl touched her clitoris, moaned, called herself a dirty name, moaned again, and got even naughtier. She stuck a finger, then two, inside, moving them around in short circles until she could feel the stickiness coating her fingers like a wet, gooey lubricant. She moaned some more, but when she eased her long fingers out, her pussy made an obscene sucking sound as if her pussy lips were smacking together. Pearl's eyes went wide, then oval, then narrowed to tiny slits as she gently gripped her clit between her two sticky fingers, smearing the morsel of flesh with her sacred juices. It felt so sinfully good, she screamed.

Now committed to some penetration, she blitzed the insides of her pussy with three of her fingers, but after a brief round of fucking herself in this fashion, she pouted. She couldn't go deep enough.

In her mind, she had been transformed into a legitimate slut, and she was quick to note how much she looked like one with her face contorted, distorted and screwed up with intense pleasure. She was really feeling the fire now. Whew!

Dropping down to her knees, she continued to relentlessly run her fingers in and out of her pussy until the inevitable happened. She got a nut! It was so powerful that it knocked her flat on her back.

But she had not had enough yet. With lust-filled eyes, she stared straight down the length of her belly into the mirror where she could see her wet pussy sparkling like a jewel. Pearl opened her legs even more. She raised her legs as she stroked the soft insides of her vagina, running her fingers deliciously slow across and over the entire expanse of her pussy entrance.

When she got her second nut, her legs crashed to the floor where they quivered and trembled for a full 50 seconds.

Then she fell asleep.

As soon as she awoke the following morning, her initial reaction was the same as any drunken bum. She wondered what the hell she was doing where she was and how she had gotten there--- butt naked. Then a brilliant recollection of the night before flashed in her mind, exploding away any remaining mystery of what had gone on. She sat up and suddenly began to hear Oops in her head. What a goddamn charming song, she thought.

She felt that she had grown up sexually. After last night, her pussy felt like a jigsaw puzzle with a couple of the pieces missing, but it was all good. Her pussy was now her best friend, a prize. It was her own private ice cream truck, one with all the flavors.

Now, if she could only decide what to fix for breakfast.

Chapter 4

Pearl was excited. She was going to chuuch! LaNisa and Angie had finally talked her into going, but she was still vaguely appalled that she had so eagerly accepted the invitation. She just hoped she wouldn't be sorry afterwards.

Studying her reflection in her bedroom mirror, she discovered she wasn't too good at hiding how she felt. Emotions, some well-behaved, others electric, threatened to burst out of her skull, ripping her braids right out of her head. For a whole 120 seconds, she stared at herself, absently wringing her hands, trying to find a sane way to deal with the anxiety. She was a total, nervous wreck.

She didn't know what to expect although evidently she knew there wasn't much chance of boring board games or intellectual conversation. Pearl's eyes rolled back in her head because she would soon be in the company of men who would attempt to fuck her.

Moments later when her doorbell rang, she got butterflies in her stomach. Could she go through with this? LaNisa had already made it clear that in chuuch there were no unattached visitors which left little room for spectators. Chuuch, if nothing else, was a 'get-in-where-you-fit-in' free-for-all. Pearl shivered.

Opening the door, LaNisa and Angie burst in. Pearl gasped in surprise. She had never seen either woman wearing so much makeup and so little clothes. It was highly unlikely they would be mistaken for the college graduates they were. In fact, Pearl, was afraid they both would get arrested because cleavage that low and skirts that high had to violate at least a half dozen ordinances against public nudity.

"I-I don't believe the two of you are actually dressed like.......hoes."

"Believe it, honey," LaNisa hissed. "And stop acting so yesterday. Damn, I thought you had finally screwed your head on right." When Pearl tried to close the door, LaNisa stoped her. "Garrison is coming."

"Garrison?!"

"Yeah, Garrison," Angie giggled. "He's parking the car."

"Garrison?!" Pearl repeated incredulously. "No."

"Girl, Garrison is a true freak. That strait-laced bullshit is for the sake of appearances."

"But he's my choir director. He sings beautiful hymns."

Angie laughed loudly. "He'll be singing a different hymn tonight, if you get my drift."

"Oh, by the way," LaNisa began, "I think it only fair that I warn you about Garri---."

"Don't dare tell me I'm being silly," Garrison lisped, prancing into Pearl's living room, "but isn't this chile a hot mess?"

"Oh my God!" Pearl fainted.

"Wh-what happened?"

"Your ass fainted, that's what."

Pearl sat up. "How, how long was I out?"

"Long-e-damn-nough to make us miss chuuch," Garrison sniffed.

"I'm sorry," Pearl apologized, "but" she cast a woeful glance at the choir director. "I wasn't ready for---"

"Welcome to the club, honey," Garrison snapped. "I'm ready for the world, but the world ain't ready for me."

"But I thought you were sweet on Sister Bernice?"

"That cow? Get real. Bitch gives me money that I, in turn, so lovingly gives to my tenderoni men friends." Garrison stared at Pearl. "It's probably best that we missed chuuch because I'll be damned if I'd be seen in public with this chile. Just look at her. Dressed like she going to communion."

"Well, at least, she almost got it right. We should give her credit for that." LaNissa smiled. "I think we should give her another chance."

"But," Garrison protested, "we were not going to communion, we were going to cum. Where her Brandy-looking ass get the union from." Turning to face Pearl, Garrison pointed his finger at her just like he did during choir rehearsal when it was time for her solo. "This is your lesson for tonight, so listen closely. Good, lil' girls and boys go to church. Naughty girls and boys go to chuuch. Do you follow me so far?"

Pearl nodded.

"Good." Garrison continued. "You go to church for communion. You go to chuuch to cum. Did you notice the distinction?"

Again, a nod from Pearl.

"Okay, here your exam and this is for 100 points." LaNisa and Angie snickered on the couch like schoolgirls. Garrison ssshed them quiet. He faced Pearl again. "If one, presumably your Brandy-looking ass, were to take the union out of communion, what would you get?"

"Come?"

"Close." Garrison sat up straight, in full choir director mode. "Cum! C'mon now, you say it. You must speak the word from deep within your diaphragm. Say it!"

"Cum!"

"Excellent. Now, get us something to drink before I perish."

"Papaya juice, anyone?" LaNisa laughed.

Garrison rolled his neck around on his shoulders like a cobra getting ready to strike. "Now, I know this chile can't be that big a Miss Goody-Two-Shoes that there is nothing to drink in this apartment but damned fruit juice. Damn, girl, you square."

Even after the first round of papaya juice was served, Pearl was still shaken up over Garrison. Her mind just wasn't ready to accept the reality. "So, Garrison, just what is it that you get at chuuch?"

"I beg your pardon." Garrison gasped in horror. "I wants

the same thing y'all heifers want. Just because I'm not a card-carrying female don't mean shit. I wants me a nigga to love me for me. Shit, honey, when the lights be off, I be making a motherfucka call me real, sweet names, and just for the record, ain't no man never called me no chickenhead. I----"

"Okay, Garrison," Angie interrupted rudely, "I think we got your point."

"And look who's talking. You like pussy."

A sharp gasp flew from Pearl's open mouth as she stared in confusion, her eyes darting from Garrison to Angie.

"Please, girl, don't faint no damn more." LaNisa frowned. "I think we best be leaving or else Little Miss Muffet here is going to blow a gasket. Another believe-it-or-not discovery tonight and we just might have to call in the paramedics."

Angie giggled. "Surprised?"

Pearl turned to stare at LaNisa.

"No, dearie," LaNisa commented bluntly. "I don't bump pussies with Angie."

Suddenly, Pearl felt exhausted. Tonight had been too much for her, and she was ready to get rid of her company. She didn't feel she was in their league, but what church girl was? Wow…A lesbian. A sissy. A ho.

Chuuch! A whole lot of dirty business must go on there.

Chapter 5

It all happened during the triumphant period between her mind-blowing self-induced orgasms and the miserable moments she spent praying for deliverance from her lewd yearnings that the news came. Angie's apartment had burned down.

Pearl glared at LaNisa and Angie who sat side by side on her living room sofa, looking like matching books ends, dressed in tight jeans and matching tops.

"I know this is so all of a sudden," LaNisa openly confessed, "but we can't let this bitch lounge at no public shelter."

"Plus," Angie added, "who would I know there?"

LaNisa patted Angie's hand maternally. "Girl, don't you worry. Pearl won't let your ass go to no shelter any damn quicker than she would put her own Mama in an ol' folks' home. Am I right or am I wrong, Pearl?"

Despite her momentary silence, Pearl recognized the very ugly business of LaNisa attempting to use her and it was this burning awareness that almost occasioned her to become infantile, pitch a temper tantrum, and show both of her friends the door, but until her life completely disintegrated, she was still a 'mistress of the gospel'. As such, she could not pretend she didn't have either the room or the heart for Angie, or else she feared she might get judged for selfishness on the day the roll got called way over yonder. She'd let LaNisa go to hell with that one because that hussy had just as much room as she did.

To Pearl, everything about a lesbian was dark and no

matter how forgiving the Bible instructed her too be, she saw no real way she, a good Christian girl, could be totally at ease with a woman whose all-consuming passion was to lick pussy. Therefore, co-existing under the same roof could mean problems, but as long as Angie didn't go sexually haywire on her then all should go well.

"Of course, Angie, you can move in," Pearl said warmly. "You're more than welcome."

"Great," LaNisa replied, smiling. "I should call the TV station 'cause this would make a wonderful human interest story." LaNisa winked. "See, Pearl, there's bonus point to being a Miss Goody-Two-Shoes."

"Recognition, LaNisa," Pearl remarked calmly, "is not my primary motivation. I'm told in the Bible---"

"Okay, okay, don't start preaching. I was just being funny."

"Like her." Pearl pointed at Angie.

LaNisa laughed. "Now, you're being funny." She kissed Pearl's cheek. "Me and Angie are going out to play with the world. I promise not to keep her out too late."

"I'm not on curfew, am I?" Angie teased.

Pearl removed a key from her ring. "Here, so you don't have to worry about me sitting up in my bathrobe, waiting on you to come home." Pearl smiled. "I've already been warned about being a den mother, remember?"

"Wish us a lot of fun," LaNisa begged.

"I can do better than that," Pearl bragged.

"You can?" Angie asked.

"Of course," Pearl replied flatly. "May God be with you?"

"Girl," LaNisa chortled, "you sure know how to bring down a bitch's party spirit, but I love your Brandy-looking ass just the same. Good Night."

It was a little after six pm when Pearl got home on Monday, and again it felt like rain. The sky was cloudless, and on top of that had turned a dirty shade of murky gray that threatened to get even more dark.

Entering her apartment, she tensed at the sound of the TV coming from her bedroom, then remembered Angie, and in the same instant the short, dark-skinned woman with shoulder length hair appeared.

"How was work?"

"You didn't miss anything," Pearl smiled. "Trust me."

Angie laughed. "Come on in the bedroom and relax." When she grabbed Pearl's hand, Pearl looked slightly agitated. "Come on, woman," Angie prodded, "I'm not going to bite you. Plus, it is your apartment, remember?"

Pearl followed slowly as it was Angie's presence, not hers, that suffused the bedroom with an eerie sensuality that made Pearl nervous, making the palms of her hands sweat. Angie interested Pearl and though she sensed a vague sexual danger with the sista being under the same roof with her, she was glad for the company.

"You might want to change that." Angie pointed at the CD player. It's something I brought with me."

"That's Maxwell, right?"

"Yes." Angie came around to the side of the bed where Pearl was seated. "Just close your eyes and listen to the brotha sing." Angie softly massaged Pearl's shoulder. "Ssssh," she whispered firmly when Pearl offered a weak protest. "Concentrate on the song, sista."

Pearl found it almost impossible not to comply, but she frowned when she felt moisture between her thighs, and although she was not overly troubled by it, she was puzzled. Arousal did not amuse her. Especially with Angie.

"You feel that?" Angie slyly quizzed, then smiled knowingly. "Feels good as hell, huh?"

Pearl promised herself not to be a fool or to let Angie get any bolder. "You've been such a great help," she almost whispered. "Thanks." Pearl stood up noiselessly. "People already think I'm a lesbian."

"Let's give 'em something to talk about. I'll bump pussies with you in a heartbeat."

"I'm honored, Angie, but no."

"I bet you play with your own pussy."

Pearl, suddenly didn't trust herself being this close to Angie having this conversation so she moved away. "I want you to know how inappropriate I find your curiosity." Both women stood silently for a second, wondering what would come next. Pearl moved away first. "Gotta pee."

Two nights later Angie approached Pearl like she was easy game.

"Guess what, Pearl?"

"What?"

I'm a president."

"Of what and since when." Pearl tossed aside the novel she was reading. "Why are you tripping?"

"I'm not tripping," Angie snapped. "I'm a president."

"And I'm the Queen of Diamonds."

"You can be so damn silly at times, girl, but that's okay. Put on some clothes."

"My, my" Pearl joked, "did I hear you right or are my ears deceiving me? Put on some clothes? What a big shock. Usually, it's Pearl, take off your clothes." Pearl looked heavenwards. "Won't wonders ever cease?"

"Just do it. I want you to go somewhere with me."

"Not to your White House, I hope."

"No, just to my headquarters."

"Headquarters?!" Pearl exploded in laughter. "What are you now, a police chief? Girl, I didn't know you had multiple personalities. Do you, sugar," Pearl joked, "it's your thang."

"Just put on some clothes and come on or else we'll be late. I speak tonight."

"You're serious, aren't you?"

"Very. Now, hurry up. I can't wait to introduce you to my friends."

Pearl sighed. "I know I may end up hating you for this, but, okay, I'll go. Give me a minute to throw on some clothes."

"Ever since the dawn of time ," Ennis lectured, "men have always pursued women."

"But how damn many of those pursuits do you believe have been high speed chases?"

"Shut up, V-Man, and drive."

"Where do you think they going?"

"Don't know. That's why we following them."

"Nigga, you mystify me with your sucka ass. Used to get plenty of pussy, but ain't had a single shot of ass since you laid your big, brown eyes on that Brandy twin. You know that if I put the word out on you, you would lose your playa's card?"

"Think I care. You can fuck all my stray bitches."

"But what about Wilt Chamberlain's record, don't you care about that any more? Wilt fucked 10, 00 women in his lifetime. Man. That's big. Every motherfucka with a dick supposed to take a shot at that record."

"I'm retiring, dawg, so I guess the only person you gotta worry about breaking the record before you do is Ron Jeremy." Ennis grunted. "They're turning, make that right at the light."

"Man, just leave the driving to me."

"Plus, I'm tired of layups. Bitches just give up the booty, don't challenge a nigga. This sista make a nigga shoot fifty footers."

"And miss."

Ten minutes later, Pearl and Angie parked in front of a nondescript red-brick building in the warehouse district of town.

"We're here," Angie announced dramatically. "It's showtime. Welcome to my other life."

Pearl wanted to ask just how many lives she had. She was church. She was chuuch. She was gay. And now this, whatever she was getting ready to turn into. But before she could utter a single word, two women---of imposing stature---rushed out, assisted Angie out of her car, flanked her like a pair of Secret Service bodyguards, and escorted her into the building. Damn, Pearl thought, maybe Angie was the President!

Twenty women, mostly young, black professionals, and nearly a third as many gay, black men clapped happily as Angie entered the room. One or two saluted smartly. Angie smiled modestly and walked to the podium. She adjusted the microphone.

"I'm late as a motherfucka, huh?"

The crowd howled. "Hell yeah."

Angie recognized everyone and immediately relaxed, feeling totally at ease. She absolutely identified with her audience who were the most comprehensive male-bashers in the city. "Comrades," she began, "men are out of control."

"The audience clapped wildly, urging Angie on.

"I may be wrong as two left shoes," Angie commented darkly, "but between this upcoming football season and the motherfucking election, it seems as though men have gotten the big head and their lil ol' imperial aura is unwelcome now more than ever. All of a damn sudden, we can't marry each other because of Amendment One. What a triumph for bigots. I have to give props to President Obama, but he needs to check his Secret Service folks. They think they can fuck a bitch and not pay her shit. This I know for a fact. If I suck a motherfucka's dick, he gonna be paying alimony or palimony or something. He's stupid if he thinks I ain't getting paid.""

"The crowd went wild, roaring its approval.

"Lately, every professional athlete and entertainer have transformed themselves in poster-children of this new kind of sexual adventurism. Motherfuckas run a few touchdowns and he think his shit don't stank no more. Remember back in the days when niggas used to brag about how they find 'em, feel 'em, fuck 'em, forget 'em. Well, that notion is somehow too complicated for these Similac sugar-daddies. These fool niggas will kill you. A bitch pussy better not be too good. Let a ho have some snapping pussy and she start that shit 'bout she tired and want to go home to Mama. Heifer end up with a pair of concrete slippers on, lounging at the bottom of some goddamn river."

For the next twenty minutes, Angie enthralled her audience, conjuring up newer and more creative ways to berate and belittle men.

"What is called for," she continued, "is less serf-like dependence on the dick as the ultimate symbol of power in this country. Every bitch in America must be re-educated and taught that she is more than a foot soldier in the war of the sexes. They must learn that male orgasms can't happen without the agency and assistance of good pussy. Women must be sexually enlightened before they can be sexually empowered."

Angie left the stage amidst cheers and applause, and when she came around the table to sit down, Pearl was mesmerized.

"Any questions?" Angie asked.

"No, Miss President," Pearl whispered. "I heard you loud and clear."

Angie smiled. "Good."

Chapter 6

Since mid-morning, Ennis had done nothing in the book store but stare out of the window, hoping V-Man would soon show up. In the few hours since V-Man had been gone, Ennis was glad the store had had few customers because he didn't want to be bothered. The one or two patrons who had come in had been waited on with the usual courtesy, but no sooner had they left than Ennis dutifully went back to the window to stare glumly down the street, looking for V-Man's red Lexus.

By the time V-Man did finally arrive, Ennis was predictably both happy and worried, but at least there would hopefully be some answers. Good or bad. For better or for worse. Answers.

"Told you you were a sucka," V-Man cracked as soon as he walked through the door.

"Go 'head on with that trouble, nigga," Ennis rasped coldly, 'cause I ain't I the mood for your bullshit."

"Damn, dawg," V-Man laughed. "You sound distraught."

"Nigga, for your information, "bitches be distraught. Niggas be----"

"What, stupid?"

"The bigger question is if you found shit out or were you out on company time fucking off?"

V-Man looked at Ennis blankly. "So that's how it is? After all the trouble I went through to find out what those three letters meant."

"What damn letters?"

"The letters on the front of that building where your girl went last night. That spot was headquarters."

"And?"

"The alphabets-----"

"Give 'em to me."

"What?'

"The motherfucking alphabets. Let me have 'em. Bet I can crack the code. Just give me a second to focus." Ennis closed his eyes, then reopened them. "I'm ready. Give them too me."

"You sure you're ready?'

"That's what I just said, didn't I. Stop bullshitting, V-Man, and give me the damn letters."

"W.A.M." V-Man paused. "It's pronounced WAM."

"Like that group George Michael was in?"

"Hell naw, that was WHAM. This is WAM. Got it?"

"WAM?"

"WAM"

Ennis closed his eye again. "They're hoes, right, so I take that to mean one thing."

"Which is?"

"The W stands for women."

"Shit, that was self-explanatory."

"Au contraire, my nigga friend, it could have stood for womb. Shit, what about wig….or better yet, weave. You know how the sistas are about their hair, so don't give me that jive about shit being self-explanatory. I figured that shit out, so give a brotha props."

"Okay, but what does the A.M. stand for?"

"There it is," Ennis yelled triumphantly. I'm one bad motherfucka---"

"Hold on, Slick, there what is?'

"The code. V-Man. You gave it away with the A.M.. WAM. Letters stand for Women in the A.M.. And since A.M. signifies morning, it is my professional opinion that it all has to do with the morning after. I know it's silly to us brothas, but we all know how bitches be withholding the pussy, scared a nigga ain't gonna respect their trifling ass the next morning."

"You dumb, Ennis."

"Dumb!? Then what do the letters stand for?"

"Women Against Men."

"You mean like in a wrestling match or something?"

V-Man shook his head. "Against men, as in opposed to men. Do you know what kind of women hate men. Motherfucking dykes, that's who. Damn, dawg, we done stumbled upon a nest of lesbians and you in love with one. Are you crazy?!"

"They're not like that, I betcha."

"What are they then, bumblebees?"

"We'll find out soon enough."

"When?"

"As soon as we find out when WAM holds their next meeting. We're attending, so feel free to bring your lil' black book."

"For what? Bitches probably got more numbers than me and you combined."

"Then," Ennis smiled sweetly, "make some exchanges."

'Fuck you, nigga. Like I said, you a sucka.

"I'm scared."

"Of what, V-Man?"

Of what?! Put on your thinking cap, Ennis. We fixing to walk into a lion's den. When those people in there see us, they might tear us from limb to limb. Just in case it has somehow eluded your attention, we are the competition, the ol' crosstown rivals. You think they--?"

"Relax, V-Man. It's all good. Damn."

"Do what you want, but I'm holding my dick."

Ennis sighed. "For what?"

"Because those bitches ain't got one. That's what they hate us for. Penis envy." V-Man frowned. "I'm warning you, soldier. Sit on your dick."

Ennis and V-Man walked up to the front door of the building.

"Good evening. May I help you?"

"Good Evening," Ennis replied sweetly. "We're here to

attend the meeting."

"You are, are you?"

"Yes, that is correct."

"I don't think so."

"Who are you if you don't mind me asking?"

"My name is Garrison. You like asking people their names? Is that how you get off?"

Ennis took a deep breath. "Are you with WAM?"

"I am WAM."

"Are you sure?"

Garrison brazenly eyed Ennis' crotch. "I'm as sure of that as I am about you having a big dick." Garrison stuck out his tongue lewdly. "Does that solve our lil' problem? Once more, though. I am WAM."

"But you're not a woman," Ennis scowled, " at least not a real one."

"You don't look so friendly all of a sudden," Garrison huffed. "Just who the fuck are you anyway?" His tone abruptly changed from soft to antagonistic, and now was more of a lion than a kitten. "Don't try to come up in here with no juvenile spy shit for the white man downtown 'cause I will deal terribly with your ass."

"Trust me," Ennis pleaded calmly, "we come in peace."

"Honey, you better ask somebody."

"I sincerely apologize. Now, may we come in?"

"Hell naw. WAM's meetings are closed to the public."

Before Ennis could respond, Garrison slammed the door and fluttered off across the room, disappearing into the back. No doubt to summon security,

Ennis turned to V-Man. "You ready to go?"

"More that you'll ever know, dawg. More that you will ever know."

Chapter 7

Pearl was in bed watching the news. She rolled over and shot Angie an evil eye, but that didn't stop Angie from peeling back the covers and sliding between the linen sheets. Pearl rolled back over to face the television.

"Nice," Angie muttetred as she fluffed the pillow under her head, pounding it into an almost oval heap.

"Comfortable?" Pearl mumbled distractedly.

Angie slid across the sheets until she was pressed into Peal's back. "Now, I'm all comfy." She draped a leg over Pearl.

"Why you gotta be so close?"

"You're less likely to run." Angie kissed Pearl on the neck. "You smell nice."

Pearl moved away. "I'm trying to watch TV, dammit,"

"Not any more," Angie intoned sharply as she wrestled the remote out of Pearls' hand and cut the television OFF. With ungodly sped, the screen went blank and the bedroom black.

"I don't believe your ass."

"Let's talk," Angie commanded.

Pearl glanced at her friend from a sideways angle. "How about let's getting some light on first?"

"Since when do we need light to talk. What are you afraid of anyway? That you might learn the truth about yourself. Is that it?"

Flicking ON her bedside lamp, Pearl hissed,. "What is the truth?"

"A damned good lesson to be learned."

Sitting up on the side of the bed, Pearl studied Angie's face. "I can't ever recall you being so....so pushy."

"And what's wrong with that?"

"It sorta hits you like a Mack Truck for one thing."

For the next minute, Pearl and Angie traded mild insults with each other, but when it reached the point where the language got stronger, they both shut up to catch their breath. Momentarily stunned by their argument, both women sulked in the silence.

Angie moved closer to Pearl, kissing the top of her exposed thigh.

"Please, don't do that."

"Stop tripping, Pearl. You know you don't mind." Angie planted a second kiss on Pearl's thigh. "There's nothing wrong with fleshly desires, so don't get all self-righteous. Sex is what makes us human." Angie sat up beside Pearl. "Plus, I want to be the one to turn you on."

"Hmmph," Pearl grunted. "And you think I'm ready?"

"Not think, sweetheart, I know. You're ready to be plucked."

"And so that's why you're so worried about my sexual health, scared you might not get none or that I might turn out to be a big freak who can't stay out of bed with a man."

"You think that shit funny, don't you? Well, it ain't. Can't nobody love you like me." Angie leaned over, trying to kiss Pearl on the mouth.

"Stop, Angie. No. You know I'm married to the church."

"That's bullshit." Angie cupped Pearl's face between her hands. "Look at me, Pearl."

"What?" Pearl's voice caught in her throat. "What's more important than the church?"

"Listen, baby, what I'm telling you is that once you're confronted with a do-or-die, got-to-get-a-nut moment, what your ass is going to find out is that you're not as obsessed with the church as you would like to believe you are." Angie paused, stroking Pearl's arm. "That won't make you a hypocrite or anything like that, but I'm just letting you know how it is. We're all weaklings when it comes to our pleasure principle, but I get the impression that you think you can compete with your hormones once they get cranked up. Well, you can't." When Pearl attempted to turn away, Angie gently twisted her head back until they were gazing into each other's eyes. "The shit that drives you to go to church and sing in the choir won't be nearly strong enough to slow your silly ass down once you bump pussies or suck a dick for the first time."

Pearl pulled away. "And you honestly think an orgasm is worth all the stress? Just look at you, as uptight as a banjo string." She rubbed Angie's stomach playfully. "Stress will make your tummy ache." Pearl laid down, stretching out under the covers, covering up to her neck. "Go to sleep, Miss President."

Angie snuggled up under the covers, pressing herself into Pearl.

"And stop grinding against me."
"You don't like it?"
"That's besides the point. I don't want you doing it."
"Let me----"
"I don't want to hear it. Just move over to the other side of the bed.....and stay there."
"Are you wet?"
"Damn, Angie, why you so nosey tonight?"
"Bet you're moist."
"Well, I'm not."
Angie gently spanked Pearl. "And got the nerve to lie."
"You think I'm turned on?"
"Hell yeah."
"Well, I'm not."
"Let me touch you and see for myself."
Pearl slid out of bed. "I'm puzzled by your behavior, Angie. You sleep here. I'll go sleep on the couch. Good night."
"Nighty-night, bitch."

The wetness between her legs seemed more like a spiritual awareness than a physical aberration, but Pearl still stubbornly refused to surrender to the sexual perceptions her brain was now flirting with. For one thing, she didn't want to remain trapped by the presence of any hormone or emotion toxic enough to make her feel that weak or passive, but even the idea of losing spiritual ground did not humble her to the point where she was willing to block out how pleasant Angie had made her feel. Pearl smiled warmly. That bitch Angie was sneaky.

Snuggled up under the blanket, Pearl struggled for a few seconds to embrace what was left of her equilibrium, but rather than awakening her belief that it was wrong to be sexually aroused by a woman, she instead became suspiciously more critical of men.

Knowing that her living arrangements with Angie had just become more delicate by the fact that she had allowed herself to get steered into some dangerously deep water didn't upset her because if things got too nasty, she would simply ask Angie to leave.

Touching her pussy, Peal suddenly realized she was wetter than she had imagined and even though Angie had done most of the work, she still played in the stickiness with the same kind of schoolgirl interest as she had when she had made the goo come by herself.

Pearl now liked to think of her pussy as a universe, a world within a world where time would stop if she put the right squeeze on her clitoris. By now, she was as familiar with the interior of her pussy as she was with the walls and rooms of her apartment, and equally at home. Her pussy was a blessing because how could doing something so simple as playing with it be such a rich source of pleasure?

She had to admit, though, that her thick, pussy hairs did look like a jungle. Maybe she would let Angie shave her---not bald, but styled like a diamond, perhaps. Who knows?

Pearl wondered what Angie's pussy looked like. At some point she had the feeling she would find out, and that thought caused her own pussy to make some more goo. How should one woman approach another woman's most private part? Pearl instantly went numb. She wouldn't even know what to do. She was sure she would 'respect the fruit' and instead of making a beeline for the clit immediately would probably opt for a well-planned ambush of it.

She would first study it, get to know it, to understand it. Every pussy, she surmised, had its own individual identity, and there were probably only a couple of things in life, she also surmised, that were as delightful as performing sexual alchemy on another woman.

Pearl got wetter and wetter, more tempted with the inspiration to make herself skeet, but getting an even more scandalous notion, she sprung up from the couch like a tigeress, and sashayed back into her b4edroom.

Angie pretended to be asleep as Pearl pulled the covers up and slid gently between the sheets. Giggling, she pressed herself into Angie.

"Stop playing sleep, hussy." Pearl grinded herself against Angie's ass.

Angie pushed into Pearl, rotating her hips in a hard circle. "Is this what you want, bitch?"

"Must be," Pearl whispered huskily, "you giving it too me, ain't you?"

Angie spun around in bed so quickly it caught Pearl off guard and before she could react Angie was kissing her and had a hand stuffed inside Pearl's panties.

"No!" Pearl shrieked, her voice muffled. "I just want to do what we were doing. I'm not ready for you to touch me there."

"Then what did you bring your ass in here for?"

"I want to…."

"Want to what, Pearl? What do you want to do or do you even know?" Angie was irritated.

"Be quiet, Angie and take of your panties."

When Angie did as instructed, Pearl moaned at the sight. It was her first time seeing a nude body other than her own, and Pearl had never seen flesh so warm and so inviting to touch. Another soft moan escaped her lips.

"What now?" Angie whispered. "Just tell me what you want me to do?"

Peal kneeled on the edge of the bed. "Just let me look at you."

"Don't be scared to touch me. I----"

"No, I just want to see you."

Angie opened her legs as wide as she could. "Look."

"Oh my God?!" Pearl gasped loudly. "Your pussy looks like

a flower."

"Touch it, Pearl."

"No."

Angie reached for Pearl's hand.

"No, Angie. Stop or I'll leave."

Feeling defeated, Angie plopped back down into the bed. "You'll drive a bitch crazy, Pearl, with that back-alley pussy-teasing shit."

"Hush, Angie, and open your legs back up."

"Like this?"

"Now, masturbate for me. Go slow because I want to see how you do it."

Angie teasingly eased her finger inside her cum-moistened pussy. "But you can help me." Angie pulled her glistening finger out and showed it to Pearl. "Let me wet your fingers, baby."

"No, Angie, so please stop asking. I want to enjoy the suspense of watching you do yourself." Pearl moved closer. "Make me feel what you will be feeling. See if you can make me cum without touching me."

Using the two fingers on both of her hands closest to her thumbs, Angie spread the lips of her pussy, rounding them into a dark O that was so deep, Pearl could virtually look inside Angie's tunnel of love.

With Pearl watching, Angie eased two of her fingers into her pussy and wiggled her ass around, humping fiercely against her hand before pulling out to spread the juice on her fingers into her pubic hair which looked like a well-manicured lawn. Then with a furious, flicking motion, Angie brushed against her clitoris. This action made her moan hungrily. In fact, it seemed to feel so pleasant it made good sense for her to keep on doing it. So she did.

Swollen, Angie's pussy lips looked like some exotic, tree-ripened fruit topped with hair that resembled peach fuzz. Pearl watched closely as Angie expertly peeled back the dark flesh of her pussy and gathered the handsome stem of her clitoris, providing herself with the dual thrill of soft caresses and deep penetration, forcing the fingers of both hands to perform different tricks at one and the same time. Angie panted.

Pearl chewed her bottom lip, but still couldn't prevent herself from slobbering like a dog as Angie's body quivered and quaked with pleasure. By now, Angie's fingers were cradling her clit like it was a guitar as she ran her sticky fingers up and down the sensitive nerve endings in the morsel of flesh until she was making joyful music of her own.

"Hold my hand, Pearl. I'm almost there."

Crouching in the wide vee between Angie's spread-eagled legs, Pearl eagerly reached for her friend's outstretched hand and found she loved the satiny texture of Angie's cum as it coated her palm. "Oooh," she squealed softly.

Leaning forward a bit more, Pearl sniffed deeply, savoring Angie's musky aroma, paying close attention to the subtle difference in their individual sexual flava. Angie's fragrance was deeper, more full-bodied, combined with a richer sexual chemistry than hers. The scent drugged her.

Angie was a talker. "Look at my pretty pussy, Pearl. Doesn't it look good?" Angie gasped, had to catch her breath. "Oh shit!, damn, it feels soooo good. Look, Pearl. Watch me, baby. Watch Lil Mama get a nut." Angie was long-stroking herself, churning her fingers round, pushing them up and down in a quick, jerky motion. "Oh, baby," Angie moaned. "I wish it were you I was…making feel…this…goddamn GOOD!"

Pearl arranged herself between Angie's legs so she could more fully bask in the experience of her friend's orgasm which was evidently about to happen real soon.

Angie blinked, not wanting to lose eye contact with Pearl, but the compulsion to close her eyes was too powerful for her to resist, so her eyelids dropped like a pair of black, silk curtains. "Oh, Pearl," she groaned. "Oh, Pearl, you bitch."

"Do it, baby," Pearl encouraged. "Play with your pussy. Cum for me."

"You want me to cum, baby?' Angie opened her eyes. "Do you wanna see me cum? You wanna hear me scream?"

"Yes," Pearl purred, rubbing herself through the sheer fabric of her peach-colored panties. "I want you to cum on your fingers and then rub it all over my titties."

"Oh, baby." Angie closed her eyes again.
Pearl removed her bra. "I-I smell you."
"You like it?"
"Yes!" Pearl yanked her panties off. "you smell delicious."
"Oh Pearl!" Angie yelled. "I'M CUMMING!!"
Pearl covered Angie's body with her own and this is how they fell asleep.

Chapter 8

    At once, Ennis found himself at it again and this time he didn't immediately rush to find an excuse to stop himself. So many times---more than he could count---he fantasized about fucking his dream girl, and automatically he closed his eyes. One time, in his fantasy, he even dreamed that she let him fuck her in the ass, and that was the best of his happily-ever-after dreams yet.

    By the time he had gotten out of bed, he had lost eye with contact the fantasy, but he wasn't worried so much about it. He had plans. Well, maybe it was more of a scheme than a plan, but he hoped it would get him either one step closer to the altar or, if not that, at least, the bed. Surprisingly, he half-believed that both were a real possibility.

    After breakfast, a shower, and a call to V-Man, Ennis was on his way to Smokey's Gift Shoppe, a rectangular, red-brick edifice next to the ABC Store on Bruton Avenue.

    Once inside, V-Man, was less interested in Smokey's than he was in the goodies next door. "Man, buy that bitch a pair of edible panties and a bottle of Hennessey, then after a few shot of Hen, you approach her like Clark Gable and kiss the shit out of her."

    "What then?"

    "Y'all knock boots until the cows come home, that's what, nigga."

    Ennis shook his head. "Occasionally, I think you really

believe some of that shit you be talking."

"Believe it! Nigga, I swear by that shit. I'm telling you, cuz, a teddy and a drink ain't nothing but the coming attractions for some freaky-deaky shit. No shucking."

Ennis shook his head once more.

"That's just how it is, but I ain't got no sympathy for a sucka, so if you don't get the panties off Miss Thang real soon, the next time you catch your breath, it'll be my dick down her throat. Understand?"

"Here," Ennis chuckled, "pay for this."

"A stuffed animal?" This time V-Man shook his head. "Nigga, you ain't about to get no leg. How the hell you expect to make physical contact behind the merits of a toy tiger."

Ennis grabbed V-Man's arm. "Just wait and see. Now, go pay for my tiger."

That same evening. 6:55pm

Ennis had been standing across the street from the apartment for nearly ten minutes. It was almost seven in the evening and he was almost ready to abort the mission, but found he couldn't. He didn't want to let this girl get away, so he rehearsed his fairly brilliant come-on. At least, he felt it was brilliant. Damn what V-Man thought.

It was time.

Walking slowly across the street, Ennis' legs seemed to sprawl out from under his torso like he was about to launch into a break-dance routine, and just as he crossed the center lane, he noticed how his feet felt swallowed up by his Stacy Adams. He also realized, too late, that his pants seemed rigged with static cling, and that the creases in them which were razor-sharp when he had left home had now somehow turned to cement, weighing him down.

6:59pm

The earliest hint of the nigga across the street dawned on Angie with the force of a concrete slab falling on her head. He was the same nigga Garrison had to curse out; the same nigga who had tried to crash the WAM meeting. And now here his ass was. At Pearl's with a stuffed animal under his arm.

Oh no the hell he wasn't! At least, not if she had something to say about it.

"Quietly, Angie credited the nigga for being cute, but damn, that posed a problem for her. With her eyes glued to his body, she studied the front of his trousers with clinical precision. "Shit!" She cursed. The motherfucka was holding.

Angie even went as far as to swiftly calculate the cost of the gear he was wearing, and she was not inspired. Nigga had bank. Lord, have mercy.

Needless to say, it was by no means easy for her to watch helplessly as the motherfucka thundered across the street. She was sick with worry, the sweat forming under her armpits, wet and sticky.

From the stubborn look of resolve on the stranger's face as he stepped up to the curb, it was clear that this was no prank call. The nigga was out to skeet. This distressed Angie greatly, but there was always the time-honored maneuver of cock-blocking so she still had an Ace in the hole. She would cock-block!

Although it consumed what seemed to be half his lifetime, Ennis finally found himself standing across the street. He strolled up to the front door. He knocked.

Rushing to meet the nigga at the door, Angie's sense of superiority quickly vanished. Damn, dude was fine.

"Yes, may I help you?"

"I'm here---"

"We don't allow strangers on premise. Sorry. That is policy and is not due to change any time in the foreseeable future. Goodbye."

"But---"

"But, what, you speak a foreign language or something? Niggas are a no-no today."

"I'll only be a minute. I would like to speak to the lady of the house."

"Who?"

Ennis sighed in hopeless resignation. "The lady who lives here."

"Didn't know you had an appointment?"
"Would you please let her know I'm here?"
"Who?"
"The lady of the house."
"No, nigga. You."
"Me, what?"
"Who are you?"
"Why?"
"Why the hell you think? I'm security, that's why?"
"You're security, huh?"
"Ain't that what I just said."
Ennis laughed. "Where's your weapon?"
"I know martial arts."

Ennis decided not to press his luck, but he didn't seem to have much choice given the woman's stiff resistance to his polite request. Growing silent, he pondered how best to deal with this immediate problem.

"Here, my brotha," Angie snarled, producing a pad and pen. "Write down your name and contact info, and I'll personally see that it gets to you-know-who."

"You're security, though," Ennis teased, "that's not your job."

"I just made it my damn job," Angie snapped. "Hurry up."

Ennis handed the writing material back. "Naw, I don't think so."

Angie scowled evilly. "I can see you a grown-assed man, but what's puzzling me is your mental age. Don't you understand that you can't see my friend this morning?"

"When, then?"

"I'm security, remember, not her damn travel agent. First of all, does she even know who the hell you are?"

Ennis gritted his teeth.

"So, it unanimous," Angie retorted coldly, "you're a nobody." Angie folded her arms across her chest. "Let's not fool ourselves. If you think you, or anyone else for that matter, can march right in off the streets without so much as a phone call, and then force you way into my sista-girl's apartment, then you better adjust your antenna.

Shit ain't happening."

"Not on your shift, eh?"

"On nobody's damn shift. Look, Mister Man, I don't see no sense in wasting no more time." Angie smiled sweetly. "Who the fuck are we to make shit worse between brothas and sistas? No more drama, alright?"

"That sounds fine with me, but you're still missing my point. I know the sista is here and I intend to speak with her or I'm not leaving."

Angie dropped her hands. "So, it's like that. Business as usual, huh?"

"I want to speak to the sista immediately." Ennis made sure his voice was controlled and steady, but he still had to force himself to pronounce each word clearly. "I hope I'm making myself understood."

Angie gazed vacantly out of the open door, breathing hard. "This could get ugly."

"I'm not leaving."

"In that case." Angie started to close the door in Ennis' face. "Get the hell away from here."

"Excuse me." Pearl emerged from the bathroom and both Angie and Ennis gawked at her. They both seemed so stunned by her appearance that their grim reaction alerted her to the tension in the air. "Excuse me," she repeated. "Am I interrupting something here?" Pearl walked closer to the pair. "Angie?"

"He's here to see you," Angie pouted.

"And you didn't tell me?"

"There were some questions," Ennis offered in Angie's defense. "She's very protective of you."

Pearl frowned. "First of all, I don't need anyone's protection and secondly, just who are you and what do you want?"

Ennis continued to stare at Pearl for a few more seconds before politely shifting his gaze. This sista was beautiful.

"Do you have business with me?"

At any other time, Ennis would have been so verbally versatile he could have, at his choosing, tossed out words of charm, ridicule, sarcasm; however on this particular evening, the best he could manage was immense lameness. "Yes, if you don't mind. I mean, er, would, if you don't mind, like to have a word with you." He gulped dryly. "It-it's pretty important."

"Come in."

Pearl watched carelessly as the stranger seated himself on the sofa and she noticed the stuffed tiger. In a flash, she realized she should offer the man a beverage, but she didn't. She chose instead to walk stiffly to her recliner and plop down. It was then that she realized that the brown suit matched his eyes. She also couldn't help but notice how his cologne suffused the room. Nice.

Still grasping the tiger, Ennis reached it to Pearl. "This is for you."

Pearl was surprised. She examined the stuffed animal. "I-I don't understand. There's no card."

Ennis held up the card, but didn't extend it. "And in case you're wondering, I'm not the delivery guy."

Pearl's eyebrows arched quizzically.

"Or a courier."

Pearl's eyebrows fluttered.

"I guess that means that the gift is from me."

"And just who—or what—are you?"

The stranger licked his lips nervously. "My name is Ennis Wallace and what I am is in love with you."

It was quite a while later before Pearl experienced the first tremors from her meeting with Ennis and they caused her to vibrate all over. The feeling was refreshing, but the most dramatic thing it did was to make her run out to buy some "stuff".

To her, stocking up on perfume and lipstick was a systematic way of coming to terms with her late-blooming femininity, but trying on a camisole was the most dynamic experiment of her life. Following her mini-shopping spree, Pearl, at last, felt as if she was finally a part of the sexual revolution even though she was still unsure if she was ripe enough for actual carnal knowledge. At any rate, a new way of looking at the world was definitely in the works. Unfortunately, Pearl was not the only one to notice her shift in perspective.

"So, you're going to become a slut." It was Angie.

Pearl was unperturbed. "Let's not bother with your childishness. How 'bout that?"

"Recovering from your guilt?"

"Chile, please. I was out shopping, not getting my boots knocked."

"Hmmph. As long as you were gone, you had time for a quickie in a cheap hotel."

Pearl suppressed a harsh laugh. "Do you actually believe that after all these years of celibacy, that some man can just walk up and either boss or bully me out of my panties? Have you lost your mind? And let me tell you something else. If, for example, I just had to dig into my pussy, I know how to use a vibrator."

"Is that..is that what you went shopping for?" Angie was curious. "Girl, don't tell me you went out and bought yourself a toy?"

"Who's to say."

"I say that it was a damn silly purchase, especially with me under the same roof with you. Now, I feel deflated."

"Shit, can't you take a damn joke, and please don't start pouting. Lord knows how evil you can get when you throw one of you lil' temper tantrums."

"So, who do you think you are now---Miss Chastity Belt. All because you managed to walk away from your first male/female sexual encounter without letting the nigga get another notch on his belt don't mean shit." Angie got up in Pearl's face. "I know what the nigga wants and you're a silly rabbit if you think it's over. You're a booty call, sweetie and the nigga is on a mission, and since you so dumb, it wouldn't surprise me if he don't fuck you in the ass."

"No, you didn't, Angie. I know you didn't go there. Anal? You have got to be kidding."

"Using your words, who's to say because the first signs of a nigga's sexual genius happens when you let him do you in the butt."

"Hush, Angie." Pearl covered her friend's mouth with her hand. "Enough is enough."

"Let's mix and mingle."

"What?"

"Let's jump in bed and bump pussies."

Chapter 9

On her way back from church on Sunday, Pearl was spiritually inspired so she decided to pay a visit to a few of the sick and shut-in, but as she turned down Colson Boulevard, she missed the exit that would take her to Miss Shirley's house. Pearl didn't particularly care for Miss Shirley, whom it was rumored was on crack, but she felt it would be less unsettling to be in the company of a dope addict than to sit at the bedside of someone who was really fucked up with a terminal illness. Despite her good intentions she couldn't dig that scene. She saw enough death on TV.

After a fifteen minutes scouting expedition, she finally emerged out of a deserted side street back onto the main thoroughfare, but by now she had lost interest in Miss Shirley. Instead she would drop by Burger King and get herself a Whopper. Then she would go home, kick up her heels, and get in Angie's shit about sitting so close to June Lincoln in church.

On a whim, since it was not that far out of the way, she decided to drive to the complex where Angie had lived to see how much, if any progress was being made to restore the apartment. Plus, she wanted to see for herself how much damage had been done. The smoke had probably messed up more of Angie's stuff than the actual fire.

Pearl turned on Kenilworth Avenue, drove two miles, and

zoomed up Fisk Road, then almost ran her BMW into a telegraph pole. There was Angier's apartment----untouched! There had to be some mistake. Pearl checked the address. Yes, this was Angie place. No damage. No fire. No shit.

Pearl parked. She dashed up to the front door. She knocked. No fucking answer. What the hell was going on? There had been no fire.

Pearl scurried around to the bedroom window and peeked in through the small crack in the drapes and what she saw both shocked and surprised her. Angie's shit was still in there.

Pausing to catch her breath, Pearl tried not to let a distorted version of the events cloud her perceptions because there had to be a plausible explanation for what she had just discovered. Instead of playing detective, which was her initial reaction, she calmly walked next door and knocked.

Pearl smiled. "Hello. I was wondering about that apartment next door."

"What about it?"

"I heard there had been a big fire there."

"When?!" the woman gasped.

"Not long ago."

The woman laughed. "Somebody lied to you. Anyway, that's Angie's apartment."

"Angie. You know her?"

"That's my girl."

"Do you happen to know where she is now?"

The woman turned suspicious. "Who are you?"

"A friend. We work together."

"And she didn't tell you?"

Pearl shook her head. "No."

"I don't know if I should tell you or not, but you don't look like the kind of sista who would break into the apartment and steal my girl's shit---"

"Trust me. I don't do crime 'cause I can't stand the time. You feel me?"

The woman smiled. "I feel you, sista."

"So where is Angie?"

"Bitch went to Africa. Ain't that something?"
"Yeah, it sure the hell is."
"You ever been to Africa?"
Pearl smiled sweetly. "I'm on my way there right now. Have a blessed day."

Pearl crept into her apartment, ready to have it out with Angie, but got that much more angrier when she discovered that Angie had not yet gotten home.
She called LaNisa.
"Where the hell is Angie?"
"Girl, you just got out of church and already cussing. When did you pick that habit up----?"
"About the same time you picked up the damn habit of setting me up."
LaNisa was calm. "Does this have anything to do with a supposed fire that allegedly burned out a certain you-know-who?"
"Dammit, LaNisa, how could you? I thought you were my girl?"
"Don't get all frantic. Wasn't no harm done. Plus Angie wanted to lick your pussy."
"And you saw fit to help her?"
"Hell no, Pearl, I know your goody-two-shoes ass wouldn't go for letting Angie between your tight-assed thighs."
"Than why did you back her story?"
LaNisa sighed heavily. "So I could win the bet."
"Bet? What motherfucking bet?"
"Okay, okay. Angie bet me an all expense paid trip to the Bahamas that she could suck your pussy within ten days and I bet the bitch a trip to the location of her choice that she couldn't."
"No, you didn't?"
"But look at how much confidence I had in your ass. Don't that count for something?"
"You bet on me like I was a damn race horse. What kind of friend is that?"
"C'mon, Pearl, as long as you don't let ol' conniving ass Angie in your bedroom what goddamn harm is done. Tell me that."

"What about the story you and the bitch concocted about her apartment catching fire?"

"Can we just call that a little, white lie and move on with our lives?"

"Just look at what you've done. You betrayed me."

"C'mon, Pearl. It's not like I sent a hit man or the big, bad wolf to live with you. Angie, when you get past her bullshit, is one of the most adorable bull-dykes in the universe. She likes watching Moesha too. Did she tell you? Did she tell about her favorite episode where your girl Brandy---"

"Later for your ass, LaNisa. Here comes your partner in crime. Y'all bitches something."

"Before you go, Pearl, I feel I must warn you about all that cussing. I know you just started, but you'll never get to heaven saying bad words."

"Fuck you, LaNisa."

As soon as Angie walked into the door, Pearl embraced her and kissed the top of her head.

"Mmmm. Mmmm," Angie purred, hugging Pearl around the waist. "What a wonderful surprise. Now, this is how you welcome a bitch home."

"Are you free for the rest of the day?" Pearl licked her lips suggestively. "I have a couple of ideas, if you know what I mean. You do know, don't you baby?"

"Should we take this to the bedroom?"

"Why not 'cause ain't no other room in this motherfucka got the equipment I need to do what I have in mind. Understand me, suga?"

Angie was already coming out of her church clothes. "And just what kind of equipment do you have in mind?"

"Oh just the kind with a big, soft mattress and a pair of cool, crisp sheets."

"Glory be," Angie exclaimed happily. "Prayer does work."

At the bedroom door, Pearl stopped. "After you, my Nubian Queen."

Angie entered the bedroom. She clasped her hands as if in

prayer. "Of all the wrong I've ever done in my life, I must have done something right."

"And you getting ready to reap your reward." Pearl kicked off her shoes at the door. She unbuttoned her blouse.

Angie reached for Pearl. "Don't stand out there. "Come on in." She pointed at the bed. "Look at that piece of equipment. Gorgeous, ain't it?"

"A real masterpiece."

"Then why you still standing out there, my sweetie?"

"Because I got a surprise for you."

Angie covered her heart with her hand. "A surprise? For me? What is it?"

"Close your eyes and turn around."

Angie eagerly complied.

Pearl slammed the bedroom door and locked it. "Bitch, you on lock-down!"

"Baby, I don't understand. What's happening?"

"Call that ho, LaNisa and ask her. Oh yes, I stopped by your motherfucking apartment today. I wish I would have burned the bastard down."

"Let me out, you sneaky bitch."

Pearl laughed. "Me, sneaky? Then what in the world does that make you and LaNisa?"

"Bitch, I'm warning you."

"Oh, and by the way, chow will be served a little late this evening. I think I will call Ennis and take his fine ass out to a movie."

Angie banged on the door. "Don't go 'round that nigga. You hear me, Pearl? You better not give away my pussy. Bitch, I'm serious." Angie kicked the door. "You let that nigga touch the pussy and I'll fuck his ass up. I'm for real. I don't play when it comes to pussy, you hear me bitch with your Brandy-looking ass."

Chapter 10

It was a hand-me-down, but it fit like a glove. Pearl had on the lilac-colored silk dress that LaNisa had given her over a year ago and though she had never worn it, she was glad she hadn't given it away. She also wore a pair of leather kitten-heel pumps that were such a sweet touch that Pearl squealed in delight at her image.

Inside her tweed clutch purse, she even had a condom, although she didn't anticipate a sexually charged atmosphere. It was just a movie date.

More than likely, Angie had taken her ass to bed. She had been quiet for the last half-hour and Pearl was glad. That bitch had really been ranting and raving, kicking and banging on the door like she was crazy. Pearl would check on her once she had finished with Ennis.

For the very first time in her life, she felt personal, sensing her own charisma and sensuality, a woman in full, ready and willing to compromise her virginity for a future filled with fable-like black heroes and mind-blowing orgasms. Suddenly, she was Miss It.

Taking one last look in the mirror, her identity seemed split in half. Was she coming of age…or was she coming apart? Or was she just ready to cum.

Ennis blew his horn

Choosing 'The Avengers' over "Think Like a Man' was a momentous, nerve-racking experience since she had never been to a movie before and had no true idea of what actually went on inside a theater. According to the church, the cinema was as big a den of iniquity as a ho house or a liquor store.

"Well, what I suggest," Ennis offered after the movie, "is that you let me get you out more. There's a big world out here, Pearl. Let me introduce you to it."

'I might just do that," Pearl replied hesitantly, "but it wouldn't hurt if we got to know each other a little better before you started showing me off."

Ennis held Pearl's hand. "If you will let me, I can make you an early appointment with love and happiness."

Pearl squeezed Ennis' hand playfully. "You know them?"

"Sure do." Ennis bragged. "Not only am I on a first name basis with both of them, but I make things convenient for them." He stopped Pearl next to his car. "You know how I do that?"

Pearl put her finger to Ennis' lips. "Take your time. Don't rush."

"Why?"

"Because I just remembered something, Ennis."

"What?"

"All the broken-hearted people in the world."

"But how do you know that your heart will ever be broken if you never offer it?"

"Why risk it?"

"Why accept loneliness?"

Pearl shrugged. "It probably hurts a lot less than a broken heart, that's why."

Escorting Pearl around to the passenger side of his car, Ennis popped the lock and assisted her as she got in. Hurrying back around to the driver's side, he deftly eased behind the wheel. He slid in a CD by Emeli Sande. "I'm not trying to be funny, but do you know anything about music?"

"I like Brandy," Pearl blurted before she could stop herself.

Ennis chuckled. "Any particular reason why?"

"So you think I look like her too?"

"Twins."

Pearl turned down the music, then faced Ennis. "Okay, now let me ask you something. Do you like Brandy?' The question puzzled Ennis, catching him by surprise. "You must think she's beautiful."

"To be quite honest, I've never been into Brandy like that."

"You mean to tell me that you have never watched her TV show or bought any of her CDs?"

"Like I said, I—"

"All afternoon, I have listened to you tell me how beautiful I am and then you just admitted that I'm Brandy's twin, so what's to stop me from believing that it's Brandy you want and that I'm merely a convenient stand-in, you know, a stunt double?"

Ennis laughed, then caught himself. "Excuse me for laughing, but I promise you that it's not like that."

"You think that it doesn't happen?"

"What, celebrity fixation? Of course, it happens but for your information, I don't think I'm the starry-eyed type."

"So I got your scout's honor that you're not head over heels in love with Brandy, and trying to get next to me because I look like---?"

"No."

Pearl looked away. "Okay."

"What's wrong, you don't believe me?"

"I not saying that although I think I have reason to be concerned. America is a star-struck society and what guy wouldn't want to be with an actress or singer…but how many will? I guess the next best thing is to get with an urban look-alike, the generic, ghetto brand."

"Let's change the subject," Ennis pleaded. "It's still early and I was hoping that we could----"

"Oh my God!" Pearl shrieked, remembering Angie. "I need to get home quick."

Imagine that! For supper, Angie had prepared an elegant, exotic meal and insisted that it be consumed by candlelight. Pearl was more than aware that the apartment smelled like frankincense, and before she could ask how she had escaped her ass out of the locked bedroom, Angie placed both hands flat on the counter-top like a military commander and stared at Pearl. "Go, bitch, and shower. I don't want you around me smelling like cheap cologne."

Initially, Pearl viewed the command with total disregard, but before long was intrigued. Feeling naughty, she blew Angie a kiss and dashed to the shower.

When Pearl returned to the dining room a few minutes later, Angie was straining an imported blend of herbal tea through a sieve. Spying Pearl, she poured a tall glass and topped it off with a pair of ice cubes to chill it slowly. "Enjoy this while I shower. Here, browse." She handed Pearl the latest edition of Essence magazine. "I won't be but a second."

To a certain extent, Pearl didn't truly give a damn how Angie had gotten out of the bedroom, but she couldn't resist asking. "Angie?"

"Yes, dearie."

"How did your lil, short ass escape out of the jailhouse I put you in?"

"To tell the truth, I didn't escape, sweetheart, I was rescued."

"Rescued? By whom, if you don't mind me asking?"

"The police."

"The police?"

"I called 9-1-1 and told them that someone had broken in on me, taken all my jewelry, and then locked me in the bedroom. They were nice enough to bring along a professional locksmith so they wouldn't have to kick the door down."

Pearl shook her head. "Girl, you a mess. Now, go shower."

Twenty minutes later, Angie reappeared and her entrance stunned Pearl.

"Damn! You look fantastic."

Angie brushed the compliment off.

Pearl ogled Angie openly and was fascinated by the purely sensual way Angie's body behaved. Every one of her luscious assets cooperated and collaborated, working in tandem to make the slinky, red gown move as though it had a mind of its own. The overhead lights played across Angie's hair and by so doing, framed her face in an angelic glow.

"You look so beautiful, Angie."

"Obviously, your blind eyes have finally been open. You need to pray."

Out of sheer self-interest, Pearl wondered how could the Angie she was used to become so radiantly and magnificently different? Never before had Pearl witnessed such a stunning metamorphosis.

"Let's eat."

Comfortably aware of Angie's perfume, Pearl inhaled deeply when Angie leaned over to ladle some of the shrimp jambalaya onto her plate. Even though she could not solve the riddle of what fragrance it was, the essence of the scent sent her senses reeling. She was sexually intoxicated.

"More?" Angie asked softly.

"Of the food, no. Of you, yes."

"Pleeze, Pearl."

By the time the meal was over, Pearl was completely under Angie's spell and was eager to spend the night with her in bed.

"How do you feel?"

Pearl said nothing.

"Well?"

"If you must know," Pearl sighed, "I feel like that old Betty Wright song. You know the one. 'Tonight's The Night You Make Me Your Woman.' That's how I feel." Pearl stared into Angie's eyes. What about you? How do you feel?"

"Like celebrating."

"Then, let's dance."

The dance was not a dance. Instead, it was a boldly provocative pressing together of all their body parts until they were a single figure; one.

Pearl listened to her breathing carefully, the only proof that she had not died and gone to heaven. The night. The dance. Angie.

"Make love to me, baby," Pearl moaned. "Take me to the other side of the world."

Pearl was highly self-conscious of her first kiss and she hoped she was doing it right. Nonetheless, she found the gesture both intimate and attractive. Angie's tongue had a vivid personality, a magic stick, but far from being only that, it was a wizard, devoted to showing off. It felt like cotton candy in her mouth, Pearl thought.

Angie's kissing was so expressive that it reduced Pearl to a whimpering mass of willing flesh. She was now prepared to do anything required to become the best piece of pussy Angie had ever had.

Suddenly, clothes became so irrelevant that Pearl was of the mind to rip hers off her body with as much speed as she could muster, but a much calmer Angie cautioned against hurry and haste, instructing her that the night was still yet young.

More conscientious now, Pearl waited until Angie was ready to expose their nakedness. The wait wasn't long. Their heavy breathing sounded like background music, but as Pearl's tee shirt was removed and her breasts freed, she howled in absolute delight as Angie flicked her tongue across the hardened nipples of one titty while rotating the nipple of the other between her vise-like fingers. It hurt so good.

"Oh Angie," Pearl moaned, "make my titties happy."

Angie licked the terrain between Pearl's breasts with such freaky zeal that Pearl would not have traded what she was feeling for anything else in the world, except for, perhaps, the pleasure she knew she was going to experience once her kitty-cat got sampled.

But first as Angie put her warm, wet lips on the nipple of Pearl's titty and greedily pulled the elongated chocolate bullet into her mouth, the loud sucking noises she made became sexual quotation marks that spoke volumes on how sweet good loving could be.

Now, using her own self-devised licking and sucking technique, Angie made Pearl's hormones whoop it up in joyful ecstasy as her breast got expertly serviced, but when Angie's hands got into the act, slipping deep within Pearl's wet pussy, the virgin-child almost fainted.

The excitement of having Angie's fingers inside her pussy made Pearl's whole body get hot. She stood on her tip-toes, trying to get away from the grip of a sensation she never knew existed.

"Stop, Angie. Please," Pearl begged. "It feels too good....I can't take it."

Angie ignored the plea. She placed one hand on Pearl's shoulder to pull her back down on the two fingers she had thrust deep into her pussy. After a second, Pearl's eyes widened to the size of quarters, getting so weak in the knees that she had to lean on Angie for support.

"I-I just climaxed," Pearl announced proudly. "I just got a nut."

"I know," Angie remarked calmly, 'and there's more where that came from. Now, lie down."

Angie had big plans. Sucking Pearl's pussy had been her fantasy/dream, and now everything was playing out deliciously according to her script. She planned to drive the girl delirious so starting slow, she kissed the soles of Pearl's feet, then gobbled each of her individual toes into her mouth, sucking on them like they were Tootsie Rolls. Next, she trailed wet, sloppy kisses all around her ankles before slowly inching her tongue up Pearl's leg. Angie blew hot air kisses at Pearl's clitoris.

"Oh shit!" Pearl moaned. "Oh shit!"

This was truly her breakthrough moment. She was on the verge of letting another woman lick her pussy. The wonderful finger-fucking she had been given was merely a introductory prelude. Getting her pussy sucked would represent a bridge too far, a point of no return because the second she turned sexually accountable with another woman, she would acquire the rookie status of a lesbian. Pearl gazed lovingly at Angie whose face was poised over the hairy mound of her kitty-cat, ready to put her tongue to work, to please her.

Pearl smiled. "Eat my pussy, baby."

EPISODE TWO

Chapter 11

It was Labor Day, and WAM was on the move. President Angie had insisted on direct action, something so provocative that it would reign as the most socially excruciating confrontation the city had ever witnessed. Everyone at WAM was terribly excited.

As soon as she had walked through the door of WAM headquarters, Pearl smiled brightly. This just might work, she thought, as she rushed over to the coffeepot to pour herself a cup of the steaming brew.

"Couldn't have asked for better weather," Garrison sniffed, turning up his nose. "It's picture perfect for this lil ol' tea party. General Pearl, I wants to do it too. I wants to participate. I'm ready. I have drunk a gallon of water."

Pearl shook her head firmly.

But why not, General Pearl?"

"President Angie thinks it's too risky, and she doesn't want to expose you or any of the other male members to arrest." Pearl pinched Garrison's cheek playfully. "This is not about showing off, honey, and President Angie thinks it can be accomplished in a more respectable way by the ladies."

"If that ain't sexist, grass ain't green. Since when did females corner the market on doing that?"

"We just do it with more finesse, that's all," Pearl teased. "With men, it's a science; to women, it's an art."

"Bullshit," Garrison spat, "and I'll challenge any of you

hussies to a personal duel. Bet I'll shut you up then."

The women all laughed.

All around the office were containers of bottled water, and Pearl grabbed the largest bottle she could find and twisted the cap slowly. "To our mission," she shouted before turning the water up and chugging down as much as she could without stopping.

Garrison and the others cheered her on, urging her to down the rest of the water in one big gulp.

"Go! Go! Go!" they chanted as Pearl took a deep breath and raised the bottle to her lips. Everyone clapped and whooped loudly when she slammed the empty, plastic bottle to the floor in triumph. Pearl pulled up her sleeve and made a muscle.

"Drink up, everyone," Garrison groaned in a wounded voice. "I'll be cheering from the sidelines."

Pearl walked over to kiss Garrison on the cheek. "Don't be such a baby. Your chance to perform will come soon." Facing the women in the room. "Drink up, comrades. It's time to go."

"Let's do this," Leah growled passionately.

"Go, girls, go!" Garrison chanted in animated glee. "Go. Go. Go. But don't get wet!"

Looking well-fed and rested, Ennis begged V-Man to ride to the Courthouse so they could watch the WAM protest. Susie Q, a blonde newslady had leaked the info to V-Man, who, in turn, had put Ennis down, and now Ennis felt compelled to see what Pearl was up too.

Privately, it bugged Ennis that he couldn't figure out what WAM was going to do, but he half-expected it to be dramatic. That was pretty much a safe bet. But what?

He also had other, more personal, questions such as why Pearl had, all of a sudden, made herself unavailable. He recounted her usual line of bullshit about being busy, but he found it difficult to believe that shit. In fact, she should have had a lot more time on her hands since she hadn't showed up for church, missing the last pair of Sundays. He knew because he had been there.

"What do you think?"

"Shit, how I know," V-Man shot back. "You the one all up

in love. Man, what kind of woman you got? Bitch stay in something."

Ennis grunted. "Ho is a trip, ain't she? I just hope she ain't too far gone with this male-bashing shit because I might have to kidnap her and find me a guru to de-program her ass."

"Cancel that, homeboy. Any sista that don't dig brothas is too far gone for counseling of any sort by anybody. As much as hoes be fixated on dick size, niggas got lucky 'cause we be holding, so women of all races naturally into us. Plus, we lay some good pipe." V-Man pondered what he had just said. "That's good money I just called, right, and the more I think about it, I'm fucked up by sistas who get with this feminist, white woman shit. I personally don't appreciate the idea of a sista who strays away from the original plan."

"Which the fuck is?"

"To treat a nigga's dick real good."

It was mid-morning when Ennis and V-Man arrived adjacent to the Courthouse, and no sooner had Ennis spotted that the place where they were parked was not a good one to observe whatever mayhem WAM was going to participate in, he nudged his friend. "Damn, nigga, this ain't no fucking stakeout, drive around to the front where we can see."

Driving around, V-Man whistled shrilly. "Look at all the cops out here. Them WAM hoes going to jail they do so much as spit on the sidewalk."

Ennis turned to look out of the window at the police who were out in full force. "Oh, shit," he muttered sadly.

V-Man gazed at Ennis woefully, "Man, forget that sista. She's a trouble-maker."

After uttering a prayer, Ennis slouched down in his seat when he saw Pearl and her fellow WAM'ers marching down the street. They were all dressed in battle fatigues, and when they reached the position where the first cordon of police were, they zig-zagged in line, south of the officers. Ennis watched as Pearl, in precise military fashion, gathered her troops in a tight circle and then did nothing.

"They well-rehearsed," V-Man confessed, "but all that

fucking goose-stepping for this. I've seen more excitement in the sandbox at the day care----"

"Shut up, nigga," Ennis snapped. "I don't need no commentary. Plus, they on the move again. I wonder what's up now?"

Pearl and the others instantly dissolved their little circle like a bunch of defensive linemen emerging from a huddle on the ten yard line. Ennis' eyes bugged out. Whatever they did, it would be virtually impossible for them to escape as another squad of cops had moved into an intercept position at a grid location where WAM was now sandwiched between a sea of blue.

"She sho' as hell didn't go to West Point," V–Man cracked, seeing how easily WAM had been out-maneuvered. "Hope your girl got a B Plan."

By now WAM had spread themselves out in a long string, perfectly spaced. Pearl was giving orders and the women, ramrod straight, went through a few harmless choreographed dance moves.

"Bitches synchronized."

"Be quiet, V-Man, damn. Let's see what's up."

Across from the Courthouse, a myriad or reporters and newspeople stood, held back by the police, but a camera crew was busy filming everything.

Abruptly, the choreography ceased, and once more the women became ramrod stiff, and after a brief pause of silence, Pearl barked a command and without the slightest hesitation, all the WAM'ers spun around, dropped their pants and pissed on the Courthouse lawn.

"Goddamn!" V-Man blurted excitedly. "Did you the fuck see that!"

Chapter 12

After LaNisa and Garrison had left the apartment, the night fell apart piece by piece until the entire night was corrupted by the tension.

"I'm serious, Pearl. If I didn't know any goddamn better, I would think that you are trying to take over WAM. And don't sit here, rolling your eyes like you don't know what I'm talking about."

"You're tripping, Angie."

"I put you in a key role and now you trying to steal the motherfucking presidency right out from under me. Is that the thanks I get or do I have to remind you on a day to day basis what your position is? Anyway, dear, in the normal course---"

"You don't have to tell me shit."

"Evidently, I do since it's obvious that you don't seem to remember that I am WAM."

"Well, maybe it's time that somebody ran against your ass."

"You don't intimidate me, Pearl."

"Maybe WAM would be a lot better off if you stepped down. You need to consider that. You could still lick my pussy when I wanted you too."

"Fuck you, bitch. I don't have to deal with your shit, and in case you haven't seen it in the mirror lately, ain't no gold trim around your pussy, and you sure as hell don't skeet platinum."

Pearl stood. "Maybe you would feel better if you slept by

your damn self tonight."

"Whatever, bitch, I'll gladly take the couch."

"No, no, Miss WAM, you keep the bed. In fact, the whole damn apartment is yours tonight. I'm going out."

Angie laughed harshly. "Yeah, right, ho. You're too afraid of the dark too be out there alone so just who do you think you're fooling?"

Pearl whipped her cell phone out of her purse. "Who said I was going to be alone?" She punched out ten digits while Angie fumed. Getting a response on the other end, Pearl smiled sadistically before spinning around, turning her back to Angie. "Hello, Ennis. Come pick me up."

Pearl was having a good time. She was on top of her Scrabble game, and after losing the first game had won the last two, but it was getting late, and both she and Ennis could sense the subtle shift in the atmosphere. The all-pervasive sensuality of the climate left little to the imagination, and it was as if she could already feel the comfort of Wamsutta sheets against her naked skin.

Feeling naughty, Pearl grabbed the pencil and ripped off a piece from the paper where they had kept the score. She quickly scribbled a single line. She folded the paper into a neat, tiny square. "You got mail!" she giggled as she pushed the note across the table with the tip of the pencil.

Ennis unfolded the sliver of paper and though the handwritten script was small, it was as bold as a full-page, color announcement in the USA Today. Ennis read it once more. "CAN YOU FUCK GOOD?!"

When Ennis tried to speak, Pearl waved him quiet. "Write me back." She handed him the pencil. "And don't lie."

"WHY, YOU GIVING UP THE PUSSY!?"
"ONLY IF YOUR DICK IS WORTHY!"
"WANT TO SEE IT, FEEL IT…TASTE IT?!"
"YES, YES…AND HELL YES!"

Ennis balled her note up, and then dramatically tossed the wad of paper into his mouth, chewing it as it were the most delightful food he'd ever tasted. "That was sooo delicious," he said, politely wiping his mouth with a silk handkerchief.

"But I got something that tastes even better, but it is in my secret garden."

Ennis slowly stood, gazing intently into Pearl's brown eyes. "Then I humbly beg your permission to get started on this dark voyage to this secret garden of yours. Maybe then, I'll see the light."

Pearl reached for Ennis. "Indulge yourself in me."

When Ennis kissed Pearl, she responded with deep animal moans. She clung to him passionately, smearing her tongue all across the insides of his mouth, but with room for more adventure, she grabbed both his hands and placed them on her titties. "Get acquainted with your new playmates," she demanded.

Peeling back her dress, the garment slid noiselessly to the floor in a silken heap, and since she had worn no bra, Ennis marveled at his first sight of Pearl's beautiful breasts. He kneaded them like they were play-dough, using his fingers to explore the compact mound of wonderfully sculpted flesh. Soon, however, he we was ready for the taste test. He delicately sunk his teeth into one.

Pearl broke out in a cold sweat.

Nibbling around the ribbed edges of Pearl's nipples hardened them until they were like pieces of chocolate rock candy. Ennis licked feverishly, allowing his tongue to slink around the brown halo surrounding the nipples before slurping on as much of her titty as he could fit into his mouth.

"Thrill me, baby," Pearl cooed. "Give me a thousand thrills."

Ennis put Pearl's hand on his hard dick. "Thrill number One," he said.

Touching dick for the very first time in her life, Pearl squealed, squeezed, skeeted. "Goodness, gracious!" she screamed thankfully. Fumbling with Ennis' zipper, Pearl felt like a slut, but the sexual delirium was tantalizingly delicious. Ennis stopped her.

"Let me take it out, Pearl begged. "It feels so…goddamn big!"

"Not yet. Play with him in his cage."

Pearl pouted. "Okay, but when do I get to meet him in the flesh?"

"In a minute, but pretty much all you need to know right now about him is that he won't hurt you."

When Ennis' dick throbbed through his pants, Pearl jerked her hand away. "Oh my God!" she panted, "it feels alive."

"Let's go to the bedroom."

"No, right here. Do it too me on the carpet." Pearl bit down on her bottom lip in pleasure as Ennis stuck a finger under the leg of her panties, and then into het soaking wet pussy. "Oooh, that's feels so good. Fuck me, Ennis. Stop me from being a virgin."

Ennis was butt-naked in a flash.

Lying on the floor, Pearl's whole body pulsated, and when she stripped off her panties, rolling them down her quivering legs like a bright, colorful rubber band, she playfully dangled the sheer fabric on her toes for a brief second before flipping them into the air over her head. They landed against the wall.

The room felt sexually radioactive.

"Taste me, Ennis. Fill your mouth up with me."

Ennis gently parted Pearl's pussy lips, inhaling her intoxicating aroma. He kissed her clitoris. "Ah,"he groaned. "Ambrosia, the fruit of the gods."

"Savor my nectar, Ennis." Pearl stuffed Ennis' head deeper between her legs. "Drink me up."

Other women, Ennis knew, could brag about having a phatter pussy, a juicier pussy, or one that snapped, crackled, or popped, but not a single one of those bitches possessed pussy like Pearl. It was of unmatched quality; a pristine flower glistening wet with its own dew, surrounded by possibly the most beautiful fuzzy hair in the history of the female anatomy.

Pearl's marvelous pussy was a moist slit that extended down the vee off the coast of her thick, dark thighs. Keeping his eyes on the pussy, Ennis used his thumbs to pry loose the lips open so he could study what was inside. Feeling the satiny softness, he lifted his eyes towards the heavens in prayerful rejoice for he had indeed stumbled upon an undiscovered paradise of the flesh.

Ennis flicked his tongue across Pearl's gold medal clit, and she wrestled with his ears, using them as though they were a set of training wheels attached to his head. She wanted to guide him.

"Welcome to my most treasured place," she purred, rotating her ass, mashing her pussy into his tongue. "Oh, shit! Make me cum on your face!"

When Ennis coaxed the first orgasm out of Pearl, it caused her to forcefully expel all the air from her lungs so that she was left gasping and panting for oxygen.

Ennis grinned. "My little contribution to your continued contentment and satisfaction."

"You just wait until I get your dick in my mouth." Pearl spoke between gasps. "I'm gonna make you beg me to stop."

"But you're a rookie, ain't never had a dick between your lips before, so how you gonna know how to make me surrender?"

"Beginner's luck, dammit. Now, let me meet my new best friend. Oowee!" Pearl exclaimed as she reached between Ennis thighs. "My first dick!" Pearl ran her trembling fingers up and down the thick meat, but just as she gently rubbed the head of Ennis' dick, her phone rang.

"Don't answer it, Pearl, Please."

Pearl thought it over, still enjoying the weight of the dick in her hand. The phone rang again. Pearl sighed.

"Please, baby, it can wait."

"It's my Ring-Master, Ennis. It's only used for emergencies. I'm sorry, this could be important."

Groaning pitifully, Ennis rolled over, away from Pearl. Already sensing that the night was over, he plodded off to the bathroom where he cursed his rotten luck.

When he came out, Pearl was sitting on the side of the bed, fixing her hair. "Come here, Ennis." Like an obedient puppy, Ennis trudged over. Pearl gripped his hand and pulled him between her legs. She stuck out her tongue, and licked the limp dick up and down until it stiffened. She kissed the head. "Gotta go. Something has come up. Angie is on her way to get me."

Pearl was not altogether surprised that Angie would contact

her while she was with Ennis.

When Angie drove up, she blew her horn and watched in anger as Ennis and Peal emerged from the house only to stand on the porch like a pair of love-struck teenagers. When they started to kiss, Angie blasted the horn again, but Pearl and Ennis didn't break their embrace.

Enraged, Angie jumped out of her car and ran up on the porch. She barged in between the pair. "Let's go, Pearl."

Ennis' body stiffened, being half-motivated to slap the shit out of Angie, but for the sake of Pearl, dismissed the notion. "Call me later," he said dejectedly.

Pearl nodded.

Seeing Ennis still standing there, Angie turned. "You don't have to watch us . We can make it to the car just fine so why don't you take your ass back inside and take a cold shower."

Pearl nudged Angie. "Be nice, sista."

"Do you need a cold shower as well." Angie sniffed Pearl. "Or a hot one to wash away the scent of fucking?"

"Let's go," Pearl huffed wearily.

Once in the car, Angie almost calmed down. "Are you still a virgin?"

"Bitch!" Pearl hissed, "pay attention to your driving and stop worrying about my pussy."

"Well, can we do something later on tonight?"

"No, not tonight."

"When, then?"

Pearl exhaled. "Who knows. Perhaps never. Who am I too say?"

"And that's it?"

"For now, yes."

Angie thought about crashing the car into a tree.

Chapter 14

Pearl giggled like a school-girl. This was the shit! Here she was, a former Miss-Goody-Two-Shoes, enjoying the best of both worlds sexually. Her virginity had vanished into thin air---thanks to Ennis---and now that she had proved her sexual integrity was no more or no less sacred than the average ho in the hood, she knew that it would only be a matter of time before she was willing to expand her sexual boundaries. She hoped Ennis didn't think he had a monopoly on her pussy. Hell, the nigga was only a test.

Again, Pearl had failed badly in her attempt to roll the perfect blunt, but since she was smoking alone, what did it matter? The weed was good, and the wine was chilled.

"Girl, you getting high already?" Angie emerged out of the bedroom, rubbing sleep from her eyes. She peeked at her watch. "I remember the time, not too long ago, when your ass would be throwing a hissy fit if you weren't already out of the door for church."

"Well, those damn days are dead and gone," Pearl said annoyingly, "and of all the people in the world, you should be the last one to bring up my past. Simple reason being that if I were the same bitch from way back when, we wouldn't be licking each other's pussies."

Angie took the blunt from Pearl. "And you wouldn't be smoking up all my reefer."

"Shit good. Be sure to buy some more."

"What you trying to do…catch up with Snoop Dogg?"

That made Pearl laughed. "Ain't I something? Looking like Brandy. Smoking weed like Snoop, and licking pussy like----who?"

"Don't even go there, girl. I'm tired of those tired-assed rumors about who is sucking pussy in the hip-hop world. At least, they have backed up off Missy Elliot, and Trina."

"Gimme that back, bitch." Pearl reached for the blunt. "You want to babysit, go to the day care. Good weed, you don't baby-sit. You puff, puff…pass."

"Don't get too fucking fucked up. You got to speak tonight," Angie reminded Pearl, "and you want to be on top of your game, baby." Angie shrugged. "I suggest that you do something to relax."

After the weed was gone, Angie retreated back into the bedroom to finish 'Coochie' the latest book by her favorite author, Gibran Tariq.

Pearl, on the other hand, wanted something more physical.

"Take it out," Pearl moaned loudly. "Stop."

"Pussy too good to stop, so throw it back and shut up."

"But I'm gonna be late. Stop, Ennis, baby. Take it out."

"Not until the cops come knocking. Now, ain't the dick good?"

"Hell, yeah, it's good, b-but….I….stop."

Ignoring the half-earnest plea, Ennis pushed even more dick into Pearl, fucking faster.

"Oooh, fuck me, Ennis. Fuck me. Don't….Boy, stop."

Now that Pearl's pussy walls had been softened up, and were slick with her vaginal juices, Ennis sexually ridiculed her request that he pull out. Instead, he slammed the rest of his dick in.

"Oh shit, Ennis!" Pearl's eyes automatically closed shut as she humped and rotated her ass fiercely against the throbbing, sensual attack of the deeply penetrating dick, now embedded inside her pussy like a thick, steel shaft. As Ennis powered-drove his dick, using a straight up and down motion, Pearl countered and took advantage of his thrusts by making her pussy pop like a whip.

"Damn, baby, the dick is good." She purred, "but hurry up and finish 'cause I gotta go."

"You want me to stop?"

"No!" Pearl yelled. "Just shoot off. I need you to wet me." Pearl bucked wildly. "Cum for Mama."

And not surprisingly, Ennis did.

After Pearl rushed from the shower and back into the bedroom, she scowled at Ennis, who still laid across the bed naked, watching ESPN.

"That was so damn selfish of you," Pearl snapped. "Just like a man, though. Don't give a fuck about nobody but himself."

Ennis hit the mute button, rolled over. "Did I hear you right?"

"Don't give me that shit. You know you was wrong as hell for fucking me like that when you knew I had somewhere to go." Pearl dressed in front of the vanity, looking through the mirror at Ennis. "I told your ass to stop."

"And I asked you if you wanted me too. You said no."

Pearl spun around. "And just what the fuck was I supposed to say with both of us about to cum?"

"I can't help it 'cause the dick good."

"We shouldn't have never started. You fucked me like that on purpose, nigga."

Ennis turned up the volume on the television. "You the first and only female in the world who complain about a good fucking. I bet if it was LaNisa, she'd be on the phone, telling Channel Nine News about it. And you got the nerve to cop a 'tude."

Pearl tuned back to the mirror to fix her hair. "But you knew I had something else to do."

"Look, the way I see it is like this. If you didn't want the dick, then you didn't have to throw the pussy back, and being that you did you couldn't have been that concerned about getting in the wind, so you need to quit it. You wanted to skeet as bad as I did or else you have ignored the dick."

"Like you made a big attempt……Shit, Ennis, you know good and damn well you got me strung out on the dick, and baby you know I ain't about to argue about getting a nut, but still your stanking ass could've made me wait."

Ennis sat up in bed. "I didn't want you fiending."

"You don't want me to go, do you?"

"No," Ennis confessed.

"Thanks, Mr. Good Dick, that's sweet. You can come and sit in the front row."

"And make myself a contender for all the bullshit you getting ready to unleash. It would probably be best if I laid in the cut, and watched your back on the DL."

Pearl kissed Ennis on the forehead. "You probably all spooked up for nothing. People talk about the President, so you know they gonna talk about everybody else."

"But this is a horse of a different color, Pearl." Ennis slipped on a pair of jeans. "Once you personally utter your first cry against the male animal, have no delusions. It will be open season on WAM. Ever since that lil golden shower incident, WAM has been everyone's darling. You got your face in the paper, been on the news, and you and Angie have become the toast of the town, but this is WAM's first ever open-to-the public meeting, and if you go through with that battle call speech of yours, you'll see just how men will rally, recruit, and seek revenge." Ennis pulled a fresh, white tee shirt over his head. "That last protest WAM did when you picketed outside of Burger King over their cruel mistreatment of animals looked so gorgeous on the late night news that some cross-town liberals ran out and bought you a brand new headquarters, stocked your treasury, and patted you on the head like a new pet, but ain't a damn thing gonna be gorgeous---"

"I gotta go, honey. Bye."

Alone, inside of WAM's new, spacious office, Pearl casually noted the time. It wouldn't be long now. Nodding her head at that realization, she began to awkwardly pace the floor. She was a remarkably polished speaker who had been well-groomed both intellectual and politically by Angie, but despite her polish, Pearl knew that what she said out there in a few minutes would make or break WAM, so she had every reason to be nervous. Maybe it would be better if she went out there, and whistled Dixie or sang a song or did a tap dance or----.

The knock frightened Pearl, and she jumped. "Yes," she croaked.

"Five minutes, General Pearl, and by the way, the damn place is packed."

"Thanks, Rebecca," Pearl warbled weakly as her knees buckled, forcing her to sit down. "What have I gotten myself into?" she groaned to herself. She felt the need to vomit.

But a minute or so later, the lights dimmed and the General stepped onstage. It was Showtime.

For a full five minutes, Pearl spoke continuously in a placid tone, filling the crowded auditorium with a melodic outline of WAM's aims and goals. Hush and attentive, the guests hung on to every syllable of her clearly enunciated speech, waiting patiently on what new revelation the next word would bring.

Leah had never experienced anything like this before. The General had the audience spellbound, eating out of her hand. She closed her eyes, imagining this was the very first time she had heard Pearl speak of WAM's lofty agenda and then on cue, she too was under the wonderful enchantment as were all the others.

Rebecca was less mesmerized because too her the General had started off a lot slower than she had expected, but at least tonight the cat would get out of the bag, and that pleased the hell out of her. She wanted the shit to hit the fan one way or the other because then WAM could openly pick fights with the male devil. She quietly shook her fist at the stage. "Come on, bitch," she whispered under her breath. "Curse men and let the chips falls where they may." When Pearl continued her tired-assed peace monologue, Rebecca got angry. "Say it, bitch," she grumbled. "Say it, dammit!"

Onstage, Pearl bided her time, plotting point and counterpoint in her mind as a foreboding sense of doom pressed in upon her. She tried to ignore it, but couldn't so she spoke on as though all was well. She was no fool. She was a make-believe General who was only minutes away from calling forth an enemy commonly recognized as the scourge of the earth, but the die had been cast, and there was little or no need to bitch about it now. It was now much too late for regrets because already, she had gone too far.

Ennis sat emotionlessly in his chair, and stared expressionlessly at the stage, hoping Pearl would stop while she was ahead because the more she talked, the more he felt obligated to rush the stage, clamp his hand over her pretty mouth, press her luscious lips closed, and shut her up. That was a bad idea, he knew, but instantly discovered one even better.

"Follow me." He reached over and poked V-Man.

"Huh?"

"Come on."

"What up? Wait, man, shit. I wanna hear this. Your girl can rap."

"Let's roll, dammit."

"But, damn, dawg, these your peeps."

"Just follow me. I'll explain later."

V-Man stood. "This better be good, brer. Drag me down here, and now you ready to go. Shit, nigga."

Outside the building, Ennis dashed around to the back, and stood in the dark until V-Man caught up. Ennis took a long, deep breath and began to search the exterior wall. "Got any matches or a cigarette lighter?"

V-Man was puzzled. "What the fuck for? What you fixing to do, nigga, break into the joint?
Fool, the damn front door wide open."

"Shut up, V-Man, and give me your lighter."

"Do you even know what you're doing?"

Using the lighter for illumination, Ennis searched the wall of the building. "I found it."

"Found what, your good sense?"

"Naw, nigga-nig," Ennis bragged in triumph, "the electrical box." Ennis paused. "Now, how do you shut down the power? Which switch do you pull?"

"Great goddamn day in the morning," V-Man cracked, "a dumb-assed crook. Move out the way, scrub, and let me take a look."

Onstage, Pearl decided it would be a great mistake not to drop the bomb now. The moment was perfect, and the timing couldn't get any better. She waited another second, then glared mutely at her notes before tucking them away.

"Essentially," she began, "this is not about BK broilers or any other animals down on McDonald's farm. It is about men and I say that men are------"

At that moment, all the power in the building went out. Suddenly.

"Dammit," Rebecca cursed.

"Touchdown!" Ennis shouted.

Pearl pouted in the dark. Her microphone was dead so no one could hear shit she said.

"You what?!"

It was early the next morning as Ennis and Pearl lay between the covers.

"You did what?!" Pearl sat up in bed.

"Saved your ass, that's what."

"Nigga, how could you?" Pearl screamed, pounding the pillow near Ennis' head. "You fucked shit up for WAM. That was supposed to be my signature moment, and you cut the damn power off!" Pearl sprung from the bed, "I'm so mad, I could slap the shit out of you. You betrayed me, nigga."

"Bitch," Ennis spat, sitting up, "you running 'round, wanting to be a big, bad WAM star, but don't none of you know what you getting ready to get your dumb asses into. You think them goddamn crackers that run shit in this country give a fuck about y'all phat asses and big titties. Hell naw. You fuck with them and it's on. Don't rock the boat, baby. That's all I'm saying."

"You a coward, Ennis." Pearl dashed to the closet, and hastily began to remove her clothes.

"What the fuck you supposed to be doing now?"

"I'm leaving, nigga. What it look like? You got a big dick, but you got a tiny heart."

"Pearl, look…wait. Let's talk."

"We'll talk when you stop being a zero." Pearl zipped her

travel bag, and slung it over her shoulder. "Are you sure you not on the Down-Low?"

Ennis jumped up, angry, started towards Pearl, stopped. "Get out, bitch, before I break your motherfucking neck."

Pearl didn't flinch. "Struck a nerve, huh?"

"Don't leave nothing, Pearl," Ennis said firmly, "because the moment you walk your silly ass out the front door, you won't be welcome in this house again."

"So long, sucka."

"Well, well, well," Angie hissed, "look what the cat just dragged in."

"This is not a good time, Angie, so don't start."

"Start what? I'm just welcoming your selfish ass back into your own apartment." Angie cut the volume down on the TV. "Did you miss me or did you finally get sick and tired of a nigga's dick tearing your lil' used-to-be-virgin pussy out the box. Oh yeah, nice speech, at least the audible part."

"Ennis----"

"Damn, Ennis, bitch. Go get in the shower and wash your ass, then come get in bed. Nigga better not be done harmed the kitty-cat." Angie eyed Pearl coldly. "When you ever gonna learn?"

Pearl inhaled, then let the air out slowly. "Maybe you can teach me when I get out of the shower."

Chapter 15

LaNisa had a serious look on her face. "Does it look like I'm trying to be funny?"

Pearl admitted that she didn't. "But-----"

"But, nothing, bitch. I'm right and you know it, and I'll suck any nigga's dick or lick any bitch's pussy that can prove me wrong."

"You'll lick a kitty?" Pearl teased.

"Won't have to," LaNisa shuddered, 'cause I'm correct. Now is the time for you to sex a baller. Your Brandy-looking ass play the field right and you'll come up real proper." LaNisa giggled. "Use your ATF---"

"ATF?"

"Yeah, ho, ATF. Ass. Titties. Face." LaNisa put her hands on her hips. "Trust me, don't nothing in the world send a nigga to the ATM quicker than ATF."

"Damn, LaNisa, I don't know."

"Be a diva, Pearl, and stop tripping. Listen to me. Once a motherfucka get injected with the right bitch's ATF, and get it into his sexual bloodstream, he'll be worse than a junkie strung out on dope. Motherfucka will bankrupt a ATM to feed his ATF habit." LaNisa shrugged. "Girl, you better charge it to the coochie, and build your empire on Pussy Power. You fucking and sucking, but you still got that church girl mentality. Unveil your Superfreak; release your inner ho."

"That's not how Angie sees it."

"And that is why Angie is just as fucked up as you are. Sometimes, Pearl, I don't know who fucked you up the most, the church or WAM. I just don't know. Sometimes, it seems like your silly ass done jumped out of the frying pan right into the goddamn fire." LaNisa stepped closer to Pearl. "This question is for all the money, so pay attention. Are you willing to fuck to get what you want?"

"Yes," Pearl responded instantly. "I'm ready."

"Then, let's go."

The 20/20 Club was reputed to be half the spot that Jay-Z's 40/40 club in New York was but with twice the attitude. The club's owner, Dirt Harris, had pulled all the tricks in the books to make sure his club was the only club that stayed open after 2 am and still sold alcohol.

Outside the parking valet openly criticized any driver who pulled up to the VIP parking section and wasn't pushing an imported whip with a price tag over six figures. Clearly, only the elite had reserved parking space at the 20/20, and it was pretty much the same inside. In essence, the joint was only for those with a special interest in being seen, and in spending lots of cash.

As soon as LaNisa and Pearl stepped foot inside the club, the one thing that became instantly apparent to Pearl was that there were two worlds. There was the world inside the 20/20, and the lesser one outside it. Pearl was awed. So all people were not created equal.

Everywhere that Pearl looked, there was an explosion of color; men and women decked out in all the latest shit from Paris and Milan that ordinary playas were not yet aware of. These high-end fashions would trickle down to the rest of the general population in another year or so at which time they would be hand-me-downs to the elite patrons of the 20/20.

Everyone at the 20/20 had a rags-to-riches story to tell about how they had pulled themselves up out of the ghetto with no other credentials than a Class A hustle game. Some had done a good job of mastering the ho game. Others the dope game. Some, the stick-up game. But all had come up. Big-time.

Moving through the club, Pearl knew her presence had struck a chord with the crowd.

"There's Brandy!"

"Is that her? Look, Brandy!"

"Wow, look how phat she done got!"

"Maybe she gonna sang!"

Ignoring everyone as LaNisa had informed her, only seemed to make Pearl's personality more potent. All at once she was the night's prized bitch, and all throughout her stroll to the bar where she would have a quick drink before heading to the VIP section as guests of Hollywood Evans, she could feel the electricity of the eyes upon her. She felt like a champion filly.

From his customized booth, Hollywood summoned one of his henchmen. "What's all the commotion about?"

"Your guest has arrived, brotha."

"Huh?" Hollywood was taken aback. "And she has caused that much of an uproar?"

"Maybe if the club had known you were expecting Brandy---"

"Moesha....That Brandy?"

The henchman winked. "Could fool everybody except me. I came up watching Moesha, and had a mad crush on Brandy, so I know the sista at the bar ain't her."

"Why you say that, dawg?"

"Two words, Hollywood. Titties and ass."

Hollywood took a sip of his drink. "What we talking, more or less?"

"More. A lot more."

"LaNisa didn't tell me all that, but I like surprises." Chuckling contently, Hollywood relaxed. "Go, escort my guests up here." Four men scrambled to carry out the command.

Upstairs, from the privacy of his VIP Elite suite, Hollywood watched in silent amusement as his bodyguards bullied their way to the bar. He smiled warmly as they politely greeted LaNisa, but he laughed deeply when Maximum, his super-sized friend, easily hoisted Pearl onto his massive shoulders and walked off with her. Typical Maximum, Hollywood mused. Nigga had his own way of doing shit. He was going to deliver the bitch in style.

Downstairs, the crowd cheered wildly. All the pimps, playas, dope-boys, and stick-up kids who knew Max was not about to fuck with him. They also knew who Max worked for, and that made it even more improbable that anyone would get in the way.

Pearl, meanwhile was game, a real trooper. She merrily wrapped her long legs around Max's neck and held onto his shiny, bald head like it was a wood grain steering wheel. She drove Max around the wrap-around bar to the mad delight of the crowd who stomped and clapped as they celebrated Hollywood's good fortune. Pearl was a number 1 stunna!

Hollywood's dick was hard already.

Pearl knew her stuff!

Hollywood's first nut had been flamboyant, an out-of-control explosion that had almost dissolved his testicles. His nut sack felt melted inside and his cum had turned so thick, it was almost as if he was shooting chocolate Milk Duds out of his dick head. The second one was even more spectacular, much more elaborate. Hollywood was pleased.

Pearl knew her stuff!

No sooner had she learned that she wouldn't self-destruct by licking a motherfucka's ass, Pearl used her tongue to navigate her way around Hollywood's sloppy butt-hole.

Eventually abandoning this sexual 'hell-hole', she went back to work on the dick, flossing it with her gloss-coated saliva. Head deep between Hollywood's thighs, Pearl served him an unpredictable medley of licking, sucking tongue-teasers until his nasal grunts and groans escalated into a mad-dog howling that sounded like Hollywood was getting a lobotomy through his dick. Pearl sucked on the dick with so much pressure that Hollywood thought she was going to pull his brains out via his pee-hole.

Pearl knew her shit!

In the days---and nights---following her introduction to Hollywood, Pearl was hardly shy about using her sexual prowess to wrap Hollywood around her little finger. He had already spent thousands of dollars on her, but Pearl strongly favored something more: cocaine. She could scarcely believe how fucking good the powder made her feel. There was little doubt that cocaine had breathed new life into her decadence, and since Hollywood had kilos of the shit, she snorted to her heart's content.

LaNisa had jokingly nicknamed Pearl 'Pawn Shop' because LaNisa said that Pearl had pawned all her dreams for cocaine, but Pearl didn't give a damn about what LaNisa thought. Or Angie. Or Ennis.

In between her fanciful cocaine binges, Pearl and Hollywood took long walks together, held hands at out-of-the-way coffee houses, and kissed passionately under the stars.

Hollywood was swept away by Pearl, and one night while they were alone in the bedroom, staring into each other's eyes, Hollywood broke down and cried like a baby.

"What's wrong, Boo?" Pearl asked, reaching out to pull the sobbing man into her arm. "What's going on?"

"Th-this is too much for me, but it's so wonderful." Hollywood's body shook. "This is all so new to me and I-I don't want it to ever end." Hollywood clung to Pearl like a long lost child. "Please, tell me, my beloved woman, that you can and will make this last forever and always."

"I can," Pearl whispered.

"You promise?"

"I promise. I promise with all my heart."

Hollywood was happy. "Thanks, Pearl. Now, will you marry me?"

Damn, Pearl thought to herself. Maybe she had carried the game a lil' too far, and had overplayed her hand because she had just sexed a baller right out of his goddamn mind. And this was merely the beginning. She now had to carefully plan her exit from this nigga, and in the process take as many keys of cocaine as she could. The nigga had just become a liability.

Next!

When Angie stepped aside, Ennis saw that as an invitation

to come in. He readily sensed that Angie was still in her disgruntled 'husband' mode, and was in the mood to get some problems off her chest. Yet Ennis distrusted her. A lot.

"I thought you and Pearl had the perfect relationship." Ennis sat on the sofa.

"Hmmph, it was a fantasy relationship," Angie sat on the other end of the sofa in the lotus position with her legs folded under her. She had on a pair of cotton shorts, and when she noticed Ennis looking at her legs, she rubbed them self-consciously. "I imagine it's both our faults. We spoiled Pearl, gave her the best of both worlds, and she turns around and gives us her phat ass to kiss."

"And it is phat," Ennis laughed.

"But so was the pussy." Angie didn't smile.

"Naw, I say the pussy was more juicy than phat."

Angie smiled. "So, what is this, the episode where two scorned lovers compare notes?"

"Not without a drink of that Alize Bleu I know you like to drink."

Angie rolled her eyes at Ennis. "Oh no, y'all didn't. I know y'all didn't lay around talking about me behind my back. That's cold. You fucking my bitch and while you putting dick in her, she giving you the 4-1-1- on me." Angie leaned close. "What the bitch say?"

"My lips are sealed," Ennis teased. "Oh, by the way, did you ever get your navel pierced?"

"She didn't?!"

"Do I get that drink?"

Angie jumped up to get the glasses. "Oh yeah," she said, speaking over her shoulder. "Your pussy-sucking wasn't as good as mine. Just so you'd know."

"Ah man," Ennis retorted, "she just put a brotha's biz-ness all out in the streets."

"And there's more," Angie giggled.

What Ennis found most interesting was that for once all the ugliness and hatred between him and Angie was gone. It was as if they now saw beyond each other's love for Pearl, and suddenly realized they had some deeper problems other than a fixation to make the same individual happy. Indirectly, it already seemed liked they could become good friends.

"The only reason I'm gonna share bedroom secrets, and I do consider pillow talk privileged info, is because if me and you ever competed for the same woman again, you'll know that you don't stand much of a chance." Angie handed Ennis his drink and sat back down, sipping hers. "Hopefully, then, you'll be smart enough to throw in the towel."

"And just let you have the pussy all to yourself?"

"Yes, that is correct. Plus, what happened to male chivalry?"

"Don't count when it comes to pussy."

Angie set her drink down. "So, what you're saying is that all in love is fair?"

"My sentiments exactly."

"You smoke weed?"

"As if you didn't know."

Angie winked. "Just wanted to see if your ass was going to lie." Angie paused. "Where do I keep my stash at?"

"What?" Ennis laughed. "Think I don't know? Want me to get it?"

"Yeah."

Ennis strolled confidently into the bedroom with Angie close behind. He went directly to where Angie hid her reefer. He removed the plastic bag. "Well, look-a-here at what I just found."

"DAAAMN!" Angie shrieked merrily. "Is there anything you don't know about me?"

Ennis sat on the edge of the unmade bed. "Nope."

Angie sat close, watching him twist up a blunt. "Well, I guess we even 'cause I know shit about you that not even your Mama knows."

"It's like that, huh?"

"I could write a book about you if I wanted to."

A sense of peace and quiet enveloped the cozy space between them as they enjoyed the blunt, and when Ennis blew Angie a shotgun, and their lips touched, she giggled.

"Stop trying to kiss me on the sly with your sneaky ass."

"Girl, if I wanted to taste those lips of yours, I wouldn't sneak and do it. You know what I'd do?"

"No, what?"

"This." Ennis leaned over and planted a soft kiss on Angie's lips. "You can open your eyes now," he laughed.

"Is that how you kissed Pearl?"

Ennis scooted closer to Angie. "For your information, I kissed our girlfriend like this. He French-kissed Angie and after the long, passionate kiss, he fell back on the bed, pretending he had passed out from the pleasure.

Angie straddled him, sitting on his chest. "Pearl must not have told you what I do to people who faint in my bedroom."

Ennis acted as if he was absorbed in deep thought. "Girlfriend ain't say shit about that." He gently pulled up Angie's tee shirt. "Aha, no ring in your belly-button. So you didn't get pierced?"

Angie yanked the top completely off, and tossed it o the floor. She cupped her titties in her hands. "Do you see any nipple rings, my brotha?" She eyed Ennis through half-closed eyes. "Wanna look anywhere else?"

Pointing at Angie's shorts, Ennis hoarsely rasped. "Take 'em off."

"Oh, so you think I got my pussy lips pierced?" Angie rolled over, putting her fingers under the waistband of the shorts. "Is that what you think, my brotha?"

"Won't know until I see what's down there."

Angie dramatically pulled the shorts off. "See!"

Ennis delicately fondled Angie's pussy, receiving great satisfaction from gently fiddling around the puffy, swollen lips.

"Your pussy is gorgeous."

"And guess what? You're the first man to ever see, and the only damn one I ever let play with it. You lucky dog. Now, stop."

"Why?"

"Because I wanna see that big dick of yours which I've heard so much about, see just what it is I've had to compete with."

"You ever seen one before?"

"Of course I have, silly. In movies."

Ennis laughed. "I mean a real one."

"Nooo, but I wanna see yours since I'm familiar with it in a second-hand smoke kind of way."

Unbuckling his belt, Ennis chuckled. "And what kind of way is a second-hand smoke kind of way."

"You know, it's like, shit, I probably almost sucked your dick myself. I wonder how many times it's been when I done kissed Pearl and the bitch just got through licking on your dick, know what I mean?"

"That's second-hand dick-sucking if you ask me."

"Well, if you don't mind, I wanna see the dick I been sucking on second hand."

"Behold!" Ennis whipped his dick out.

"It-it's hard."

"As Chinese arithmetic. Wanna touch it?" Ennis grabbed Angie's small hand. "Pearl was scared at first."

"Whooo!" Angie panted. "It feels like steel. What makes it so hard?"

"These." Ennis kissed each of Angie's breasts. "But especially this. He gently pushed Angie back onto the bed. He put his mouth on her pussy. "Understand now how the process works?"

Angie nodded.

Ennis stripped off his clothes.

"I-I can't let you fuck me, Ennis."

"Why?"

"I just can't, that's why. I won't like it." Angie's voice trembled.

"How you know that when you ain't never been fucked before?"

Angie moved away. "And I don't think I want to know, either. My life is complicated enough as it is, and the last thing I need is some dick drama." Angie closed her eyes and stuck out her tongue, barely grazing the head of Ennis' dick. "Understand?"

"Well," Ennis sighed, "kiss him goodbye."

"Who said anything about goodbye. Tell me that?"

"But----"

"That's the problem with niggas, always thinking wrong." Angie grinned wickedly. "If I let you get the pussy, then you take away what I've been all my life, and I don't want that. I wanna die without a dick ever going in my coochie." Angie touched Ennis' dick. "Light that blunt back up, and listen to what I'm saying. I don't want no dick in my pussy, but it wouldn't necessarily be cheating if you fucked me in the butt." Angie rolled over on her stomach. "Can you handle that?"

Ennis put the blunt down, and kissed Angie on the cheeks of her dimpled ass. "The pleasure would be all mine."

"Be gentle, nigga."

"Let's finish this blunt so you can relax."

"And when you fuck me, fuck me just like you did Pearl."

Ennis suddenly felt blessed.

Chapter 16

Two weeks later

The restaurant, though out of the way, was quite popular and Ennis wondered not so much as to why LaNisa had chosen such an upscale place just to meet—but why she had even wanted to meet with him to begin with.

The conservative lunch crowd was perfectly at ease with the pricey menu and the classically trained pianist who plunked out standard jazz tunes at noon on Wednesday. Technically, it was a BUPPIE joint where all the Black Urban Professionals thought their shit didn't stink. The sistas, in their button-down power suits, all imagined they were Black American Princesses. Ennis grunted. The only BAP he had ever known was Pearl.

Spotting LaNisa at a booth in the back where she sat alone, putting on airs, Ennis instantly detested the jive phoniness of The Lunch Spot, and thought of a thousand reasons for having no reason to ever visit the place again.

"Hello, LaNisa." Ennis politely kissed LaNisa's hand.

"Have a seat, Ennis, and thanks for coming." After Ennis was seated, LaNisa glanced around furtively. "Look at these Negroes," she cracked cold-bloodedly, "droning on about their 401(k) retirement packages."

On a personal level, Ennis felt that LaNisa was just as phony as anyone else in the restaurant, but he remained silent.

"These dizzy dames, smart though they may be, are more exploited than the average street corner ho. Look at that bitch, will you, and what the fuck is that the hussy drinking?" LaNisa was gearing up to launch into a tirade until she noticed the look on Ennis' face. She quickly switched topics. "You seen Pearl lately?"

Ennis indicated that he hadn't.

"Bitch look bad."

"Pearl?"

"Ho thin as a dime."

"You have got to be kidding," Ennis huffed. "A woman just doesn't lose that much titties and ass overnight."

"She will if she on crack."

"Crack!?"

"Bitch smoking like a Navaho chief."

"Damn." All the air went out of Ennis. "You seen her?"

"Yeah, she done lost it. Don't work no more. Quit. All she want to do is hit the pipe."

Ennis recalled what Angie had told him about Pearl having practically abandoned her own apartment to live with some rich nigga. "Where is she staying?"

"Nigga named Hollywood fucking her now. Nigga a big dope boy, gives the ho everything she wants. Bought her a Benz straight off the showroom floor. He's the one that pays all the bills at her apartment; rent, lights, cable. Shit, all Angie gotta do is buy food. Angie gave up her place a long time ago, sold all the shit in it and moved in." LaNisa sighed. "I'm worried to death about Pearl. If she gets any worse, I'll have to start calling her ugly."

Ennis laughed aloud. "Pearl, ugly. Never."

"We gotta do something to save our girl. Wanna hear my plan?"

"You got a plan?"

"Yeah, we kidnap the ho and throw her trifling as in rehab. I can lure her to lunch, and then you and your dawg can snatch her ass and go." When Ennis failed to respond quickly enough, LaNisa quizzed him. "You do still care about her, don't you?"

"She kicked me to the curb, remember?"

"Niggas and bitches break up all the damn time, and then get back together down the road so that ain't no legit excuse. Wanna try again?"

"How 'bout if I told you that I ain't trying to go to jail for kidnapping Pearl or if that don't grab you, how 'bout if I tell you that I ain't wanting to get shot up by no dope dealer over kidnapping her dope-smoking ass. Let Pearl get her own ass out of this shit. Maybe she happy. You ever thought about that?"

"You a damn coward, Ennis. You'll gladly give your dick to a bitch, but you too damn trifling to give her a helping hand when she needs it."

"My bad, LaNisa, but I ain't kidnapping no grown woman who should've known better than to trade her Bible for a crack pipe."

"Thanks so much for coming by, Ennis."

"But what about lunch?"

"Eat dog food, nigga."

"Okay, okay, damn. I'll holla at my boy and see what he thinks, but I want you to understand one thing right now. I ain't doing this for no damn Pearl. I'm doing it for you."

"Oh, you don't say."

Ennis looked LaNisa over lovingly. "And one favor deserves another."

"Well, I'm paying for lunch and this ain't exactly a Jack-In-The-Box."

"Keep your money. I got lunch. I want you in my debt."

"How do you want me to pay?"

"In flesh."

"Oh my goodness, boy. Do you know what you're begging for?"

Ennis nodded.

"Well, we'll just have to see about that. You might not be ready."

"Ha. Ha. That's funny. I know girls talk, so I know Pearl told you how handy I am with the dick."

"She did, but what the fuck she know? You was her first dick so she will always give you props, but to a veteran bitch like me, you gonna have to put in work. Now, shall we order lunch?"

"Only if this conversation can be continued at a more appropriate time and place."

LaNisa batted her eyes, flirting. "Your house or mine?"

The matter was discussed at work over coffee and doughnuts.
"I want you to help me and LaNisa kidnap Pearl."
"That's funny, Ennis. You and LaNisa gonna kidnap Pearl." V-Man sat aside his plastic cup. "Oh, by the way, who got Pearl----the church choir?"
"Shit ain't funny, V-Man. Pearl fucked up bad, in deep with some nigga named Hollywood---"
"Hollywood? I've heard that name. From all the talk around the barbershop, nigga notorious. He got Pearl?"
"Yeah. He the motherfucka that introduced her to cocaine, but evidently she promoted her own damn self to crack-head."
"Wow, that don't sound like Pearl."
"Tell me about it," Ennis lamented. "Bitch changed."
"Like you didn't help change her. Nigga, you should have left that girl in the church where she belonged." V-Man pointed an accusing finger at Ennis. "You opened the door for all the bullshit that she going through right now, so don't act like you so innocent."
Ennis moved away. "You full of shit, nigga."
"You turned that girl on to sin, and she couldn't handle it."
"Before you get up on your high horse, just remember that I stuck my dick in Pearl's mouth, not the crack pipe."
"For a church girl, one was just as bad as the other. Both of 'em brought out the devil in her." V-Man stood. "But because I don't like to see no woman strung out on that shit, I'll help you get Pearl away from that fool Hollywood if you gonna put her in treatment or something."
"That's what me and LaNisa gonna do. Put her ass in rehab. LaNisa say that Pearl look bad. Can you imagine that, V-Man?"
"It's crack she on, Ennis, not Botox. What do you expect? Anyway, how we gonna pull this rabbit out of a hat?"
"LaNisa gonna invite Pearl out to eat. Me and you snatch her ass and get missing."

V-Man took a long, deep breath. "Sounds simple enough. Okay, when will it go down?"

"Let me holla at our girl, LaNisa, and set things up. Then I'll get back at you. Bet?"

V-Man watched Ennis strolled away. He thought for a second. Once they had rescued Pearl, he was going to have to step back from Ennis. Nigga was becoming a nuisance.

"I feel like we on a police stake-out," Ennis crowed, "like we getting ready to take down Scarface." Ennis glanced at V-Man. "Why you so quiet?"

"You can learn a lot just sitting around thinking."

Ennis punched V-Man on the arm playfully. "Your ass sitting there trying to solve the riddle of the universe. That's deep, dawg. Damn, you the man."

From every perspective he could think of, V-Man scorned the idea of allowing Ennis to drag him into any more of these high-risk capers, but he wouldn't bring it up just yet. "What time LaNisa say she was expecting Pearl?"

Ennis glanced at his watch. "Any minute now, so be ready."

V-Man pulled on a pair of black, leather gloves.

"Damn, dawg, you done went all the way gangsta for real. Black gloves and shit." Ennis laughed. "You ain't got no piece, do you?"

"Naw," V-Man intoned flatly, "and I got the gloves so she won't bite me when I cuff my hand over her mouth. You just make sure you sweep her off her feet just as soon as I grab her so we can get in the wind."

"10-4, good buddy, it's almost showtime. Bitch should be coming 'round the mountain in a short short."

V-Man licked his lips nervously. Once this caper was over, he was putting Ennis on a long leash. The nigga really was Ennis the Menace.

Pearl had spent the better part of the morning, bragging to the mirror about how good she looked. and how she would look even better in her sexy, red dress. The weather would be changing soon and this would represent one of her last chances to sport something from her summer wardrobe.

Spinning around, she studied herself. Her ass was coming back a little bit and her titties weren't half bad, so maybe she'd give LaNisa a dose of her own medicine. Bitch talking that nonsense about her and a skeleton being the same size. Pearl admitted that she had dropped a few pounds, but she could always gain them back if she starting drinking some high protein fruit smoothies.

Fully dressed now in nothing less than her sacred diva gear, Pearl put on her lipstick. Fire engine red.

Off she went to lunch.

One hour later.

"Being that I'm so fair-minded, I would be the first to admit that confinement can be a very terrifying experience, but people live through it."

"But my friend, LaNisa, is going to be worried about me. I was supposed to meet her for lunch." Pearl shivered. "She might think something happened to me."

"Something did happen to you, Miss Washington."

"But you said I wasn't under arrest, that I would be able to go after I answered a few questions."

"See there, Agent Moore, she's confused." Ronald Hawthorne, a black FBI agent, addressed the female agent present in the interrogation room. "Evidently, Miss Washington has no idea what I mean when I say something that I don't really mean."

"I call that lying," Pearl sobbed.

Hawthorne patted Pearl's hand. "Let me explain what I meant so there won't be any misunderstanding between us, okay? What I didn't mean is that you could simply answer some questions and then just fly out of here like a bat out of hell."

"That's what you said," Pearl shouted angrily.

"Correct. That is what I said. It just wasn't what I really meant."

Pearl started crying. "What did you mean, then?"

"What I meant and I mean this, is that you can go if you

give me the right answers to my questions."

"The right answers?"

"Yes, Miss Washington, the right answers. We know that you have been living with Hollywood Evans, a man we have been interested in for quite some time. And we need you to assist us with our operation to bring him down."

Pearl cried some more.

"Don't cry, honey," Agent Moore whispered. "Everything will be just fine. It's not you we want, It's your boyfriend."

"I want to go home."

"And since you are a smart woman, you can. Soon." Hawthorne was all business now. "Earlier this morning we arrested your old housemate, Angie."

"Oh my God! For what?"

"Obstruction of justice, for starters. Doesn't sound like a big deal right now, but once we tack on a few other offenses, she will be facing a boatload of time."

Pearl groaned pitifully.

"So if you want to keep your friend out of prison, we can make a deal." Hawthorne gazed unblinkingly at Pearl. "Let's trade. I'll give you Angie if you will give me Hollywood. You do that and all will end well. You can go home---"

"Angie?"

"She can go as well. I give you my word on that."

"Okay," Pearl sobbed, "what do you want to know about Hollywood's operation?"

"You willing to talk?"

Pearl nodded. "And you won't bother me and Angie again."

"No."

"It's a deal," Pearl said.

"Great," Hawthorne gushed. "Now, all you have to do is to tell us everything you know about Hollywood, and then give us the security access code to his home."

"But I don't know the code."

"No problem. You can just open the door for us."

"When?"

"Tonight, once he's asleep."

"Where will you guys be?"

"Outside. We'll show up. You tell us the time."

"Around midnight. We don't usually stay up past one."

"Midnight, it is, then." Hawthorne made notes on a pad. "When Hollywood is sleep, I want you to turn off all the alarms and slip out of the front door. We'll take it from there."

"You're not going to kill him, are you?"

"That, I'm afraid will depend on Hollywood, but you can lessen that risk. Does Hollywood sleep with a gun close by?"

Pearl nodded.

"Take it with you. Without a weapon, chances are good that he'll go peacefully. If we don't have to shoot, we won't. Once you leave, check into a hotel and spend the night there. Anything you want out of the house, take it."

"Honey, get all the money," Agent Moore chimed in. "All the bling."

"Whoa, on second thought, that might not be such a good idea?"

"Why," Agent Moore asked Hawthorne. "Sounds like a plan too me."

"What if she wakes Hollywood up while she's on her prowl for goodies. That could get ugly and if we didn't get in there on time, there's no telling....I just got a better idea." Hawthorne paused. "Just take the gun. Leave everything else. Money, jewelry, whatever. Leave it. What I'll do as soon as daylight hits will be to draw up the paperwork transferring the house and everything in it over to you."

Pearl gasped in total surprise. "Everything?"

"Lock, stock, and barrel. Now, do we have a deal?"

Pearl extended her hand. "We have a deal."

That night Pearl gave up the pussy like a woman possessed, using every trick she knew to make sure she wore Hollywood out. Everything hinged on him sleeping like a baby. Hawthorne had suggested drugging Hollywood, but he rarely, if ever, drank at home. He saved that for the clubs and even then it was primarily for show. Same thing with weed. Cocaine was different, but it had the opposite effect of what she wanted, so she had to rely on pussy power to knock his ass out.

After the sex, they snuggled in bed watching a movie. Pearl had chosen one that was inexcusably bad, hoping that it would bore Hollywood to sleep. Pearl made certain she kept the conversation to a bare minimum since a long, drawn out debate was also at odds with what she wanted.

About a quarter of the way through the boring movie, she dove under the covers to suck Hollywood's dick, knowing that another nut would damn near sexually cripple his ass. Working tirelessly, she was able to coax the limp dick to bone hardness, and running it in and out of her mouth, she applied intense pressure as her head ferociously bobbed up and down. At the same time, she used her fingers to massage his balls so within a minute, the deed was done.

Hollywood got a nut.

Minutes later when she heard Hollywood gently snoring, she was filled with a horrible sense of guilt. Hollywood Evans was not the best man she had ever met, but he had treated her good and had lavished expensive gifts upon her. Growing up in the church, she had been taught to return good with good, but sadly enough, this was not Sunday school, and she imagined that it would be best for her to get out while the getting was good.

Afraid to breathe too loudly, she sipped small mouthfuls of air as she raised up from the bed. She had been careful not to get back under the covers after she had sucked Hollywood's dick because she didn't want to go through the task of attempting to strip the sheets off her without rousing Hollywood who generally was very sensitive to every move she made. If she tossed and turned too much, he would wake up and groggily ask her what was wrong. She couldn't risk that tonight.

Almost immediately, she reached for the gun. It felt heavy, but if something went wrong she would rather it be in her possession than his.

She dressed quickly and quietly, and after taking one last look at the sleeping figure in the bed, tip-toed out of the bedroom.

The house felt eerie, too quiet and much too dark, and even though she knew where everything was, she still used her hands to navigate through the blackness. The gun grew heavier.

Down the stairs she went, going slow, taking one step at a time, stopping to catch her breath each time. At the bottom, she discovered just how thirsty she was, how she desired a cool glass of water, but she dared not detour to the kitchen. Shuffling across the thickly carpeted living room floor, she turned somberly introspective, but knowing it was too late to change the course of events she had set into motion, she exhaled. She de-activated the alarm, blinked the lights three, quick times in succession, and then stepped out into the night.

The cool, fresh air helped stop the buzzing in her ears and helped sweep away her dizziness, but suddenly she felt tired. Looking around so her eyes would adjust to the darkness, she was startled when, from out of nowhere, a firm hand gripped her shoulder.

"Ssssh." It was Agent Moore. She crooked her finger, motioning for Pearl to follow her. Moments later, dark-clad men appeared from everywhere. "Wait here with me." Agent Moore had led Pearl over to where Hollywood's cars were parked. "Which one is yours?"

"The white Mercedes."

"When I give you the word, get in and go."

Suddenly, jittery, Pearl fidgeted. "When will that be?"

"As soon as they have Mr. Evans under control. We can't allow you to leave before then. Your car would awaken him."

Pearl knew the woman was right, but still she was ready to go. She couldn't bear having to face Hollywood again. She sure had traveled a rocky road since she had left the church, but that seemed like two lifetimes ago. This was now. Hell.

Standing there, Agent Moore got some kind of signal over her radio. "That's it, Toots, drive safely."

Unlocking the car door, Pearl's hand felt drained of all blood. Her head pounded, but she wanted to be gone when they escorted Hollywood out.

Even though her head was reeling, she handled the Benz

smoothly, pushing it up beyond the speed limit until she reached the exit. Damn, she needed a blast of cocaine. Rummaging through her purse, she jumped when her hand touched the gun. She snapped the purse shut. She'd wait until she got to the hotel to get high. One was just beyond the next exit.

Pearl put a Brandy CD in and she sang along. In the distance, the city lights soothed her and suddenly she relaxed. Everything was going to be all right in the morning.

But, oh what a night!

Staring back at the city lights, Pearl decided that she wasn't going to a hotel. Why struggle through the night in such antiseptic surroundings when she could go home to sleep in her own bed?

According to Hawthorne, he wasn't going to sign the release papers for Angie until around 8:00am so that meant the apartment would be empty. Pearl could hardly believe how long it had been since she had actually slept in her own bed---alone. Well, the bed was all hers tonight. Talk about a small miracle.

Reaching her apartment, she literally jogged to the front door. She slipped the key in and happily entered her personal domain. She felt blessed.

She kicked off her shoes and taking a second to sit down on the sofa to knead the stiffness out of her calves, she grabbed her purse and wearily trudged to her bedroom.

She opened the door and flicked ON the overhead lights, flooding the bedroom with brilliant, white light. Pearl couldn't believe her eyes. She stared in disbelief. Her knees buckled. In her bed were the three people she had been the closest to….fucking!

She stared. Ennis was fucking Angie in the ass doggy-style while LaNIsa laid under Angie getting her pussy licked.

Pearl reached inside her purse. "Having fun?!"

Ennis, LaNisa, and Angie looked back at Pearl, their eyes wide.

"Is this a joke or something?"

Ennis patted the bed. "There's room for one more, baby. Join us."

Pearl pulled out the 9mm. "I don't think so." Peering coldly into her friends' eyes, she pressed the trigger. The gun bucked once, twice, three times and kept right on bucking until the clip was empty. Feeling nothing, she walked back out of the house.

Driving down the highway, she laughed insanely at how Hawthorne had played her. The bastard had never arrested Angie. Lying cocksucker.

But what hurt worse was how she had gotten played by her friends. Maybe it was time for her to get back into church. Lord knows, she had sinned.

EPISODE THREE

Chapter 17

Sunday.

Pearl pushed through the church door hurriedly, gladly shutting out the strong, blustery winds left behind by a late-night storm that had swept through downtown. Pearl had been frightened by the storm and felt certain that it was a sign from God to her----and everyone else in town---to get in line in time. She had stepped out of the old year convinced that time was running out for her, and if there was any salvation to be had in the New Year, she wanted her share. And then some. Lord knows, she had sinned.

As she strolled down the aisle of Big Rock AME Zion Church, she felt consumed by angry stares and the cold glare hit her like a slap of freezing ice. All eyes were on her, and she instantly experienced the almost uncontrollable urge to spin around in her Steve Madden suede heels, and to run out into the driving force of the wind. Better that than this, but by now a church usher was at her side guiding her to a seat.

The head usher, sensing that Pearl was going to be seated where she could be seen, jumped up and rushed to intercept her.

The congregation watched.

"Those seats are reserved," the head usher said, smiling saintly. She patted the younger usher's hand. "I'll show her to her seat." The woman roughly gripped Pearl's hand as though she wanted to squeeze the blood out. "This way, please." Pearl was spun around forcibly.

"Reserved seats in a church?" Pearl whispered. "Have I

been missing from action that long that God had started to play favorites?"

"Ssssh!" The head usher tugged at Pearl's hand violently.

What did it matter, Pearl thought. She knew how church folk were. Following the head usher, Pearl suddenly realized that soon there would be nowhere to go but outside if she was escorted any further into the bowels of the cavernous church, but just before they reached the big, swinging doors, the usher---with a measure of immense pride---pointed Pearl to the far end of the last pew in the church.

"Enjoy the program, chile," the head usher uttered sweetly. "God bless."

Pearl felt ostracized, but didn't want to think about it, yet it was hard to mistake the "hate" vibes the church members were sending her way. In fact, the more she thought about it, the more she recognized that everyone in the city had turned against her. She was an outcast!

Throughout the whole service, Pearl looked for diversions to help counter how totally numb she felt in the company of church folk whom she had believed would welcome her back with open arms. God, had she been wrong.

The whole time the preacher had verbally steamed up the gospel, whipping his flock into a near spiritual hysteria, Pearl had never felt more alone. Heads---with colorful hats---fully turned around to cast hate-filled eyes at her, but would dutifully look away after a second or two. This Pearl could deal with. What really disturbed her was the choir. Their collective eyes never looked away. They were all on "Hater-Aid" and suddenly, all at once, Big Rock seemed to be the last place on earth for her to get shown some love. It was like Whoa!

Pearl had had enough and was ready to go, but halfway through the closing hymn, the head usher came rumbling down the aisle in her direction.

"Don't go nowhere," the old sista snarled like a thug out of a movie.

"Why not?" Pearl whispered. "Am I under arrest?"

"Don't you worry 'bout no reason why I tole you what

I just tole you, chile. You just do it." The head usher moved her body into the pew, nudging Pearl over, and when she was sure she had Pearl completely blocked in, she stood stiffly and sung the remainder of the hymn in a rusty contralto.

Departing the pulpit with a dramatic, "Thank you, Jesus," the preacher beat a hasty exit to the back of the church so he could be on hand to personally see the congregation out. It was a cruel world out there, sheer madness in certain places, so Reverend Arnold was real touchy-feely because he never knew what fate awaited some among his worshippers. In the hood, the seven days between services was time enough for anything to happen.

Like a dressed-up congo line at Shoney's buffet bar, the congregation paraded down the aisle, all eager to get a hug or hand shake from the preacher who certainly knew how to work a room.

"Hey there, Sista Martha. Jesus surely must have taken the calories out of the food he's been blessing Brotha Joe to bring home and put on the table. Looks like you getting all the taste, but none of the weight. Hallejuiah!"

Next was Brotha Calvin. "Reverend Arnold, you know we been praying that my boy get out of jail."

"Yes," Reverend Arnold said eagerly, "and what miracle has our prayer wrought?"

"Fool boy confessed to the crime," Brotha Calvin cracked, "and now they gonna give him life."

"But at least, he'll be out of jail."

"Yeah, he'll be in prison."

"Our bad," Reverend Arnold snapped. "We forgot to be specific, but you tell that boy about Joseph. He went to prison behind some woman to." He dismissed Brotha Calvin, stepping around to stoop down to greet a little boy. "Now, I hope you have stopped saying bad words."

"Some of 'em."

"And why haven't you stopped using them all, son?"

"Because I know too many of 'em."

"Oh, Jesus, have mercy on the children," Reverend Arnold wailed loudly, "because if the devil don't get them, the white folks will. Have a little mercy on the babies, please, Jesus."

Within minutes, the reverend had whittled down the crowd to zero, and without warning stormed off towards his office next to the choir box.

"Well, what you waiting on?" It was the head usher speaking. "Go."

Pearl started towards the door.

"Not that way." The usher placed her wide body between Pearl and the door. "You keep right on, chile, and something bad gonna happen up in the Lord's House this morning."

"Hmmph" Pearl huffed, "and they think the streets are unsafe."

"Like they say on TV, roll out. I don't be liking for nobody to keep the reverend waiting."

Pearl rolled out.

When Pearl and Sista Benson arrived at the study, Reverend Arnold was slouched against the doorway. His robe was flung carelessly across a chair. "Come in," he said to Pearl. To Sista Benson. "Close the door."

"I don't have long," Pearl announced softly.

Reverend Arnold lit up a cigarette, still leaning against the wall. He inhaled, exhaled, talked. "You make it look too easy."

"I beg your pardon."

"Just look at you, Miss Washington, all fly in your Givenchy gear, strutting up in my church, plumper than a Thanksgiving turkey. Hard for me to tell if you came to repent or to show off." Reverend Arnold took another drag off his cigarette. "We all know what you've become. Where's your remorse?"

Pearl dropped down in a soft-back chair. "My goal for this year was to get my life together. I felt the church would be a good place to start. I just didn't know I had to bring any other ingredients with me."

"Believe me, you do." The preacher snubbed out his cigarette. "Beginning with a contrite heart, and in your case, a special prayer line, you could've look more the part of a prodigal sista. But no, you come sashaying up in here, according to your own whim, looking like a paid ad for sin."

"I-I don't believe you just said that."

Reverend Arnold chuckled. "The one thing you should know about me is that I have perfected the art of not playing around when it come to this church. That alone is enough for me to ask you to stay away from The Rock." He tapped another cigarette from his pack. "Now, what I do suggest is that you join the ministry up at the women's shelter. They serve up a lighter fare of the gospel there which has a great appeal for junkies, prostitutes, and women who take off their clothes for money." Reverend Arnold smiled. "I even recommend that you try out for the choir."

"No, thanks," Pearl said firmly. "I think I want to attend this church. And sing."

Reverend Arnold paced the floor. "Consider this, if you would. We just started a new program where we attempt to teach the youth of the church how to survive as a Christian in a pornographic world. Now, how would it look if they stare up in the choir and see you every Sunday? That would defeat our purpose."

"And how is that?" Pearl cracked.

"You just might remind them that's it's easy to bounce back from sin and drugs. They see you sitting up there in your designer gear, and that might be a big enough endorsement for them to go out and get high or sell booty." Reverend Arnold blew smoke rings. "You feel me, sista. Your mere presence could be corrupting, and I can't allow that to happen."

"So what am I to do, stay in the gutter?" Pearl was close to tears.

"Jesus, no," Reverend Arnold protested. "I applaud your efforts to get back on your feet, and God knows nothing will alter that perception, but I feel the most crucial element in your full recovery will be to not ever step foot in my church again."

When Pearl raised her voice in protest, Sista Benson burst through the door like SuperWoman. "Is she sassing you, Reverend Arnold?" The usher towered over Pearl menacingly. "She done been warned. It just might be that she think I'm playing so it might be necessary-----."

"No, I don't think so, Sista Benson." Reverend Arnold wrapped his arms round the usher's big shoulders. "Everything is fine."

"You sho' 'bout that, Reverend, 'cause this whole situation done set my soul on fire." Sista Benson stared at Pearl's expensive outfit, then snarled. "Chile, do you know how much it will cost to steam the blood out of that pretty dress you got on?"

Pearl stood.

"What that mean? You standing up. You trying to cross my path or something? You trying to get showed something?"

"By who, sista?"

"By me, that's who."

"Be quiet," Reverend Arnold shouted wearily. "Both of you."

"No!" Sista Benson yelled. "I want a piece of this hussy."

"I'm going to have to ask you to leave, Sista Benson."

"I'm not leaving."

"But you're upset."

"And what God-fearing woman wouldn't be, standing face to face with a hand-maiden of the devil."

"Well," Pearl began, "I can't help how you feel, but I ask you to say some prayers before you even think about putting your hands on me----"

"Stop it! Both of you. Up in here acting like heathens."

"Don't worry," Pearl smiled, "I'm leaving."

"Good riddance."

Pearl sighed, glaring at Sista Benson. "If fate would ever be unkind and have us meet in a dark alley."

"Ain't got to be no dark alley, chile. The next time I see you, it's on. We can be in the mall, at the grocery store, at a PTA meeting. Wherever we at, when we meet again, I'm bringing it."

Pearl opened the door. "It's official, then. We got a date."

"Lord, have mercy," Reverend Arnold wailed. "Mercy, mercy, mercy."

Once Pearl was out of the menacing company of Sista Benson, she struggled with the inner turmoil she felt. How could the church be so vengeful? All she had wanted to do was to regain the innocence that had been stolen from her so long ago. Tears welled in her eyes, but she realized that crying would not remove her pain or take away her disappointment. She simply had to play the hand she was dealt. It was now or never.

Driving through Center City, she opened the car window, letting the wind blow over her. She had a lot of problems in her life that needed fixing, and if the church had the nerve to turns its back on her, then she would make it on her own. She would take her fight to the streets, and compel this bitter earth to teach her its secrets so she could get in where she fit in. She had no other choice. The streets loved her. Everybody knew her name.

By the time she drove past the Harvey Gantt Center, the tears were streaming freely down her face and she didn't try to stop them. Where had all the sunshine in her life gone? Why hadn't her prayers been answered? Was it because she got high? Or because she just didn't give a damn anymore.

Turning right at The Bojangles on South Tryon Street, Pearl visibly flinched as she watched the sky over West Boulevard erupt into a spasm of dazzling lightning so white hot that it looked like God was stir-frying the heavens. The thunder BOOMED with wondrous might as though it was a majestic passage from God's own autobiography, but when the rain came and the wind picked up, Pearl grew extremely nervous.

God was after her.

Dashing into the lower-level apartment in Little Rock Homes that she shared with two strippers, Pearl closed the door quickly, and fired up a blunt. Soon, she no longer felt powerless. Nor did the thunder and lightning scare her any more. She then made up her mind. Since God had apparently forsaken her, she would raise hell for the rest of her life. Pearl didn't give a damn if the devil liked it or not, but he had just gotten a new sidekick, and he had better not try to stop her from being bad!

Pearl put the blunt out, then lit it up again. She had an idea. Laughing, she took a big hit and held the smoke in. She ran over to the hole in the wall and blew the cloud of reefer into the small opening next to the raggedy-assed stove. She giggled uncontrollably. She had just hit the rats with a blast of the best weed on the block. What about the roaches, she wondered? Did they want to get high as well? The apartment was full of them.

Motherfuckas acted like they paid the damn rent or something. Didn't even try to hide when she had company over. Motherfuckas would disrespect her by popping out like a nosey next door neighbor, all up in her business like she owed them. She wasn't giving them shit.

    It was just past dinnertime, and Pearl was still slightly agitated at the notion she entertained. She was tired of living like this. She vacantly stared at the paint chipped walls of the apartment for a second before she had to look away. The apartment was dreadful; ugly. The carpet on the floor had at one time been beige, but now it was stained with so much shit that wouldn't come up that it was a shade of some color that hadn't even been invented yet. Not only were the floors and walls depressing, but the stove wouldn't get hot and the refrigerator wouldn't stay cold, and she couldn't decide which she hated more, the roaches and rats inside the apartment or the dope-selling niggas outside the apartment. Both had now became a big joke to her. This was not how she wanted to live although she couldn't honestly say that she regretted her decision to move in with Diamond and Pepper because at the time the choice for her had been simple. She had to either live in Little Rock or to live under a rock.

    Last week, when she didn't have anywhere else to go after she had become a suspect in the murder of her friends, Little Rock had seemed like a great opportunity, but the joy had quickly faded. How much of a blessing was it when the first thing you smelled when you stepped outside the door was piss? For some strange reason, the local dope-boys acted like it was a rite of passage to piss under the stairway in front of the apartment where she stayed. Shit was crazy. Motherfuckas could at least piss in one of the beer bottles that littered the hallways and front entrance to the apartment. How fucking hard could that be?

    As she munched on a stalk of celery, she pushed her bowl of Ramen noodles to the side, mentally considering what would come next. She thought shit over for a brief second or two, and out of the blue, she made up her mind. She was leaving. At first, she felt a little guilty about leaving Diamond and Pepper, knowing damned well that both those bitches would view her departure as an indictment against them, but that would be untrue. If those bitches wanted to live like dogs, then they could have Little Rock, and all the bullshit that came along with it.

    Sitting in front of the TV watching Jerry Springer, she temporarily basked in the glow of her decision, but then she popped the big question too herself: when was she leaving and what was she going to do? That question, though simple and straightforward shook her up, knocking her down mentally. She tried to shake it off, but couldn't because the question begged her, like a hungry puppy, for an answer. She poured herself a shot of the left-over Alize as she sized up her options. Then she clumsily got up from the worn, torn sofa and flicked the television off. What it boiled down to was elementary. If she was going to stop cheating herself out of the finer things of life, then today was the best time to get started. She also knew that if she was smart that she would leave now. Staying would only expose her weakness for not getting up, getting out, and getting something. Starting today, she was a bitch with a mission. She might not have had much of a motherfucking plan, but at least, she had a goal. Pearl smiled. She had just enrolled herself in Head-Start for bitches who didn't have shit but wanted to have something. She frowned because she would either graduate with honors or die trying.

    Even though she couldn't guarantee what would happen to her once she walked away from Little Rock, she knew that neither Diamond nor Pepper would ever go to bat for her again, but so what? If she was ever going to establish herself as a dancer, ho or anything else a broke bitch could become then she sure as hell couldn't fall apart, worrying about bitches that had even less common sense than she did.

    "This is not going to be easy," Pearl muttered softly to herself, and with that in mind started to put together her strategy. She was either going to have to dance or start hoeing, the two basic job options for a broke, black chick.

    It was time to either put up or shut up!

    Pearl felt energized. She didn't know if it was inspiration or desperation, but what she did know was that she was thrilled to become a work-in-progress. She jumped off the couch like the energizer bunny. She thought about going to the Red Door on Independence Boulevard, but remembered a new shop in University City. Then she also remembered she had no money.

Slipping on a pair of Apple Bottom jeans, she headed to the door. Ignoring the smell of piss and the eyes on her ass, she stuffed her bags into the trunk of her car. Then she happily drove away. She threw back her head and laughed. Some things just never changed.

Arriving at her location in a small strip mall on City Boulevard, Pearl was ready to steal. Once inside the store, she cleverly concealed her purpose behind vacant eyes and a pretty smile, but the guy who owned the store moved leisurely towards the counter to greet her.

"And just what might I interest you in?" he grinned.

"A suit of armor," Pearl dead-panned.

The man's grin broadened. "In today's world, a sense of humor is invaluable." He started to say something more, but halted with his mouth still partially open. "You're the young lady that was on the news, aren't you?"

Pearl was surprised the man remembered. "Yes."

The owner boldly looked Pearl up and down as if he was ready to go on a treasure hunt to discover just what goodies her clothes hid, but he quickly lowered his gaze once he recognized he was being rude.

"I apologize for staring."

"Where's yo' ho gear?" Pearl asked tonelessly. "Boots, undies, stuff like that."

The man examined Pearl again with his eyes, but looked away when he noticed Pearl biting her bottom lip in annoyance. "Is this ho gear, as you call it, for you?" The question was undeniably personal. "Or perhaps for a friend too bashful to shop for her own needs?"

Pearl laughed. "A shy bitch can't sell no pussy. The shit is for me."

"In that case, whatever you want, it's free."

"Free?"

"Let's just call it the Shop-owner's Discount." The man

bowed slightly at the waist. "I am Andre Pierre, your humble servant, but why are you still standing there Miss Dark and Lovely? I just gave you a free shopping spree." He smiled. "Welcome to my world. I think you will find everything here that you will need."

At the simple mention of the word "free", Pearl was ready to get busy. Like a little girl in a candy store, she dashed wildly from aisle to aisle and from row to row, snatching skimpy articles of clothing off the shelf as if the pieces would disintegrate.

When she returned to the counter, her arms were loaded with gear. She hoped the man wouldn't think she was greedy, but what did he expect? Free was only one of the two things she valued more that getting a nut. The other, of course, was money.

The man didn't flinch at the amount of clothes she had. He simply stuffed all the gear into four shopping bags. Pearl studied the man. His exceptionally pale face revealed nothing, but she understood it to be a mask behind which he hid. His dark, doe-shaped eyes radiated a quiet strength. Andre Pierre was confident and also very tall; over six feet. His hands were expressive and his long spiked hair fell over his massive shoulders.

"Everything in here is spectacular," Andre Pierre bragged, "no doubt you have learned that." He winked slyly. "The only thing these outfits leave to the imagination is how much a hotel room costs."

Just in case he hadn't noticed her first smile of appreciation, Pearl flashed a second one. A nicer, more ear-to-ear kind. He had just saved her some money she didn't have, and like any other broke bitch, that was good news. Pearl's smile grew even brighter.

"I don't know what your finances are like," Andre Pierre said casually, "but if you need money, I know of some--- er--- developments that could help out. You think you might be interested?"

"What woman you know who's not interested in money? What's your scheme?"

"No scheme, I assure you."

"That just makes me even more interested."

Andre Pierre's voice sounded more high-pitched, more excited. "Come with me, please."

Pearl was led across the shop, past racks of shoes and accessories to a door next to a water cooler. Through the door on the right, Pearl could hear muffled sounds, strains of animated voices. A moan.

"Don't pay that no mind," Andre Pierre suggested, opening the door on the left. He held the door wide so Pearl could step through. "After you, please," he mumbled courteously.

The room, though a somber grey, was bright and airy compared to Pierre's affinity for black, and after taking everything in, Pearl saw no clues that this room was used often. It was spotless.

Sinking into a wicker chair, Pearl savored the possibility of getting her hands on enough money to get a new apartment in some faraway city. She silently prayed that Andre Pierre would turn into her financial savior, a spiked-haired Santa Claus.

Across from her in an identical chair, Andre Pierre crossed his long legs and smiled. He looked away as he rubbed his stomach nervously. He made eye contact. "I know this doesn't sound like the perfect thing for one stranger to say to another, but what the hell, you can correct me if I'm wrong."

Pearl smiled nervously. "I've heard it all before so if you think you might hurt my feelings, don't sweat it." She placed her arms across her bosom. "Tell me," she purred, "what's on your mind?"

Andre Pierre smiled. "You look like an operator to me."

Pearl saw no reason to let on that she didn't know what the hell he was talking about, so she played along. "Everybody's an operator."

"So it has been said." Andre Pierre rubbed his stomach nervously. He looked off into the distance. "When it comes to sex, white people blew right past black people; left you guys standing on a corner way back in the dark ages." He made eye contact. "For some reason, black people think they were born sexually enlightened."

"I never heard that before," Pearl shrugged, "but I can see

where there could be some truth to it. Who needs the Kama Sutra when you have rhythm and endurance?"

"But that's just my point. Sex shouldn't always be about strength because there are a list of other options to be tried. Nuances that succeed where power never could."

Pearl laughed. "No one yet has complained about the way I get things done in bed."

"I bet they haven't," Andre Pierre chuckled. "Who am I to question technique, but that's not the reason I invited you back here." He winked. "There is something else I could recommend."

Reaching into his jacket pocket, Andre Pierre rolled off a single, one hundred dollar bill from what appeared to be an impossibly huge roll. He handed the money to Pearl. "It's yours. I value your time."

Pearl plucked the crisp bill out of the man's hand. "And I value money." She stuffed the bill in her bra. She smiled. "Now that money has exchanged hands, why don't we stop beating around the bush? What do you want?"

"I was wondering if you understand the value of your body?"

"Aha," Pearl laughed. "Now, we getting somewhere, but let me ask you a question. When you say body, do you mean my body body or do you mean my pussy?"

Andre Pierre threw his hands up in the air defensively. "Whoa, I wasn't expecting that, but I meant just what I said, but let me clarify. You are a dancer. Am I correct?"

"Not yet?"

"Okay," Andre Pierre conceded, "I see, but what would it take for me to tempt you to try something a wee bit more experimental?"

Pearl laughed nervously. "What are you talking about?"

Andre Pierre leaned forward. "What if I told you of a brand new world of exotic entertainment where you can make fantastic amounts of money?"

"Sounds good, but what's the catch?"

"There is no catch"

"Really?"

Andre Pierre jumped up. "Let me show you something."

Pearl followed the older man to a wall at the rear of the room. They stood in front of an oil portrait which presented a stunning view of a vase of sunflowers. Andre Pierre took a deep breath and then removed the painting. Pearl audibly gasped, involuntarily taking a step backwards.

"Come," Andre Pierre pleaded. "They can't see or hear us."

With her hands demurely clasped behind her back, Pearl walked up to the one-way mirror and clinically observed a pale, buxom woman about her own height, beating the naked ass of a white man with a leather hood over his face. The woman sweated. The man swooned.

Andre Pierre moved closer until he was standing shoulder to shoulder with Pearl. He whispered her name and when Pearl didn't respond, he gently tapped her on the shoulder to get her attention. "The woman is called a dominatrix. See how well-conditioned she is, almost muscular; a real performer. She's good, can really whip some ass. Look at how hard the man's dick is. He loves getting beat, it turns him on." Andre Pierre seemed pleased. "He adores it."

"Apparently, so does she." Pearl studied the woman, noticing the intense passion and emotion that was etched across the face of the female. Pearl also took note of the woman's nipples which were rock hard and fully extended, protruding from the woman's breasts like huge rubber erasers. The woman was visibly excited.

"She has made a fortune doing that, although administering beatings is just one of the services she performs. She dances as well" Andre Pierre eased behind Pearl and casually began to massage her shoulder. "Just relax and enjoy the show. Sybil is a pro and is paid well. Most of her other appointments will take place in two thousand dollar a day hotel suites, but no matter where she performs, men love it." Andre Pierre turned Pearl around so they faced each other. "I know you have the potential, but first you must learn how the game is played. Are you willing to, at least, see what I'm offering you?"

Pearl nodded slowly.

"Good. I'm ecstatic."

On the other side of the mirror, Pearl watched the man masturbate as the woman tickled him with a feather. Finishing, the man politely thanked the woman, and dished out what appeared to be close to a thousand dollars. Within minutes, the room was empty.

Andre Pierre flashed Pearl a cool smile. Grabbing her hand, he kissed it delicately. "Welcome to the world of S&M".

"S&M?!"

'Yes, S&M, the wonderful world conjured up by the illustrious Marquis de Sade. It is a wonderful mix of Ringling Brothers and Girls Gone Wild. You'll see. It's amazing." Andre Pierre paused. "Have you, by the way, ever heard of Marquis de Sade?"

"No, not really."

"No background on him at all?"

Pearl slowly shook her head.

"Don't worry," Andre Pierre said with relief in his voice, "most black people haven't." Andre Pierre winked. "There is a big difference between being freaky, and in being daring, and white people are way more sexually daring than black people could ever begin to imagine."

Pearl smiled. "You get with the right black freak, and I think you just might change your mind about how sexually daring we are."

"Let's not debate, but I do want to say that our Marquis de Sade was quite a character, and we, the adherents of S&M, emulate him in mind, body, and soul. I wholeheartedly invite you to become one of us. I personally feel it is time to export the teaching of de Sade into the bedrooms of black America."

"Why, do you think that black people are doomed sexually and need to be rescued?"

Andre Pierre chose his next words carefully. "Please excuse my bluntness, but fucking is so ordinary, the cut-rate thing to do in the bedroom when you have no other options." He shrugged. "I find it both crude and comic that two people would waste time in bed simply copulating which they, oddly, find so delightful."

"Beats a vibrator and it's a lot better than masturbation" Pearl laughed.

Andre Pierre didn't crack a smile. "First, I want the sanctity of the teachings respected and preserved. I want them protected at all costs." He glared at Pearl coldly. "I dare you to name for me one thing your people have cherished. Jazz belonged to black people. You abandoned it. You invented the blues and what happened. You walked away from it. I know of no other people in history who so easily part ways with their traditions than black people, so is it any wonder that I don't want the ways of the beloved Marquis de Sade trampled upon.

"Show me the money," Pearl giggled happily, "and you won't have to worry about me."

"In that case, I imagine, we see eye to eye."

"Of course," Pearl responded, "eye to eye and dollar to dollar."

Both Andre Pierre and Pearl, for a brief moment, sat in the vibrant chemistry that was silently simmering between them, pleased that a strong trust had been instantly established.

Andre Pierre stood. He peeled ten one hundred dollar bills from his roll. "This is a gift, the rest you will have to earn, but you'll be filthy rich before you know it. That I guarantee." He smiled. "Are you ready?"

"Why not," Pearl quipped. "I'm one broad that's been in the storm too long."

Andre Pierre extended his hand. "Good. Your training will begin Monday."

Chapter 18

Monday

"You haven't been doing your homework, dammit," Sybil cursed, "or else your fucking technique wouldn't be so lousy. You have got to concentrate if you expect to get it right." When Pearl started to say something, the blonde Amazon stopped her. "And I would appreciate it if you wouldn't interrupt me. I'm the one who is familiar with this shit, not you. Therefore I strongly suggest that you give me your undivided attention or else I'll have to inform Andre that you're not working out."

"Just give me a little more time," Pearl begged. "I can do it. I know I still have a long ways to go, but I really want to learn."

"You sure about that, kiddo, because if you ask me I think Andre has made a mistake." Sybil glared at Pearl with a sneer on her pale face. "Personally. I don't think you have the character or the heart to be a dominatrix. Sure, you have the body, but S&M is a way of life so let's be real about what's going on here, okay?"

"I told you I can get it."

"Look at how many chances you've had already, and you still keep fucking up. Why don't you just run back to whatever street corner you were on when Andre found you, and jump in and out of cars for twenty dollars a pop. That's more your style."

"Bitch!" Pearl rasped in a cold, hard voice, "you don't know shit about me, and if you don't want yo' white ass kicked, you better stay out of my personal affairs."

"And if I don't?" Sybil, in one amazingly quick movement,

was standing almost nose to nose with Pearl. "You, kick my ass. That'll be the goddamn day. I wish you would try it."

"Don't either one of you even think about it." Andre Pierre paused, letting his disengaged voice sink in.

Sybil stepped back, looking in the direction of the one-way mirror. "I'm sorry, Master. It won't happen again."

It amazed Pearl how quickly Sybil had gone from being aggressive to becoming so passive she was virtually limp with submission. She should have guessed that Andre Pierre would be in his observation room, watching every move she made, analyzing her every response and reaction. Her defiance softened.

"Now, get back to work, both of you. Understand?" The speaker-box squawked off.

With that, Pearl relaxed. "Look, Sybil, I'm not asking that you indulge me or even try to be my friend. Just teach me. Would that be asking too much?"

Sybil didn't look like she absolutely approved of the idea, but she nodded just the same. She recognized the danger involved in giving Pearl too much knowledge because she wasn't particularly pleased with setting up a rival for herself, but her Master had spoken. She had to obey. "Okay, let's go over this again."

For the next thirty minutes, Sybil schooled Pearl in the fine art of tying someone up.

"You don't just lash them to the bedpost. That's not what de Sade would like. In all honesty, tying up is not merely tying up even if that is what it does look like, but what's harder to explain, I guess, is the pure art of it. You have to have a love of bondage or you will never be a true virtuoso." Sybil sighed. "In order to succeed, the entire act must come from out of the darkest recesses of your imagination and must be plotted beautifully because if you're going to draw people into the wonderful world of bondage, all the intricate parts must be perfectly assembled."

Pearl gobbled up the teachings like Ms. Pac-Man. Sybil spoke with such effortless passion, detailing her obsession with de Sade which had developed while she was still a young girl in Scandinavia, the country of her birth, that Pearl suddenly wanted to be tied up.

"Enough of this talking," Pearl whispered sexily, undressing herself. "Show me what it's like."

Sybil's seduction was a drama that didn't unfold. It bloomed, blossoming into a vast intersection of soft, sensual turmoil where Pearl felt both arrested and excited, and even though she had experienced women before, Sybil heightened the aura, the mystery…..the possibilities.

By the time she was completely naked and spread-eagled on the bed, Pearl understood that Angie and her other female lovers had been woefully inadequate bed-partners. Sybil was more of a perfectionist whose fingers and tongue had been well-tutored in a sexual tradition that went far beyond the challenge of producing an orgasm out of nothing at all.

In reaction to Sybil's heat-generating kisses, Pearl's body felt so sexually enriched she was convinced she could climax simply by whispering Sybil's name. It felt just that good.

Being the champion she was, Sybil's aggressiveness became even more pronounced after she had rounded up enough energy to provide Pearl with her first O.

"It's time to get tied, baby." Sybil kissed Pearl's mound. "Let me lock you up."

Lifting up her hips for another pussy smooch, Pearl moaned. "Do me, baby."

Pearl took a special delight in the way the lips of her swollen pussy felt like the sun had risen between her moist thighs, seductively igniting a flame of passion previously unknown to her. Compared to any other sensation she had ever experienced, being tied up seemed vaguely futuristic, and despite black folks' well-known reputation for being hesitant to try anything new sexually, Pearl was more than eager to see just what would come next. She gawked in wide-eyed lust as Sybil eyed her pussy like it was a bejeweled metropolis of utter pleasure.

Feeling a jolt of electrified excitement, Pearl was wildly amazed at how her sexual fortunes had now changed. She hoped that while she was being tied up that she would be blessed with the chance to recruit an even bigger orgasm out of her pussy than the one that had just exploded out of her insides like an atomic bomb.

Getting tied up was going to be such fun.

For what appeared to be long stretches of time during the next ten minutes as she was being expertly lashed to the bedposts, Pearl moaned and groaned in a purely spiritual tone, as she plunged head-on into her new best-thing-in-the-world-to-do. Feeling so good as the silk rope seemingly caressed her soft skin, she wondered aloud if Sybil still viewed her as a protégé or a worshipper.

"According to all the black non-believers in the teaching of de Sade," Sybil teasingly scoffed, "It would appear that you are about to become the exception to the rule." The sexual sarcasm was apparent in Sybil's voice. "And it's about damn time." After Sybil had completed her task of tying Pearl up, the blonde Amazon purred. "Are you ready for your crowning?"

Since Pearl realized that the question was not some out-of-the-blue quiz, all she could manage was a smile.

Sybil would not back off. She was in hot pursuit of a more welcoming reaction so she decided to push her luck. "Are you ready, bitch!?"

"Yes," Pearl whispered, "I am ready."

"The mask cannot harm you."

"I-I'm ready."

"No. No, you're not," Sybil countered sharply. "I can feel the fear in your voice." Sybil straddled Pearl's chest. "Release your inner fears. The mask is your friend, your protector…another part of you." Sybil's tone was now tender and dreamy, coming from afar. "Are you ready now?"

Pearl took a deep breath. "Yes, Master, I am ready."

With her fingers intertwined in the gaping holes of the mask, Sybil leaned down and planted a wet, smacking kiss on Pearl's lips. Then when she had finished, she carefully unhooked the twin gold clasps on the back of the "executioner's" mask and when she had spread it at its base, the grotesque mask seemed to yawn. Then, slowly, Sybil extended it forward, towards Pearl's face. "The mask will make us one."

Pearl inhaled.

Going over her head, the mask smelled like lemon-scented leather as if someone had sprayed it with Pledge. Gulping air, she overcame the first wave of fear, but when the mask settled full over her face, the emotional impact was so explosive she wanted to yank the leather contraption from her face and to fling it to the floor.

"Breathe…..slowly." Sybil made the announcement like a movie director conducting auditions from the casting couch. "Your fear will recede." Sybil gazed at Pearl. "Look into my eyes."

Looking at Sybil was difficult as the peep holes in the mask restricted her vision. Even worse was her breathing. Her nose felt packed with cotton, and the hole designed for her mouth was so extraordinarily constricting she wasn't sure if she could even utter words. Generally speaking, she felt vulnerable and powerless, a feeling that slowly engulfed her.

"Close your eyes, black woman."

Teasingly deliberate, Sybil sucked Pearl's engorged clit into her mouth and gently nibbled on it with her teeth, rocking her blonde head back and forth in a numbingly hypnotic way until Pearl commenced to moan, slurring her ooohs and ahhhs.

When Pearl's clit was moist and slippery, Sybil pushed two fingers into the pussy. Pearl shamelessly humped, wanting another finger. Or two. The whole hand.

Pearl's sweat oozed from under the mask.

Chapter 19

10 and a half days later.

The city's top detective clenched his eyes shut, but he still listened attentively to the report even though he had heard more than he cared to hear about the new underground movement taking place in black America's bedroom.

"It could be worse."

"How many so far?" Epps' voice carried an edge.

"Four."

Epps blew air through his nose like an enraged bull. "One is too damn many."

"All the people I've interviewed provided info only on the condition of anonymity."

"Of course, of course," Epps snorted, shooing away the remark. "Who in their right mind would want their name associated with something as sordid as this." Epps paused. "They'll remain confidential, but I'll tell you this, I'm going to order a full-scale investigation."

"But did you hear what I said about who's involved in this? God know, sir, a scandal of this magnitude would destroy the city's black elite."

"Damn those upper-crust Negroes, running around with their noses in the air, pretending their shit don't stank. They disgust me."

"It's a terrible thing, I admit," confessed Al Lindsey , a

portly, black detective with Al Sharpton hair, who had just celebrated his thirty-fifth birthday on Sunday, "but we must move with caution on this----"

"Why....because the Mayor's wife is involved?" Epps' voice bristled with emotion. "That woman has always been out of control."

"Still, I don't think it would be our smartest move to jump to any conclusions, and hey, I'm not defending Tammi Duncan, but just because there seems to be a fast growing pool of sexually aggressive brothas and sistas isn't enough to jump down their throats. They're sexual predators, sir, not murderers."

"Not this time," Epps chortled, "but I wouldn't get too comfortable. This is not The Dating Game." Feeling almost embarrassed to hear the story again, Epps threw his hands up in the air. "Okay, once more from the top."

Lindsey spoke. "Kid comes home from school early, sneaks in the house, creeps upstairs to surprise his Mama, but peeks into the bedroom and sees a strange man tying his naked Mama up. Kid rushes back downstairs, dials 9-1-1. Cops arrive, but instead of finding a robbery and rape in progress, they stumble upon a small S&M cult. There was another couple in the guest bedroom representing the Marquis."

"Tammi, Tammi, Tammi," Epps lamented, "when will you ever learn to leave well enough alone." A devilish grin crossed his face. "Probably never."

Lindsey nodded in agreement. "The sista is a live wire, but it did kinda bug her out that her son saw what he saw."

"No doubt she sold him on the robbery/rape angle. Probably talked him into believing he was a hero, but I don't believe the Mayor is going to fall for it."

"Tread carefully, boss-man, because a lot of eyes will be watching this one if you pull the covers off the bed. The niggerati in this town is legendary in their appetite for revenge, so if you cross them in any way, they will be out to crush you. I was born and raised here," Lindsey conceded. "You're new meat still. Yeah, you better be careful. I'm telling you personally."

Epps's eyes narrowed. "And I'm telling you to tell them

that I intend to expose their upper-crust perversion."

For best results, Pearl decided to take the info for what it was worth. She figured she would be untouchable, the premier prima donna in the S&M world soon. She had the discipline and the eagerness to learn. Plus, being black set her apart, giving her a distinctly exotic flava that she was sure would drive the crackers---men and women---wild. Pearl felt thrilled.

Her performance this afternoon was going to be so electrifying that Andre Pierre might call a press conference to announce the unqualified success of her coming-out party.

This was going to be an occasion.

Twenty minutes later, Pearl parked out front of Girl Gear, but didn't enter. Instead, she went next door, and had a seat at the far end of the bar. The bartender winked knowingly, providing her with a free drink. Pearl, in return, raised the glass in toast.

Gulping down the drink, Pearl could feel the warmth snaking down her throat like a liquid tongue. Another drink was sent over by a secret admirer. Pearl faced the crowded establishment, and raised the glass in thanksgiving. Already she felt like a diva.

From the moment she had walked in, she instantly become the center of attraction, and she smiled approvingly at all the attention. And she deserved it. She hated to think she didn't. The pink leather pants fit her like a glove, and her phat ass was indeed worthy of all the back-slapping and whistling. She was a dime-piece. Again.

Through Sybil, Pearl had been informed that Andre Pierre also owned the bar, and that it was more than a mere watering hole where working stiffs on a lunch break came in to hammer away their mid-day blues. It was a S&M depot.

On Wednesday---the up and over the hump work day----the doors at Wet Willie's were locked for thirty minutes, commencing at noon at which time, the man (or woman) of the half-hour would leave the packed room, and exit down a long hallway only wide enough to accommodate one person. At the end of the corridor was the green room where to enter meant throwing aside all inhibitions, and to get ready for one incredible bout of perversion, kink, and sex.

Pearl was impressed with the whole set-up. Respectable men who would not be caught dead in Girl Gear could gain entrance through the forbidden green door. No one would raise an eyebrow at a man stepping into Wet Willie's, never suspecting where his real destination was: The Green Door!

When the bartender locked the door, the crowd cheered wildly. They whooped and clapped even more intensely when Pearl exited, walking the green carpet towards the green door.

A crimson light flooded the corridor with a blood-red glow that seemed to stretch the carpet out for an entire city block, but at the end was a bathroom where Pearl entered to change into her gear. By now, she was breathing fast.

The spartan john reeked of sexual fantasy, and for a scant moment Pearl felt as though she was a camera-toting tourist trespassing on the carnal knowledge of the countless others who had used this bathroom as a way-station to the green door. Staring into the squeaky clean mirror, she attempted to channel all the collective wisdom of all the sexual goddesses who had come before her, the prized bitches of S&M whom she one day hoped to outrank. Today, she would get her start.

The door opened.

"Are you scared?"

"Of what?"

"Making history." Sybil moved closer and planted a soft, wet kiss on each of Pearl's bare shoulders. She rubbed Pearl's flat stomach. "I can feel your butterflies."

"That's hunger," Pearl lied.

Sybil spun Pearl around. "You can do it, Pearl, but you must have supreme confidence in yourself."

Pearl kissed Sybil on the lips. "Thanks, but I got this here."

"Well, let's go. It's show-time."

As soon as Pearl entered through the green door, her dancing music, 'Who Is She Too You' by Brandy blared through invisible speakers. Dressed in black, studded biker shorts and a matching leather halter top, Pearl danced, entertaining herself until a second later, Sybil led a man in on a leash. He was on all fours and was naked except for a black, leather diaper and a black, silk hood. The man barked.

"WOOF! WOOF!"

Sybil, the Mistress, was dressed in a tight, black leather jumpsuit, her sadistic eyes hidden behind a pair of dark sunglasses. She carried a riding whip in her left hand. She flicked it at the air.

After commanding the man to lie on his back on the floor, Sybil roughly grabbed Pearl by her arm and with icy efficiency, positioned Pearl over the man, straddling his chest. Then stripping the shorts from Pearl's hips, Sybil made the man lick Pearl's pussy.

Disappearing for a second, Sybil returned with a bottle of warm champagne, and yanking Pearl from over the happy, masked man's face, Sybil roughly pushed Pearl's stomach in until her ass poked out at a forty-five degree angle while her back was arched upwards. Sybil then poured the beverage down Pearl's neck. Letting it roll slowly down the black woman's back, down over the crack of her ass into the man's open mouth.

The masked man drank greedily.

When Sybil had decided the man had consumed enough of the flaming liquor, she cracked the whip in the air, and made the man lick Pearl's ass which he did with such incredible force and power that Pearl involuntarily emitted a high-pitched shriek.

Squatting over the man's face, Pearl hugged her knees with her arms while at the same time, deepened her squat, spreading her ass cheeks wider.

At the sight of the puckered, black, pear-shaped crack, the man released the demon in his tongue as it crawled all over Pearl's backsides, moving faster, then slow, but always in constant contact with her inflamed flesh.

Pearl felt the man tasting her.

"Take off his diaper," Sybil instructed gruffly. "Turn him over." When Pearl complied, Sybil handed her a paddle. "Now, spank his naked ass."

Trembling with excitement, the man muttered. "Please, hit me hard."

The very next day.

Standing in the middle of the townhouse, Pearl took in the scenic view outside the window and noticed how majestic the city looked from this height. From The Arlington, the wide, open spaces in the far distance seemed so lush and tropical, illuminated by a dazzling sun that tinted everything with a sparkling glow. Right up the street, all the skyscrapers that stretched out around uptown were decked out with sleek curves, domes, and crowns. The splendor of the highly-polished buildings was very impressive.

When the realtor walked back into the spacious living room, she apologized. "Sorry, it took so long." She gestured at her phone. "Work, work, work." She gazed out of the window admiringly. "The view is almost so breath-taking that it almost feels like you have died and gone to heaven." The blonde woman chuckled. "And so you do exist?"

Pearl smiled slightly. "I sure as hell hope so."

The woman blushed, suddenly feeling uncomfortable. "Anyway, Andre Pierre is a close friend and if you want this place, as a favor to Andre, I'll make sure that you get it."

Pearl gazed at the woman with brazen awe. "So you retired and ran off into the sunset"

"Well, actually, I didn't get tired of the life. I just wanted to do something different"

"And this is it?"

"For right now, yes. Tomorrow, who knows."

Pearl nodded in understanding. She wanted to ask a lot more questions, but her phone rang. She ignored it. "I want this place."

"Great", he blonde realtor smiled. "It's yours. I will get all the paperwork ready."

And just like that, Pearl knew she was finally on top. She smiled. Andre Pierre was truly her Santa Claus.

Chapter 20

The first day of the next month.

"So, whaddya say?"

Ernest Epps stared at his hands for a second before returning his gaze to FBI Agent Jonathan Hawthorne. Still, he offered no immediate reply to the question asked.

Hawthorne had shown up in Epps' office only thirty minutes ago, and this time had come bearing gifts. It was a good start to a second career, but he knew what he would come up against, and he disliked the idea of becoming a trained guard dog. Officially, that would be a big problem for him.

When Hawthorne saw the crushed look on Epps' face, he silently cursed himself once he realized his offer was about to be rebuffed. "It's a great opportunity," he reminded the black detective. "I have been working for the FBI since I left college. Can't say that I regret the decision either." He paused. "If you need a few days to check things out, go ahead, think it over."

A little more than five minutes later, Epps had sent Hawthorne on his way. He had already given it enough thought, and basically what his decision amounted to was not so much an indictment against working for the Federal Bureau of Investigation. It was that he had something else he had to do. Catching murderers was what he did for a living, and out there--- somewhere---was one he had to bring down: Princess Washington.

Sitting at his desk, he poured himself a cup of strong,

black coffee. He sized himself up, but rarely had he felt so ancient. Although fifty-five, there was still enough lean muscle packed on his six-foot frame that he had the tendency to lie about his age, provided the right female was inquiring. Years ago, he had started to use hair coloring to hide the grey that had started around his temples, but had slowly invaded his entire head. Epps hated his grey hair because it aroused his vanity, but youthful bed partners made the efforts worthwhile.

By the time he had finished the coffee, he had completely gone over the short history of his case against Princess Washington. He almost laughed aloud.

The girl was smart. Epps acknowledged that. Plus, she could think on her feet whereas most dames would fall apart under pressure, however slight. But not Princess Washington who was turning out to be a real cool customer.

After the murders, Miss Washington had checked herself into a hotel which was, Epps conceded, a high value option considering that Hawthorne would go to bat for her since he had been the individual who had ordered her to do so. Epps studied the time variables, but they gave him nothing by way of a guarantee because in his efforts to establish the time of death for the three people in the apartment, the Medical Examiner could give only an approximate time. What bothered Epps, though, was that the time of the murders, when put to closer scrutiny, came very close to the same time Princess Washington had gotten herself all cozy at the hotel.

Another thing that was a source of irritation to Epps was Hawthorne. The fucking guy was too neutral, and was so damn quick on the draw with the standard response of how he would deny any fucking knowledge of the situation if Epps pointed him out to anyone who could directly affect his anonymity. Hawthorne had laughed, insisting that there was not enough at stake for the FBI to get involved, so all the secure info Epps had was the time Princess Washington had left Agent Moore that night, the time she had checked into the hotel, and the approximate time of death in the triple murders. Surprisingly, all of them happened within minutes of each other.

This was not going to be easy, Epps told himself.

The black detective realized he had to keep his guard up. It was the first of the month, and he was good and tired of playing games with Princess Washington, but there was still a lot of loose ends to be tied up. On the one hand, he felt he was building a strong case against the former choirgirl, and that he had her skating on thin ice, but on the other hand, he and Lindsey didn't have shit. To be honest, he had grown a bit restless living in the parallel world of Princess Washington, and it was time the shit ended, but under the circumstances, he felt there was not much he could do. Still, he would get the bitch one way or the other.

Without thinking, he reached for the magazine article, and thumbed through it until he found the page about black sexuality. A lot of it disturbed him, but he couldn't argue with the facts as the article had been thoroughly researched. What was shaping up, according to the article, was a trend he didn't particularly care for. While the man on top was still the favorite position in black bedrooms, more sistas and brothas were venturing out into sexual territory where they were willing to experiment with porno, whips, chains, blindfolds, handcuffs, dildos, vibrators, and a host of other sexual goodies. Epps frowned. This was the hardware of de Sade, and if he was invited into the bedrooms of black America, then the country would have a real crisis on its hands. Hoochie Mamas gone even wilder!

What was wrong with today's generation of brothas and sistas? Was old-fashioned sex that tired that straight up fucking was too much of a handicap for them. In times gone by, fucking was natural, a totally conclusive act based on the action and reaction of two people in heat. Now, niggas wanted bonus points, and fucking was no longer conclusive, but suggestive, a sort of foreplay before the whips and chains came out. Shit had surely changed.

Sadness shadowed Epps' face because from what he had read, and from the increased level of sexual perversion going on right under his nose, it was a fact that black people were taking an interest in the mysterious de Sade and his kinky sex. This surprised him because he had never believed that brothas would allow anything to steal their 'dick thunder'. The myth/reality of the great nigga stud had been a long time in the making, and for centuries the white man had killed to conceal the existence of the black man's sexual prowess., but now a nigga's dick would pose about as big a threat to white America as a nigga's brain. Thanks, de Sade.

He had never been more disgusted in his entire life. Urban America---niggas---were in a sexual quagmire, and if something wasn't done quickly, the 21st century would become the era where black folks lost all their morals and decency. He had never viewed himself as a savior, but since his people needed someone to rally behind, it might as well be him. Yet how did he rescue someone from pleasure? Where did he start? How did he start?

He raced flat-footed across the room to search in his chest-of-drawers to pull out the Bible he had never read. At least, in there he knew of a similar thing happening. And when he turned to the pages about Sodom and Gomorrah, he read greedily, searching for instructions, but soon he tossed the story aside, disillusioned. The people were struck down for their patriotism to perversion. They were too fragile to turn away from sex and sin because they felt they had earned the right to indulge their passion as they damned well pleased. And so did black America. The parallels were frightening.

Epps puckered up his face. At least he had Lindsey to depend on. He phoned the younger detective, but again received no response. Epps mused. Perhaps Lindsey was tied up.

Lindsey was tied up!
Strapped naked to a straight-back wood chair, Lindsey stroked his dick as the lady of the house playfully moved from behind the bed, dancing sensuously to the reggae beat of the Caribbean rhythms.

Stripping off her silk robe, the beautiful almond-colored woman guided herself to the center of the bedroom, tip=toeing across the floor, caressing the insides of her thighs.

"Faster!" she ordered Lindsey. "Do it faster."

Lindsey complied instantly. He sat rigidly upright, his legs trembling as he raced his hand up and down his dick, in short, quick spurts. He gulped air through his open mouth.

"Slower!"

"Oh my God, Miss Tammi," Lindsey yelped. "I can't slow down."

Tammi Duncan slapped Lindsey hard across his mouth.

"Alright, all right," Lindsey groaned. "I'll do it. Look, Tammi, I'm going slow."

Tammi slapped Lindsey again. "Now slow enough, dammit."

"Okay, okay," the black detective cried out. "How's this?"

Tammi kicked the chair over. "Did I tell you that you could talk to me," she yelled. "Did you ask my permission to speak?" Tammi stood over the man and placed one of her stiletto-heeled feet into Lindsey's heaving chest. She applied pressure. Lindsey yelped in pain. "Have you forgotten who the Master is?"

Lindsey looked up into the sneering face. "May I speak?"

"What is it, slave?"

"Can-can I touch myself again?"

"Why?"

"I like it and it feels good."

"No."

Lindsey pouted.

Smiling lewdly, Tammi unbuckled the leather restraints that bound Lindsey to the chair. "Stand up. I have something else for you to do."

"What is it, Mistress Tammi? You know I'll do anything for you. Anything. Want me to lick your feet?"

"Stand up!"

"Your wish is my command, Mistress Tammi."

The voluptuous woman stared at the man. "Would you like to put on my panties and bra?"

Lindsey's eyes lit us instantly. "Can I, can I, Mistress Tammi? I have been good, haven't I?"

Tammi rocked back and forth, thinking; her arms folded across her chest. "You can wear my black lingerie."

Lindsey's face fell.

"What's wrong, slave?" Tammi asked.

"Nuthin'"

"Don't lie to me." Tammi stood in Lindsey's face. "I'm going to ask you once again…..What's wrong?"

"I want to try on your purple teddy or something in red. Red makes me feel soft and sexy. Please, Mistress Tammi, let me wear red today."

Pearl felt like the most miserable bitch in the world, and she hated the sensation. She didn't want to celebrate, or cheer her good fortune, or to count her blessings even though she had become a successful dominatrix. She felt empty inside.

In a million ways, she wanted her former life back, but she called herself a fool for entertaining that notion. Lord knows, she had sinned. Big-time. And on top of that, she felt condemned. That feeling was unmistakable.

Even though she still possessed a fear of God, it almost broke her heart that she also possessed an even bigger love of sex. She was glad to belong to the fraternity of those she fucked, but she resented being into S&M. It made her feel like a dirty pervert, but it was the only job she had. And now she had work to do.

Pearl gave in a little. She hummed a tune by Brandy, and thought of all the new possibilities not being broke gave her.

Driving up Westinghouse Boulevard, she stopped for gas, and then headed to the side of the convenience store, pulling into the automatic car wash. She rolled up all the windows, and then carelessly watched as the big, fluffy roller brushes wiped the dirt from her car. For some reason, the swishing, sloshing water usually had a calming effect on her, but since the wash only lasted a short instant, she drove out the other end in the same mood.

Shortly, Pearl parked in front of a magnificent solar home whose front entrance was flanked by thick, egg-shell white Ionic columns. The grass on either side of the well-swept walkway was immaculately cut, and the expensive garden was still alive with patches of colorful flowers.

At once, Pearl was met by a maid, and grandly ushered inside the polished interior of the mansion. The maid turned Pearl over to a smartly-dressed butler who led her---awestruck---down a long, richly carpeted hallway and up a short flight of steps that winded around to the den. Pearl stood at the door, her mouth dry as the butler rapped softly on the burnished wood.

Invited in, Pearl's mouth grew even drier because seated behind a beautiful maple desk----was the Mayor! Immediately, Pearl couldn't help but think that some dreadful mistake had been made; however when their eyes connected, she was absolutely certain she was in the right place. She knew a freak when she saw one.

"Ah, Miss Washington," the Mayor said casually, so we finally meet. And the pleasure is all mine or will be." He smiled. "Your reputation precedes you."

When the Mayor stood to greet her, Pearl received a second shock. Despite wearing a suit coat, a silk shirt as well as a tie, he wore no slacks or underwear, and his dick jolted out like a rod of iron. It was huge.

He grasped Pearl's hand. "I want you to spank me until I shoot off."

Pearl instantly found herself wondering about the tall, handsome, dark-skinned man who had just four years ago became the city's first black mayor. Normally, she was never intimidated by any of her clients, but she did have some difficulty believing the Mayor was into spanking and submission. Her stomach churned.

Following this brief bout of unpleasantness, she assumed her role and her spirited work ethic returned. It was time to get busy.

Oddly reassured, Pearl lashed out with her left hand, and administered three quick slaps to the Mayor's hard dick. Though the stinging smacks made the Mayor howl in pain, he did appear genuinely pleased.

"What is this silly thing?" Pearl gripped the Mayor's dick and squeezed it until he yelped in anguish, but before he could say a word, Pearl had wrapped his tie around his neck, pulling it so tightly the man could scarcely breathe.

The Mayor gasped for air, but Pearl, feeling no remorse, yanked the silk tie even more forcibly, but at the exact moment when he would have passed out, she released the tie. While she stroked his dick, a thick wad of cum exploded from the Mayor's penis.

"Goddamn!" the Mayor exclaimed, gasping for breath, "that felt good!" Still gasping for air, he checked his watch. "Now, maybe you'll volunteer the remainder of my time by making me get off like that again." He rubbed his deflated penis. "Are you capable of that?"

Feeling challenged, Pearl backed away and in one swift motion, ripped the tear-away sweat suit from her statuesque body. More buff now than ever thanks to her gym regimen, she looked menacing and imposing in her black studded leather undies. The Mayor's breathing increased.

Pearl made a silent gesture with her hands that both prompted and invited the Mayor to consume her with his eyes. Then she blew out all the air and frustration she had pent up inside her body.

The Mayor, taking his fill of the black Amazon, glanced furtively over his shoulder as if he preferred some help, but after a second shucked off his suit-coat, shirt and tie. He stood. "Bring it on, bitch," he growled, "don't be shy."

Shaken by the dark malevolence of the man's voice and the animated twinkle in his eyes, Pearl shuffled across the carpet to where her black bag sat by the door. Instinctively, she reached for the heavily-braided riding whip and the silk hood, but then she saw the Mayor walking towards her, rubbing his hands together greedily as if in anticipated celebration. The man showed no fear. Not one bit.

Pearl snapped. As a dominatrix, it was her job to inspire fear, even if both parties understood their roles. Yet the Mayor's response seemed unnatural as if he craved punishment. If so, he was in for a damned big treat. Fuck the staged bullshit. She was fucking this nigga up.

Dropping the whip and hood, Pearl balled up her fists, and without warning hit the Mayor in his face as hard as she could, and although she was unable to knock him down, the blow did cause him to stumble backwards. Standing mute, she watched for his reaction.

"That's a new trick," he rasped, caressing his jaw. "Any more where that came from?"

Enraged, Pearl leaped at the man like she was a big cat, swinging hard, but the Mayor, aware of the danger, didn't even flinch.

"Motherfucka!" Pearl screamed.

The Mayor shook his dick at her. "Of course, but why is my dick still limp?"

In stark contrast to all the other men she had dominated, none had ever welcomed pain is such a jubilant, exhilarated fashion, and the more Pearl administered blows, the more outwardly reserved the Mayor became. The glazed expression of sexual bliss forced Pearl to wonder what would come next when she applied the fur-lined handcuffs. In case that gesture wasn't drastic enough, she would strap on the thumbscrews for good measure.

Following another timed minute of stinging slaps to the Mayor's face, Pearl removed the beaded leather gloves when a subdued whimper of approval echoed throughout the den. She clapped her hands at this overtly emotional response, but graciously smiled when she noticed the man's dick was hard again.

When the Mayor saw Pearl eyeing his dick, he rasped. "Later," he taunted. "That's what in it for you."

Pearl had never seen a dick as big as the Mayor's. She slapped him across the mouth. "And what exactly is that supposed to mean?"

The Mayor caressed his dick lewdly. "Just that. You give me pain. I give you pleasure." He held his dick up for inspection. "Just look at this piece of beef, will you?" The Mayor's tone was challenging. "Pain excites me so I want you to hurt me, and in return I'll ram my dick so far up your pussy that you'll nut for days."

Despite the fact that she was supposed to be in control, Pearl was weakened by lust, and she stood by meekly watching the Mayor play with his monstrous dick. Intent on taking command, she took a step forward, then froze when the Mayor's dick throbbed, threatening to break free of his iron grip. She desired to see what would come next.

"Do you have rings?"

Pearl nodded.

"I like those." The mayor stuck out his chest. "I would like for you to attach one to my dragon." He pointed at his dick. "I hope you have the extra-large ones."

Pearl could feel the tension, knowing the Mayor spoiled for a fight, that he desired surrender, to become submissive but she also knew she would have to pay the psychic costs of his submission.

The Mayor rolled his eyes impatiently. "Well, I'm waiting, bitch." Recognizing Pearl's reluctance, the man repeatedly emphasized how unfit Pearl was to be a real dominatrix. He laughed gruffly. "And I heard you were a rising star in the S&M world. Evidently, your skills were over-hyped, but then again it's easy to dominate those white boys, huh?" He laughed. ""I'm a real man. I can take everything you got."

Pearl punched the Mayor in his mouth with her fist.

"That's weak, bitch. I demand corporal punishment."

In a rush, Pearl was upon the man. She kneed him in the groin. The Mayor yelled out in pain.

"The whip, bitch, the whip!"

But Pearl had other plans. No longer concerned with over-reacting, she ignored everything Sybil had taught her about discipline, and it was at that moment that she became dangerous. Everything fell apart, and she wanted to kill the Mayor. He had pushed her over the edge.

"MOTHERFUCKA!"

"I agree wholeheartedly."

Pearl spun around at the sound of the female voice, and found herself face to face with a stunningly beautiful almond-colored woman.

"Ah shit, Tammi," the Mayor groaned, "we were just getting to the good part."

"She would've killed you." The woman extended her wonderfully manicured hand. "I'm Tammi, his ex-old lady."

The Mayor relaxed. "Too much dick for her, run 'em away

every time. Young tenderonis don't want their coochies stretched."

Tammi laughed.

"Since we've already met, you can call me Lee." The Mayor kissed Pearl on the cheek. "You're a diamond in the rough .What do you think, Tammi?"

"Pay her, that's what I think." Tammi turned to Pearl. "You can get dressed, sista, while I fix us all a drink. You have earned it."

"I'll say." It was the butler.

"You're good," the maid smiled. "We saw you on the monitor."

"Oh, I see the gang's all here." The Mayor slipped on his slacks. "Come introduce yourselves."
"I take it that you're not real house servants."

The butler laughed. "Is that a trick question because we're all servants. I'm Al."

"But we're also superiors. We play it both ways." The woman dressed as the maid smiled. "That way we experience both ends of the spectrum. I'm Alice."

"Essentially," Tammi said, setting the drinks on the desk, "we represent the crème de la crème of the African-American de Sade society. There are others of us that we hope you'll be willing to meet later." Tammi passed out the beverages. "White S&M ain't shit because once you try black, you'll never go back."

Pearl laughed. "I never thought the day would come when somebody would use that line on me."

Mayor Duncan suffered a few scrapes and bruises, none serious enough to require medical attention., but to his friends, the cuts were ooohed and aaahed over as though they were souvenirs.

"I have never had to be hospitalized," Mayor Duncan bragged proudly.

Pearl smiled glumly, wondering if she was missing something or whether it was that she was too big a fool to understand the enjoyment quotient in getting your ass beat.

"S&M is an individual's sense of stern sexual justice." The Mayor must have noticed Pearl's bewilderment. "It's a sort of personal atonement for our private sins, and it beats the hell out of being stressed out with a guilty conscience."

Without a word, Tammi kissed Pearl gently. "And I think it's time you joined us. You look stressed out of your mind. Plus, what's your argument not to?"

Pearl's voice surprised her. It sounded small and soft. "It's not easy to explain."

"We're not deliberately trying to overwhelm you, but we're serious enough to do whatever it takes to convince you that you have a home with us." Tammi smiled. "And if that doesn't sound like much of an inducement, just think about having one of the biggest dicks in town at your disposal." Tammi smiled at Pearl. "And size does matter. Trust me."

Tammi made it sound as if there was no sane way why any sane female could simply walk away from the promise of good dick, but Pearl was uncertain. "S&M is cool, I guess," she said matter-of-factly, "but it's not the real world for me sexually. Too me, it's nothing more than a job."

"Well, for us, it's a way of life."

"But I just don't get it."

"What's to get?" The Mayor replied. "We're all God's children and all are church members, but we also enjoy sin. S&M is our preferred method of redemption. It's how we purge ourselves. The pain purifies us, the humiliation readies us for absolute submission to the cross. You see, Miss Washington, corporal punishment is simply tithes, a tithing of the flesh."

Al Lindsey spoke up. "S&M helps us fight back against the evil snares of the devil. When we sin, we just don't step in it or lay down in it. We enjoy it, but we atone for it. It's the way of the cross. It's just that we don't wait on divine accountability for our wrongdoings, we mete out our own punishment."

Pearl's mind tried to circumvent the active connection between S&M and religion because the notion disturbed her. What bible did these people read? And on top of everything else, this was even more inappropriate than chuuch, and Pearl was left wondering who had started all these unconventional, controversial church practices. Who was the ambassador for such spiritual madness where it was not uncommon for people to engage in sin and then indulge in S&M as penance? It was almost as though the devil himself was in charge of church affairs because who else could stir up such a brew of spiritual and sexual controversy?

"Confused?" Alice quizzed. "Or do you have a problem with good Christians handling our own repentance----?"

"But that's where prayer comes in," Pearl blurted.

"Prayer!?" Mayor Duncan laughed. "Have you prayed for anything lately, Miss Washington?"

"Yes."

"Wasted energy, am I correct?"

Pearl sputtered before deciding to remain silent.

Mayor Duncan couldn't resist smiling knowingly. "People, good Christian folks, mistake prayer. They view prayer as a magic lamp that is supposed to grant them all that they pray for. If that were the case, then there would not be any problems in the world, now would there? Prayer is nothing more than a formal statement, but humans have a history of challenging God in prayer. Either that or they beg and bargain, none of which serve any real purpose."

"Then, why pray?"

"You tell me, Miss Washington. Why pray when it is a known fact that you can't petition the Lord with supplication. The new theology is that each individual is responsible for his or her own salvation."

"And S&M is the way?"

Mayor Duncan nodded. "It may make you uncomfortable, but nothing else addresses both sides of our personality so fully. Sadism and masochism are nothing more than the psycho-sexual manifestations of our passive/aggressive human nature." The Mayor unzipped his pants. "As you can see, just talking about the new theology turns me on." He confronted Tammi. "Have you been a bad girl lately, dear?"

Tammi slipped out of her dress. She was naked underneath. "I'm always bad," she purred, "but that's what makes me so damn good."

"Then come let me punish you with my dick. I'm going to fuck you hard, you know that, don't you?"

"Yes, Master, I understand. Fuck me real hard."

Black Pearl | Gibran Tariq

Chapter 22

Pearl felt dirty.

Standing inside the door of the Mission Ministry on Fontana Street, she shuddered. Despite the tattered look, this was still God's House but that revelation only made her feel more dispirited and deflated. All of a sudden the small, dark-skinned minister came out to greet her just as she was ready to run from the building.

"Greetings, fellow traveler, welcome back to the Mission." The man's voice sounded too loud for his slight body. "How may I serve you this most blessed evening.

Pearl looked away uneasily, speaking softly. "I have money to donate to your church."

She would have preferred to just hand over the three hundred dollars, and to have left immediately, but the man wouldn't hear of it. He insisted on a brief discussion. "You will surely be blessed, my child." He moved closer to Pearl, taking her hand in his. "But I could never accept your contribution without first knowing more about who you are so that I can pray for you."

Pearl mumbled a hushed thanks as she fumbled around inside her purse for the sealed envelope. She handed it to the man.

"And you are?"

"Princess Washington."

"What a fitting name for you are indeed a princess. Do you have a second to chit-chat. I won't talk another hole in your head. I promise." The man's eyes twinkled. " Come, let's sit for a moment because your eyes tell me that something is troubling you. Who knows, I may have advice, but if not, I'm a great listener."

Following reluctantly, Pearl stepped into a partially renovated office, and had a seat in a chair that clashed with the purple drapes.

Characteristically, a king-sized bible laid open on the cluttered desk, and on the shelves behind the minister's head were long rows of feel-good Christian books by some surprisingly popular authors. A donated 27" Zenith TV was on mute. CNN.

"We all have a mission," Minister Bob lectured, "so that means we are all crusaders for something or another." He smiled. "Where's your manifesto?"

Pearl smiled shyly. "I have none."

Pearl silently wondered what Minister Bob, the street preacher, would think if he knew her crusade was S&M. That would surely cook his goose because underneath all his ghetto toughness, she knew he wasn't prepared to deal with a mess like the one she was in. Her first impression of the small, black man was that he was one for spiritual debate and not direct action.

"At some point, we must all come clean about our crusades."

"You sound like you want a confession." Pearl smiled nervously.

"Confessions are not essential to God, but they do sometimes help humans spot the flaws in their lifestyle. Can you believe how difficult it is to explain the difference between what we want to do and what we actually end up doing."

Pearl stared at her feet.

"Many of today's youth are openly critical of the postmodern black church," Minister Bob began, "and what they disapprove of most are the mega-churches with their impersonal aloofness. The old-timey neighborhood churches did a much better job even though they were a little strapped financially."

"What about the black sexual experience back then? How did the church deal with that or did they?"

"Back in the days, sex wasn't a black predicament like it is today. Sistas didn't run around half-naked, and we lived light years away from the historical fiction that women of color were hot-to-trot. Anyways, back then the church had a way of reaching the youth mainly because it wasn't hobbled by competition from mass technology. What didn't fit into the black experience was omitted. And then came integration. "

Pearl was nervous about asking questions about oral sex because she assumed Minister Bob would rebuke her for her curiosity, but if she was going to get a shot at eternal salvation, she would need to know how to cure her sex addiction. She was honest. She knew she possessed what some might term a psychological dependence on sex, but she also knew that it didn't stem from a sense of personal worthlessness. She engaged in sex because she liked to fuck, and she had discovered nothing eccentric about that. Nothing at all.

"An argument can be made," Minister Bob continued, "that church folk themselves had never been unspirited in sexual matters, but the difference between then and now is that there was no nascent sexual revolution brewing. That happened in the 70s W. F. T."

"WFT?"

"White Folks Time." Minister Bob smiled. "The thread of sexual perversity that rocked suburban America in the 70s didn't take root in urban America....until later."

"Why?"

"We didn't savor the same things privately that white folks did."

"You mean sexually?"

"I like privately better, but, anyway, some of the white bedroom practices did become a little bit more interesting to us decades later. Black people were late-comers to freaknik."

Pearl laughed. What do you know about Freaknik?"

"Ah, the sweet rebellion of youth. I recall it well."

By now, it was clear to Pearl that Minister Bob had some clue that she was attempting to direct herself through the urban, sexual minefield of the new millennium. What he didn't know was if she was an accidental tourist trapped in the maze or whether she was a sexual predator. Nonetheless, some of the points he made recognized both approaches, but most of what he transmitted was the unspoken warning to leave the field.

"I recall a newspaper article about pedophiles. Used to be that automatically I would assume he was a white person, but nowadays, more and more, the pervert is black. That makes me nervous for the children. It seems these days that everyone is obsessed with one sexual curiosity or another until the America Dr. King dreamed of is a X-rated one."

Pearl winced. "Do you view the world like that? I don't."

Minister Bob Shrugged. "To each his own, and like they say, beauty is in the eyes of the beholder. Did you know that in America, porn brings in more money than the revenues from all the professional sports team combined? That's quite a haul. Actors and actresses legitimize adultery on the silver screen as Hollywood glamorizes an act that is a sin."

"But God gave sex too us."

"Yes, He did."

"Then what is the problem?"

"The problem is that God's original intent is dismissed, and this insures immorality."

Pearl stood. "I'll bring you more money next week."

Minister Bob grabbed Pearl's hand, holding it tightly. "I pray that you, my child, are not flirting with disaster. Don't destroy your soul because you can exempt yourself. All you have to do is to communicate with God."

"It-it's too late"

"No!" Minister Bob wailed. "It's never too late. Never!"

Pearl pulled her hand back. "God has forsaken me."

"No, my child. No. God forgives."

Pearl ran out of the Ministry.

Deep down, Epps understood that for the time being, he had no choice but to remain on good terms with Al Lindsey, but there was little doubt that he would ever be able to forgive the detective. Well, if the man decided to come clean and mend his ways, that would be a good enough start.

Anyway, he had made up his mind to end the silence between them and to bring everything he had found out in the open. Everyone in the game knew that Epps had complete confidence in his skills, and that he was a battering ram once he got going, and that he wouldn't let go no matter whom he had to bully.

"I have no intention of letting you off the hook that easily." He eyed Al Lindsey coldly. "You know what I mean?"

"I'm sorry if you feel I have insulted your intelligence, sir, but I don't think it is any of your business what I do after-hours….. or with whom I do it."

"So you don't think it was your duty to report that you were getting your dick sucked and your ass spanked by a prime suspect in a triple murder case? I find that laughable." Epps snorted derisively. "Putting you in charge of this investigation was like putting the fox in charge of the hen-house. I should have suspected something a long time ago."

"Do you actually believe that the case against Miss Washington is compromised?"

"Hell yeah. If you're fucking the suspect, how the hell are you going to make a convincing case against her?" Epps shook his head. "Boy, you sure know how to fuck a case up. You ain't worth shit." While he maneuvered his way between phone calls, he made a distasteful remark about S&M and glared evilly at Lindsey. When the phone calls were ended, he smirked. "What the hell do you get out of being a pervert?"

Since Lindsey wasn't looking for an opportunity to further inflame Epps, he merely answered with a noncommittal grunt.

"You don't give a fuck now, do you?"

Lindsey was sure a response was expected this time so he made sure his voice was clear. "Where's the law that says I can't be a freak and a detective at the same time?"

"Don't give me that shit, man." Epps was all fire and brimstone now, as caustic as acid. "So that was the idea all along, huh? To fuck Princess Washington and me at the same time. You dumped this case off just to get you in better with your S&M buddies. What kind if shit is that, man?"

Lindsey exploded angrily. "And just who the fuck do you think you are to try to tell me what to do with my dick? I'm into S&M and I love it. I'm the fucking smart one here and don't you ever forget it. I'm the man, goddammit!" He barked a few more obscenities and then took a deep breath. "Must be driving you wild just knowing that Tammi Duncan lets me lick her pussy." When that tirade went unchallenged, Lindsey gloated. "You think I don't know that you got a thang for Tammi. Can't blame you. The bitch is all that, delicious." Lindsey relaxed. "As best as I could, I tried to tell you that this was bigger than it appeared to be. I tried to tell you, man, that this shit was going to blow up in your face. Told you it was only a matter of time."

Epps shook his head. "If you help me nail Princess Washington, I'll go the distance to make sure that your involvement is never disclosed."

"Excuse me," Lindsey said calmly, but evidently you haven't heard a word I said. I don't give a damn any more. If you want the Mayor. If you want the choirgirl, get them yourself." Lindsey beat his chest in triumph. "You want me, I won't be hard to find."

This time Epps was deliberately blunt. "You ain't shit!"

Chapter 23

In a rapid fashion, the pain turned to pleasure. "Oh my God!" Pearl shrieked. She couldn't believe the sensation she was felling. She pushed back, self-conscious that her thighs were trembling. Tammi leaned further into her, sliding the rest of the 14 inch dildo up Pearl's stretched ass.

Realizing that his was as good as it got, Pearl squirmed and bucked wildly against Tammi's torrid gyrations, wondering if she would have any luck getting an O this way. She didn't see why not. She was highly receptive to every grind and thrust that Tammi put to her, and settling into a no-nonsense rhythm, Tammi rammed the artificial dick in and out in quick, monstrous, heart-stopping strokes. Pearl obediently fucked back.

When the Mayor entered the bedroom, Pearl instantly got goosebumps, hoping that he would ravish her pussy, while Tammi continued to pound her from the rear. She wanted to be in the middle of a sex sandwich. Getting a tremendous O would be no problem then.

To her dismay, Pearl pouted as the Mayor made Tammi pull the dildo out of her ass, making them both suck his dick. They took turns and before long had the Mayor wheezing and rasping loudly, almost ready to cum, and when his dick produced a series of spurts, wetting their faces, the women licked each other clean. Softly, the door to the adjourning bedroom opened.

"Behold!" Mayor Duncan yelled dramatically. "The Horse!"

With fairytale-like excitement, both Pearl and Tammi gasped in awe at the well-known porn star with the 15 inch dick. On screen, the Horse was highly regarded as an artist who was always sexually correct, exceedingly professional, essentially a fuck-on-command actor. He did only what he was paid to do although the quality of his work had elevated him to cult status. For years, it had been rumored that he was into kink, but nothing had ever been proven. Until now.

The Horse was chocolate, looking like he had been chiseled out of a mountain of the stuff, and that every facet of his body had been sculpted and molded simply to bring pleasure. And his dick. Since the day he had first dropped his pants for the cameras, that one feature of his anatomy, in particular, had been the subject of both raves and curses. It was a shrine.

Tammi and Pearl looked at each other, then at the Mayor.

"Hey, I don't have anything to do with this." The Mayor threw up his hands in resignation. "He's all yours."

From the very start, the woman easily knew that the Horse was a disciple of bondage, but he let it be known that he was a competitor. He was a man who loved to be punished. It wasn't enough that this was the ultra-black S&M community on the East Coast, the Horse wanted to find out if it was the best.

When Tammi attempted to secure the Horse's hands behind his back with a pair of plastic handcuffs, he howled at the insult. He would only be manacled with real steel. Even though he was willing and eager to be humiliated and tortured, he felt duty-bound to defend his honor by submitting to only the best, using only the finest techniques and equipment.

"He's devoted to suffering," the Mayor hinted. "Pain is his goal. In fact, he's the only fucka who's a bigger masochist than I am. I'm good," the Mayor bragged, "but I'm not worthy to have my name mentioned in the same breath as the Horse."

In acknowledgment of the accolade, the Horse threw back his clean-shaven head and howled like a wounded beast. The ear-piercing sound unnerved both women who knew they had their hands full.

"Come on!" the Horse yelled. "Give me pain."

"Let's break this motherfucka down,' Tammi screamed.

"You unworthy bitches. What are you waiting for? An invitation?"

No longer fearful or intimidated, Tammi and Pearl sprung into their most severe dominatrix mode, ready to push the Horse to his limits because they knew they wouldn't be allowed to enjoy the dick until he was totally obedient to them. That was the beauty of submission. Both sides of the whip won.

And then two hours later, the glory of submission. Total. Complete. For one thing, both women were glad it was over. The Horse was endowed with incredible resistance and his pain threshold was superhuman, but now Tammi and Pearl stood in the presence of a man sexually disembodied. It had taken a lot of work to diminish him, but the task had been accomplished. The Horse had been diminished, but in no way reduced. And therein rested the greatest achievement because the point had not been to mechanically take the man apart, but to spiritually dissemble him so that not one iota of his strength and beauty would come up missing. Now, all three of the participants felt wholly absolved, wonderfully free.

"What an exhibition." The Mayor was impressed. ""A tour de force." He kissed Tammi and Pearl happily. "You two have restored my faith in the fine art of submission. Today, you have made a slave. Bravo!" The Mayor approached the Horse who was still bound, gagged, and had on a blind-fold. "And how do you feel?"

"Joyful!"

The Mayor smiled. "And that is precisely how you should feel." He embraced Tammi and Pearl. "You have elevated yourselves. When there is no contempt on the part of the slave for his submission, but rather celebration, a remarkable breaking-in has taken place. Now, enjoy that big dick of his. You have earned the privilege."

The bulk of Pearl's guilt came from deep inside the aura of her love/hate relationship with S&M. She hated the magic of it, yet had little faith in anything else sexually. S&M possessed too much mobility and so easily adapted to her erotic consciousness that she worried obsessively over her worthiness because few times in her life had she aspired to be anything as much as she wanted to become a top dominatrix. And she was well on her way.

Suddenly remembering the CD Tammi had given her, she decided to listen. Tammi had told her it was an undercover S&M song by a black group called Foxy. The name of the song was 'Get Off', and as soon as she heard the lyrics, she smiled. The song only deepened her understanding that the black S&M movement had been gathering steam since the 80s, but that only a very small audience had the sexual mentality to keep it real.

There was something deeply mysterious about S&M, about a sexual culture that was as thoroughly interested in pain as well as pleasure, where orgasms were big and special....And noisy.

Ennis had introduced her to sex that was charming and modest, but Pearl had now discovered that she was better-suited to bedroom drama where the step-by-step road to gratification could assume the seriousness of a blockbuster movie.

S&M was a thousand times more interactive and more stylized than pointless copulation because fucking was too painfully stereotypical. Pearl laughed. She was a self-made dominatrix, but, at heart, she was still also a choirgirl.

What a goddamn dilemma.

Epps had to agree. He had been given fair warning, but he still felt duty-bound to find the facts that would send Princes Washington to prison.

The District Attorney fixed Epps with a cold glare. "That's off the wall and I'm not about to risk the reputation of this office while you play fill in the blanks with your lack of evidence, and for the record, for the damned last time, I want it repeated that I am not going with anything unconnected to the brutal triple murders." The D.A.. shrugged. "If this Miss Washington person committed the crimes as you say she did, then go get her ass."

"May I suggest----"

"Now, you may not suggest a damned thing."

"That's fucking sad, Kirke."

"Be that as it may, but I refuse to help you bust up a S&M ring. Personally, I don't care what the Mayor does in his spare time. More power to him is what I say and I don't intend to use him as a lure to draw out your personal venom against him. So what I'm saying is this. If you think you have sufficient evidence, then I want you to go out and arrest Miss Washington---for murder."

"A lot of what I have is unproven."

"Then, let it go, ol' buddy." The D.A. smirked. "S&M is the farthest thing on my mind. I can live with a little kinky sex since it only affects a handful of people, but how can I turn a blind eye to murder? You the man, Epps. You know enough shit to go out there and get the goods to slap the handcuffs on Miss Washington. Or else she will walk away."

"Naw, man," Epps shook his head. "The bitch ain't just walking away. Never"

"Then get the arrest over with."

Epps grinned. "In the immortal words of Smokey Robinson. I second that emotion."

Chapter 24

Pearl prayed up a storm early Sunday morning. It had been a while since she had fallen to her knees and had prayed with such fervor. It felt marvelous.

Now, with a contrite heart, she felt once more like she could wheel and deal with God. She was 100% certain that she had broken it all down for God in her prayers, and had presented her case in such a flawless way that she could privately strike a deal with God for absolute forgiveness.

Pearl sighed, knowing that although a lot of her after-the-church activities were questionable, she could always point out how it was Ennis and Angie who had misled her. She smiled at the merit of that assumption.

With so much at stake, she had taken a bath in salt water and had burned scented prayer candles. She fasted.

Whew! She had truly been a bad girl and with evident reluctance, she prayed that God would strip her of her fascination with bondage. She argued prayerfully that her meteoric rise in the S&M world wasn't because she was a bad girl. Rather it was because she was so damned good at it.

Another Sunday

Pearl pushed through the church doors hurriedly. There was no problem with the wind this time, but she was anxious to be seated, and she wanted a good seat because, in a large sense, she felt she deserved it. She was back and what this meant among other things was that she fully intended to win back her prima donna spot in the choir. What a vicious paradox between her as a choir soloist and a dominatrix, but the past no longer mattered now. She had been forgiven. The ugly parts of her life had been destroyed and buried. Joy had finally come, and she felt ecstatic.

Yet she soon spotted a problem. Sista Benson. Pearl watched as the head usher thundered down the aisle as though Pearl had a bull's-eye painted on her chest. Pearl, stood in place, muttering a brief prayer of deliverance.

Sista Benson rumbled on like a Sherman tank.

The church watched, waiting on the collision.

This, after all, was church. Surely Sista Benson wouldn't pick a fight during services, but as the big woman passed pew after pew, Pearl sadly noticed Sista Benson deliberately rolling up the billowing sleeves of her frock. No clearer advertisement for a battle was needed.

Sista Benson looked both frightened and silly as she prepared to shed blood in the Lord's House, but suddenly feeling God's presence, Pearl decided not to fight back. God would protect her since there was no longer a crisis between them. The usher was almost upon her.

"Sista Benson!"

At the booming voice of Reverend Arnold's caustic voice, the head usher staggered back as if she been struck by a bolt of lightning. Pearl smiled. God was great. And right on time.

"She defiles the church, Reverend Arnold."

Pearl smiled.

"Who among us is without sin?" Reverend Arnold intoned from the pulpit. "Who among us is pure?"

Pearl smiled even more, feeling totally vindicated. Suddenly, finding it undignified to stand, she looked around for the perfect seat, but as she brushed forward two strange men accosted her. Pearl glared at the men, ready to demand that they release their grip on her arm, but her speech grew frozen when she saw their gleaming badges.

"Princess Washington, the oldest man uttered flatly, "you

are under arrest."

"God is great," Sista Benson mumbled. "My prayers have been answered."

BOOK TWO

CHAPTER 25

The last days
The darkness of night ushered in the prospect of something from a made-for-TV movie, but Pearl saw it differently. The blackness, though frightening, offered her a new dawn, a second beginning, one last chance to save herself.

The mood of the night was so evil that the darkness, becoming even more black, stimulated her. Suddenly, she felt heroic as if she could do anything and that no one could stop her. Not even The Big Man Upstairs. If He was even upstairs. Pearl felt ready to take Him on.

It was getting late and by now both ends of the sky as far as she could see were twisted into a flawless strand of fight-for-your-life nothingness. But all that tended to do was to make her more courageous, more war-like. More I-don't-give-a-damn. She wanted to taunt God, to get back at Him for not answering her prayers.

She drove on.

Riveted by the awakening ugliness of the stark blackness, she, for some unexplained reason, experienced the sensation that the night had eyes, and that they were watching her. She smiled. She was the star of the show.

"Stop me!" she screamed in defiance at the heavens. "Stop me!"

Her plan was to expose God's total neglect of His creatures by killing one of His servants tonight, that is unless God Himself stopped her. This was her plan, her private experiment to prove that God did not answer prayer.

She pulled into the church's parking lot. She took a moment to reflect. It had only been a week since the Superior Court judge had dismissed the three murder charges against her and she had walked out of jail a free woman. Now, came the big question. Did she really want to go through with this? Hell yeah!

Pausing just inside the church's door, she smirked. Damn places all smelled the same, like they had just been sprayed with wood polish. She turned up her nose.

As she now moved quickly through the quiet sanctum, she numbly recognized how the edifice reeked of all the passages in the bible dealing with the Ten Commandments. She cringed and for a brief second stopped, standing mute in the eloquent silence.

On the move again, Pearl's blood stirred. Creeping forwards, she removed the gun from her purse, and snatching open the door to the pastor's study, she confronted the preacher. "Pray!" she ordered coldly.

The preacher spoke calmly. "There is no need for the gun, my daughter. I will pray for you because I love you."

Pearl scowled. "The prayers are not for me."

"No?" the preacher said quizzically, "then what family member are they intended for?"

"They're not for anyone in my family."

The preacher was clearly confused. "Then who?"

"You!"

"Me? But I don't understand."

Pearl exhaled. "You do believe in the power of prayer, don't you?"

The preacher nodded.

"Then you must believe that God answers prayers, that He is kind…and good….and great?"

The preacher remained silent.

"Well, dammit," Pearl snarled, "do you?"

"Why yes, of course."

Pearl smiled. "Then pray to make Him stop me from killing you."

"W-what?"

Pearl nodded. "You heard me right. I say that God does not exist."

"That's blasphemy. God is."

Beginning to enjoy herself, Pearl pushed the study's door closed with her foot. She skillfully fitted the silencer onto the gun, and winked her eye. "Then you should be more than willing to participate in my little experiment."

"Miss------."

"Shut the fuck up and listen." Pearl hooked a chair with her foot and not taking her eyes off the man, dragged it towards her. "The experiment is simple, very uncomplicated. I am going to kill you unless-------."

"Unless what?"

"Unless," Pearl said casually, "you make God kill me. Rather simple, huh? Personally, I don't give a damn how you pray to get the job done. Hell, surprise me. You can pray that I have a heart attack or just drop dead, right here, of natural causes. How about this, with the bad weather outside, what about a lightning bolt through the neck?" Pearl smiled evilly. "Now, that would be creative. Anyway, the choice is yours. It's your prayer, but I'll tell you this, let you in on a little secret. Now, if your prayer doesn't get answered and God doesn't kill me in one of the infinite ways at His disposal, then this is precisely how you're going to die. You ready for this?" Pearl chuckled. "If God lets you down, then I'm going to stick the muzzle of this gun down your fucking throat and blow the damn insides of your head to Kingdom Come." Pearl leaned back in the chair. "Does that sound fair to you? It does to me." She got comfortable. "Don't mind me....Pray!"

"You better pray harder than that, preacher-man," Pearl wailed. "I don't feel like I'm dying or nothing. If you can't get Him to kill me, then tell Him to send you a guardian angel to knock the gun out of my hand. If not, then well, you know……."

After another five minutes, Pearl cursed, declaring religion a fraud. She waved the gun like it was a baton. "Do you hear me, preacher-man?" she ranted. "Where is your God? Why doesn't he deliver you? You know why?" she shrieked. "He doesn't exist, that's why. It has all been a big hoax."

Pearl stuck the gun behind the head of the kneeling man. She laughed fiendishly. "What has all your foolish praying brought you? Nothing." She took a deep breath. "Prepare to die, fool," she snarled viciously. "It's gonna get a little rough from here on."

"Don't play with God," the preacher whimpered.

"First time playing this game, huh?" Pearl laughed.

"Oh my God!" the preacher shrieked. "You're insane."

"You worrying about the wrong thing, preacher-man. You need to say your prayers harder. I know some of you preachers are so dumb that you can't recite Mary Had A Little Lamb, but I hope you one of the smart ones." Pearl made a dramatic gesture with her eyes. "Then that would mean that I'll be the one who'll get fucked up." She frowned. "To be truthful, though, I don't think that will happen."

"I believe in God," the preacher shouted angrily.

Pearl cleared her throat, then blurted. "Make Him kill me, then. That's what I want you to do. I want you to pin your hopes on prayer. I'll pin more on this pistol." Pearl's shoulders sagged appreciably. "Let's see if God is on your side."

After what had seemed like an eternity, Pearl felt faintly masculine and when she demanded to know if the man sensed he was about to be saved, she spoke in a voice that sounded like ironed darkness.

"Your time is up!"

Predictably, Pearl unconsciously brought her right hand up and in one quick sweep leveled the gun on the back of the preacher's head. Breathing rapidly, she hovered over the kneeling man, and with the gun nudged the man's head deeper into the carpet. "Pray, motherfucka! Make God kill me! Pray!

Slobber dripped from the corners of Pearl's lips as she appeared caught up in some devilish rapture. Her inflamed eyes glowed with a perverse fire that burned as if they had squeezed out all the sparks from her soul. She howled with outrage. "Ha! You preachers are the so-called steward's of God's divine promise and yet He won't even answer your prayers." Pearl laughed wildly. "Some God."

    Over coffee the next morning, Pearl considered what had happened the night before, and she started to pace back and forth across the kitchen floor. With the first thoughts, her old fears crackled back to life, but she was not surprised. It just gave her butterflies in the pit of the stomach.

    As usual, she had been all business once she was convinced that God was not listening to the preacher, and had held the gun firmly against the man's head. Yeah, she had knocked him around some, but it had been relatively painless. A few loose teeth, a fractured rib or two. That was the extent of it. Playground injuries.

    But it had gotten worse. Since the man had been larger than she was, it had required a lot more energy to win his surrender. And it hadn't been a completely bloodless affair either, but Pearl couldn't have helped that, not with the seeming super-strength.

    The pastor's study had been small and when she had knocked the preacher over, he had put up a valiant struggle. Pearl had always known that problems could occur if any of her victims fought back, but the excitement of a life-and-death battle only added a new, more breath-taking dimension to the adventure. And she had loved it.

    After the first shot to the man's shoulder and a second one to his leg, the preacher had sadly learned how unfit he was to play hero. Then it had gotten ugly.

CHAPTER 26

The doctor told Detective Epps to sit down, and he wouldn't leave the hospital room until he was sure his patient was as comfortable as possible. Once satisfied, Dr. Melton stormed off.

"Don't be long," he said. "The patient needs-----."

"Now if you will excuse us, Doc." Epps stared coldly at the broad-shouldered man. "This shouldn't take long."

"Make sure that it doesn't."

This was Epps' second trip to this room, and he couldn't avoid marveling at the man, who, by all accounts, should have been dead. Talk about a miracle. The man smiled weakly.

Epps took it upon himself to fling open the blinds on the window. It was a beautiful fall morning and Epps felt that a little sunshine would be perfect for someone who had just experienced a three day coma. As the sunshine pierced the room, the man smiled more fully, welcoming the glow.

"What about that night?" Epps asked.

The patient jumped, slightly unnerved, saying nothing.

"Tell me about it?"

The patient stared at Epps, wondering what words he could use to describe that night. How could it ever be explained? "It was evil." The patient spoke with enough crispness so that he barely had to breathe. "Evil."

Epps walked closer to the bed, had a seat. "But there has to be more."

The man openly wept.

"Has it reached the point where you've forgotten?" Epps coldly ignored the man's tears.

"No."

"All right, then," Epps whispered. "I need to know what happened." He looked at the weeping man as if he was a spoiled child. "Do me a favor and pull yourself together. I need you to talk about that night without falling to pieces."

The man pursed his lips, but made no response.

"The problem with your silence could mean that the man who did this-----."

"Man? It wasn't a man."

For a brief second, Epps looked embarrassed. He became more guarded. "You mean it was a....a woman?"

The man nodded solemnly. His eyes fluttered wide open. "Surprised?"

A light instantly came on in Epps' head, but he just as quickly turned it OFF. "Tell me more, please. I'm sorry if I appeared surprised, but it's just that-----"

"She was pretty, a pretty devil."

Epps removed a micro-cassette player from his briefcase. He touched a button on the player's silver front, and a red dot in the tiny corner shimmered ON, and after informing the recorder of the day, date, and the nature of the business at hand, he looked into the minister's eyes. "Tell me everything."

The preacher got chills just from thinking about that night. His body tingled. He felt light-headed, and wished over and over again that that night had never happened. Looking back in time, his blood pressure surged as the events of that night leaped out at him, slamming into his consciousness. Trying to remain calm, he saw his hands transformed into fists, but how did he protect himself from a nightmare that had already come and gone? Still his heart hammered.

The preacher wanted to hate his vivid recall of what happened, but the memories were there, gleaming and glistening with terrible fright, frozen in his mind's eye. Every time he took a breath, the fear inside his heart seemed to gather momentum, tightening up its psychic noose until he wanted to yelp like a sick puppy.

Cradling his head in his hands, the preacher groaned miserably. "Her voice was full of hostility. It sounded like darkness, like nature gone crazy."

"I understand," Epps commented blankly.

The preacher doubted.

"What did the woman say with the voice?"

"She was ranting, raving, saying blasphemous things like God didn't exist, and that she was going to prove it."

"How?"

"By making me pray."

"For what?"

"For God to kill her."

"Huh?!" Epps exclaimed. "To kill her?" He was puzzled. "So the woman wanted God to kill her. Why?"

The preacher sighed wearily. "Because that would be the only thing that could prevent her from killing me."

"I-I-------"

"The point, detective, was that the woman wanted to prove to me that God didn't exist, and what better way to demonstrate that than by showing me that my prayers for my life would not be answered."

Epps got the point. "And who else should God respond to quicker than one of his stewards." Epps turned thoughtful. "Still, it appears from everything you've told me that the proof was not so much for you as it was for the woman. The issue seemed to be that the woman was the one seeking confirmation that God----"

"Suit yourself," the preacher butted in. "Either way, it almost got me killed."

Epps switched OFF the recorder. The city was going crazy. A woman?!

Just past his second drink, Epps was still visibly agitated at the notions he entertained. He was alone in his small office-at-home, and he was paying no attention to the Presidential debate except when President Obama made a valid point. So far, he was kicking Romney's ass.

He clapped his hands merrily when Candy Crawford, the moderator, stood up to support and defend President Obama on the question about Libya. Epps liked that. Candy Crawford was a real ride-or-die chick.

He flipped through his electronic phone book. He was pretty sure his longtime friend, Reverend Walter Bridges, might lend him a sympathetic ear. Epps had never forgotten the best-selling book the minister had written four years earlier on the power of prayer.

As soon as Epps recognized Reverend Bridges' voice on the phone, his first reaction was to play a joke on the man, and while he had absolutely no problem with doing just that, he considered the danger playing around would pose to the serious nature of his call. He spoke with solemn dignity. "This is the Big E, old pal. What's new?"

"Epps!" the minister said with genuine pleasure. "Well, I'll be a monkey's uncle. You still running with the devil?"

"Naw, man, he stopped chasing me as soon as I stopped gambling and chasing loose women."

Reverend Bridges laughed. "Don't go to thinking you're home-free just yet because anyone who is not saved is always cruising for a bruising......You haven't been saved yet, have you, Epps?"

"The truth is----."

"No."

"In capital letters. But enough about me. I was wondering if we could exchange some info."

"Sounds good to me."

"Would you enlighten me about prayer. You know, how it works."

"Glory to God!" Reverend Bridges exclaimed, "finally coming around to your senses, huh?"

"You think prayer works?"

"Don't be silly, Epps. Of course, I do. Prayer is the

cornerstone of Christianity. I will have you know that the answer to our prayers is our personal connection to God's existence."

"So what you're saying is that if someone could demonstrate that prayer didn't work, then that person would effectively prove that God doesn't exist, wouldn't he?"

"That-that's impossible," Reverend Bridges stammered. "It's-it's blasphemy. God exists. He is real."

"I'm not in a position to argue either/or, but meet me for lunch tomorrow and I'll blow your little boat right out of the water."

It rained the next day.

Reverend Bridges waited inside the doorway of the restaurant and when Epps arrived, greeted him coldly. "God exists."

"Please, Walt, let's sit down."

The two men seated themselves at a black-lacquered table near the bathroom to accommodate the minister who suffered from a weak bladder. Epps momentarily soaked up the tranquil vibe of the tiny corner where they sat. He enjoyed the handsome wood and glass interior with the dark checkerboard tile floor. No wonder that every time he was here, he wanted to play a good game of chess.

"No offense, Epps, but you really got me in a fighting mood right now and I'm peeved at you, to be quite honest, for being so gullible. You may not believe in the scriptures, but you have good sense." He glared across the table. "Hold on for a second. Gotta go."

As his friend criss-crossed the floor and headed into the bathroom, Epps surveyed the depths of what little info he had, and was compelled to admit that something notoriously fiendish was going on. He had a real problem with that. There was, for starters, his ominous awareness that Reverend Baker would not be the only preacher murdered. For some reason, he had been certain that the 'pretty devil' would strike again. And he had been as right as rain.

"Four ministers have been murdered, Walt," Epps said as soon as his friend had returned to the table. "I think they're connected. Someone is snuffing out men of the cloth in an attempt to prove that God is dead. Get it?"

"Quite frankly, no."

Epps sighed. "Okay, remember on the phone when you said something about prayer being central to knowing God, and that God answered prayers as proof of His existence."

Reverend Bridges wiped his hands on a napkin and then shook his head. " That's not what I said."

"But admit it, Walt, to get your prayers answered---"

"Yes, yes," Reverend Bridges retorted abruptly, "an answer to a prayer would serve as God's most compassionate gesture given the circumstances that we, mortals, love to invent for Him."

"Still, Walt, there's much to be said about a God that couldn't keep His promises to His servants. Not only that, but I bet no one will say that praying for your very life is trivial." Epps leaned forward slightly, as if to strengthen his thoughts. "At the very same time that all good Christians are singing the praises of their Lord's greatness, He allows four of His ministers to get snuffed out as they begged to be saved. Can you possibly imagine how real those prayers must have been? They probably highlighted everything that needed to be said in a prayer, but yet God was silent."

"And that's proof that God doesn't exist?"

Epps gave a polite shrug. "For someone like the person I'm chasing, I would think that it might be. Come on, Walt. Begging God for your life while some fool has a gun pointed at your head would very well have to be the mother of all prayers. God knows what I would have said in prayer under those conditions, and I'm willing to bet that in the closing seconds of each of those ministers' lives, they also questioned God."

Reverend Bridges was quiet for a second. "Self-help precedes prayer."

Epps laughed aloud. "I have a big problem with that, Walt. Self-help implies some sort of future, but what kind of future do you think anyone has with a .45 pointed to his head. And that's just it. The killer wanted to make sure that the preachers knew they were in a position where they couldn't help themselves, where it was clear that they realized that only God could save them, and

God struck out four times."

"God exists!" Reverend Bridges uttered passionately. "God is!"

"Then why didn't He save His servants?" Epps voice became a bit more strained. "And I really think you should think hard about that, Walt. You're a minister and until this killer is caught, no one can predict who'll bite the bullet next."

"Men of God need not despair of God's mercy," Reverend Bridges remarked in a voice filled with spirited animation. "Besides, it is not the genius of a man's prayer that awards him the favor of God, it is the favor of God Himself."

"Men are dead, Walt."

"Death is the final call of life. None is immortal that walk upon the earth."

As great as the remark was, Epps could still see that his friend was troubled, and that he wanted answers. He reached out and gripped his friend's hand. "There is a madwoman out there trying to personally dispute the existence of God." Epps composed himself. "So far all the ministers killed have been black, but who's to say that she would soon come after white ones."

The minister didn't like that idea. "No seriously, Epps, what if this girl exists?"

"She does, and if you think about it for a second, it makes sense. If this killer is in the business of finding out just how effective prayer is, then who could be a better candidate than a white minister? Who, in America, the whole world in fact, that doesn't know that Jesus is white. Heavens knows there are enough portraits of him and the belief is that......

"If the son is white------."

"Exactly," Epps interjected. "It will be only a matter of time before the killer makes this connection and when she does, she might feel compelled to see if a white minister's prayers are more potent than his black counterpart. Doesn't that make sense? Blacks, she'll know, have always been victims, and may conclude that there is no such thing as divine justice either. She'll also know about white privilege or what is made of it in the African-American community. Considering that, what's to prevent her from believing that black prayers are discriminated against also, and where will that lead her?"

"To white ministers……to me."

"Wait, Walt," Epps muttered, "let's not get carried away here."

"I'm not. I wrote the book on prayer, remember?"

"I know," Epps groaned.

Chapter 27

11:27pm

Unable to sleep, Epps pulled Reverend Bridges' book from his library and went into the kitchen. Leaning against the refrigerator while the coffee brewed, he studied the words and then without warning began to feel sick on his stomach, his mood darkening. Staring out of the window with its bright yellow curtains, he saw the moon, the only key player of the heavens out and about, working the night as it slowly spread across the horizon like a spool of creamy golden butter.

As he poured himself a cup of the coffee, the hot steam fogged up his reading glasses. Then true to his habit, he dumped two packets of sugar into his cup and threw in a splash of milk for added body and when he gently sipped, he found that it suited his taste. He sat the coffee cup down.

He understood how badly he needed a battle plan, and while the book wasn't nearly enough to send him scurrying on the offensive, it was a clue. Not much, yet a start.

Night after night, in an all-out drive to find the ultimate edge, countless men and women petitioned the Lord with prayer, begging for divine assistance. Some knowing it was a long shot, simply smiled and moved on when their hope for a lucky number or a pot of gold didn't pan out. Others, simply began to view their prayers as a spiritual trek with no frequent flier bonus rewards points, but this was probably the first time a person had the nerve to use his discontent to make a case against God Himself. Epps grunted obscenely. There actually was a fool out there who fancied herself as some type of spiritual insider who was out to publicize that God didn't exist.

By the time he had finished the coffee, he was all fire and brimstone, but still visibly tense. Reluctance hung over his head like a haze of stale cigarette smoke and his initial enthusiasm over the potential of the book had lost so much of its earlier appeal, he now felt almost chilled. First off, he persuaded himself to think positive. Then he wanted a drink.

However just as soon as he discovered his need for a drink, he countered with a new line of thought, the notion being to mentally mount a make-believe attack with what he knew now. And within seconds, he stood on his imaginary beachhead.

He moved quickly, going after his target, a middle-aged black woman, more than likely demented, who believed there was no God. He settled deeper into enemy territory, but moved more cautiously now and instead of striking fast, he stood sentry over his meager ration of hard facts and attempted to infiltrate the enemy's defenses by outflanking her mentally. More often than not, he conjectured, a rabid disbeliever in something, was at some earlier point a true believer and what that meant was that the killer had once been a devout Christian. This excited Epps. This info was ammo. The killer had been involved in the church. But who was she?

He suddenly wanted to retreat so he could totally reorient himself and become more precise because if he moved beyond where he now stood, he would get buried. In war, he knew that not knowing if you were coming or going was not a good strategy. The light came on in his head and he moved back into real time. All that remained now was to get something going, but the thing was----what?

Thursday.

Two years earlier, Epps had made the acquaintance of a black Baptist preacher from Atlanta at a rally against the World Trade Organization. The man, Augustine Mayfield, had impressed him as a solid, God-fearing individual even though he was going full blast at the time with a radical liberation theory. He wasn't even sure the preacher would remember him since so much had gone on at the rally, but his call was returned as he had hoped it would be.

As they spoke, the reverend sounded much more subdued and introspective than Epps had remembered him. Reverend Mayfield even mentioned, without a trace of irony, that he was now more spiritual in a worldly sense.

The inevitable chit-chat had Epps acknowledging that his life had not changed much. This, however, followed the confession that he had been momentarily thrust back into the action. Next, Epps popped a big question.

"How do black Christians respond when their prayers go unanswered?"

"The same way white ones do," Reverend Mayfield laughed. "They rant and rave and throw temper tantrums."

Epps took another leap. "And it's over with?"

"Why not?" Feeling that response was not sufficient enough, Reverend Mayfield explained himself. "Prayer is so much more involved than say, the dogma of Marx or the positive affirmations of Iylana Vanzant. Prayer is no grand adventure with a million dollar payoff as its triumph. Prayer is balm for the soul."

Epps could scarcely not help feeling that the minister had misunderstood what he had asked. He didn't care to know what prayer was. What he wanted to know was if blacks would kill when they found out what it wasn't.

"Please excuse all the questions, but I'm trying to get a feel----."

"Don't worry that you might be making me uncomfortable. You're not." Reverend Mayfield chuckled. "I enjoy intellectual pursuits, religious or otherwise." He chuckled again. "My faith won't be shaken no matter what you ask."

Epps actually wanted to know whether or not black people thought God was white, but he was scared to ask even though the question strained to burst from his mouth. He painfully calculated the question's overwhelming racist overtures and couldn't believe the odds against him getting a logical explanation, so, in the end, he refused to voice it.

"Please forgive me for having such a miserable spiritual I.Q."

Epps begged politely, "but are there real big differences in the black and white practices of Christianity?"

"Well, black folks sing louder," Reverend Mayfield offered lightly.

"Besides that?"

Reverend Mayfield took a steadying breath. "Personally, I think both races should get a standing ovation for our long tradition of doing God's work in America, but truthfully there are a lot of faces on the white church's yearbook that are truly racist. For a long, dark moment, the black church seemed destined to remain tied with the white church until we evolved our own rituals that grew from our unique African heritage."

"Just how far did the black church stray from the legendary teachings of Jesus and I know it may sound silly, Reverend Mayfield, but do black Christians believe that God dies?"

In the middle of the ultra-quiet that ensued, Epps was almost certain that the minister had probably stopped breathing. More troubling was that there was nothing he could do about it, but just as he started to panic, he heard signs of life on the other end. He sighed gratefully.

"If we believed that God dies, then we would hardly be Christians, would we?" Reverend Mayfield snorted in dismay. "That really put my heart in my mouth, thank you."

"It wasn't intended to be rude or anything, but this is a need-to-know situation of vital importance."

"To whom, Lucifer?"

For long stretches during the next ten minutes, Epps conversed in a purely antiseptic tone, plunging head-on into his new investigation but divulging only as much as was convenient. Still, it began to get to him when it appeared the conversation was not going as he hoped it would. More proof of this surfaced when he wondered aloud if white Christians didn't still view black ones as their spiritual protégés.

"According to all the white nay-sayers," Reverend Mayfield scoffed, "it would appear that we blacks are too busy killing each other to have the time to harm God. Not even the toughest, meanest thug in the neighborhood would have the heart for a high-risk mission like that despite how big a rep he wanted." The sarcasm was apparent in the minister's voice. "The time has yet to come in the black community when anyone would feel confident enough to accept a challenge that big. We might be bad, my brother, but not that bad."

Since Epps knew the preacher realized the question was not some out-of-the-blue quiz, he easily managed the audacity to press the issue. "Well, I imagine that to insist that someone could kill God is pretty nuclear, so would it be more suitable to ask if black people in the church can believe that God can cease to exist?"

"Truthfully, Mr. Epps, that bit of blasphemy differs little from the first, both are fantasy. God exists and can never die or cease to be."

Epps did not back off. He was in hot pursuit of a better response and he had the guts to push his luck. "Can you identify for me, reverend, what it would be like for a good, black Christian in mean, old America, who prayed day in and day out for relief from the racist, white man, and never got it? Wouldn't God be in big moral trouble? For an African-American with no earthly power, prayer is like swinging for the bleachers in the World Series. It's the only chance he has. He's down, out, and not driven to prayer by the thrill of the hunt. He's in it because of its hoped-for pay-off and it's his only opportunity and he knows it. He also knows that with prejudice being what it is, only God can help him make his mark in the world, and when God ignores the prayers of his righteous servants, isn't God non-existent to that servant?"

Fifteen minutes after the phone conversation, Epps routinely discovered that he hadn't had much success. Dutifully, Reverend Mayfield had told him, quite clearly, that black people didn't keep track of their win/loss record when it came to prayers. They understood, he had said, that it was their distinction to serve without reward as black theology sustained itself on the old pie-in-the-sky theory, the age-old belief that they would get their crown 'over yonder' where everything would be set right.

Epps turned that belief over in his head and as vibrant as it appeared to be, he trampled on it because he was certain that at least one African-American didn't believe in that sort of spiritual hocus-pocus, and that was the woman he wanted. She was a true killer.

Chomping down on a thick, chicken sandwich, Epps sat in his living room scanning the local newspaper. This was his way of searching for clues to the events or incidents that may have triggered the killer's murderous rage. As of yet nothing significant had caught his eye, but he was committed to the idea that something, possibly tragic, had happened that had forcibly compelled the killer to abandon her belief in God.

He looked away from all the clippings about the last election, Michelle Obama's bangs, and the high unemployment rates. None of these were strong enough to destroy a man's faith in God so it had to be something more personal. Only a divorce or a death would have enough muscle to gain that much venom, yet nothing of that sort had gotten his attention yet. It was out there, though, somewhere.

By the time he had finished off the sandwich with a glass of cold, sweet tea he was convinced that a religion with a tradition of plush bunny rabbits, brightly-colored baskets of candy and toys where millions around the country, such as the thousands in New York, who paraded down 5th Avenue in gaudy Easter bonnets, was also capable of producing a serial killer. To Epps, it seemed like a package deal. One insanity breeds another.

On the short trip from having a full belly to being fast asleep, Epps had a new premise. The killer was a female preacher. By the time he started snoring nasally, he was in no mood for any other alternate pet theories. Without even attempting to conceal his optimism, he almost prayed that this would pan out since it was much less complicated than anything else he could come up with. Epps liked the advantage he had just given himself. Somewhere out there was a big, bad, black female preacher who was also a big, bad, black female killer.

Pearl had made up her mind. She was buying herself a book, a gift to herself and for this esteemed occasion, she opted to visit a string of high-end stores at a high-priced strip mall out in the 'burbs. This was not simply shopping as usual, and she had a tremendous amount of difficulty masking her excitement as she patiently studied the extravagant, colorful coffee table pictorials at BooKs R Us. She liked them all.

"Is there anything in particular you are looking for that I may be able to help you with?"

Pearl glared at the man. "No."

"I have more books in the back. I'm the owner."

"You do?"

"Sure. Lots of them."

"If it's not too much of a problem---."

'None at all," the owner replied. "Follow me."

"Now that I think about it, I'm really quite interested in

books with a church theme."

"No problem, I have the ultimate in Christian literature."

The storage room was behind a red curtain, and down a pair of cement steps. The owner flashed a smile of triumph when he pointed to all the boxes. Pearl was ecstatic. There were nearly twenty crates loaded with hundreds of magazines and books. Pearl smiled widely when she spotted "CROWNS", the quintessential picture book about black women and their Sunday church hats.

"What about this one?"

As soon as Pearl touched the slim volume, she felt like she was suffocating, that she might die from a lack of air. She also developed a slight fever, but glancing again at the book, she instantly developed something else, a renewed fondness for her experiment. She smiled weakly. This was the mother of all prayer books! This was the book for her.

Too bad she would have to kill the clerk.

"I know this may sound a little far-fetched," Pearl explained, hoping to elicit sympathy "but do you know much about the author of this book?"

"Who? Reverend Bridges?"

"Yes."

"They say his theories on prayer are cutting edge stuff and when done right, well you know, your prayers get answered."

After Pearl had confessed to the owner that she had a certain fascination with prayer, the young man gave her a strange look. "Reverend Bridges even had a book signing here a few years ago. People love his work."

Pearl felt clever. "I bet you have some contact info around here somewhere?"

The owner beamed. "Indeed I do." The man made a meaningless gesture. "I don't usually do this, but you do seem mighty interested."

"I'm a Sunday School teacher and in today's cruel world, urban children need any advantage they can get. It might be that Reverend Bridges could come speak at my church."

The owner stepped around Pearl and yanked on a silken blue cord that dangled from the ceiling. "It's against my policy to-

---."

"No one will ever know. I promise."

"Well, since no one else is in the store and it's the slow time of day, okay."

"Thanks," Pearl mumbled sincerely, "thanks a lot."

"Come on."

Wrestling with the cord made the overhead hatch pop open, and when the man pulled on the underside of a metal handle, a set of fold-out access stairs angled down through the vent.

Craning her neck, Pearl watched the owner ascend into the black hole above them where all she could see from her vantage point was absolute darkness.

"Well," the owner asked loudly after reaching the top, "what are you waiting for?"

The stairs rose like a metallic jig-saw puzzle into the upper reaches of the floor directly above her, and near the top step she noticed how a sheet of artificial light hung around the neck of the hatch. At the top, she climbed into a fairly spacious room where stacks of books and magazines were scattered all over the place.

"Over this way is where I keep the contact info you was asking about." The man picked up a footstool and handed it to Pearl. "Have a seat, this may take a minute."

The room was tainted with the odd mixture of decaying paper and patchouli as though someone had recently burned some incense, but what Pearl appreciated most was the heft and weight of the footstool. "You owned this long?"

"Seems like forever, but actually, I inherited it from my father."

"Interesting."

The man looked away, sifting through a stack of business cards and change of address forms. Pearl was glad she was sitting because her legs got rubbery when the owner stopped thumbing through the papers, and stared at the card held between his fingers.

"That it?" Pearl asked quietly.

"You bet."

Ripping the card out of the owner's grip with one hand, Pearl swung the stool with the other, slamming it brutally against the man's head. She swung again. And again. And once more.

Once it was a confirmed kill, Pearl checked herself to make sure no blood had gotten on her clothes, and once satisfied there wasn't she made her way back down the stairway and out of the store.

No doubt, the owner's body would be found whenever someone thought to look up in the attic for him. Actually, she didn't give a damn. What now interested her was Dr. Reverend Bridges. She would soon personally find out just how much he knew about the power of prayer. That got her to thinking.

Pearl totally adored her ideas. God had taken a lot of hits lately. The Supreme Court had outlawed prayer in school and all of the so-called faith-based initiatives had come under fire from both the left and the right. Plus, at the moment, the world seemed increasingly angry, and it wouldn't be too much longer before everyone was ready for the truth, but Pearl had one more experiment to conduct. She wouldn't go public with her announcement until she had sealed her experiment by testing a renown white clergyman. It still got on her nerves that the Pope was out of her reach, but the more she thought about it, Reverend Bridges would substitute rather nicely. After all, the man was considered an authority on prayer and had travelled the globe teaching others how to drill for a miracle with their prayers. He also was a highly-acclaimed professor at a well-known seminary school, and in his free time operated a prayer hotline that attracted callers from all over the United States and beyond.

Pearl smiled. One of God's so-called made men if there ever was one, and Pearl would soon see just what it was exactly that he was made of.

The week following.

Pearl took a special delight in the way the sun had set with such an angry snarl, and sliding out of her car, she politely waved at a small throng of visiting ministers who had come to town to attend a Christian gala.

Compared to her real hometown, Atlanta appeared vaguely futuristic. Despite its well-earned rep as being 'nigga heaven', everything seemed haunted with the ravages of BOB C. (Black On Black Crime), but Pearl still gawked in wide-eyed awe at the metropolis as it gleamed in the darkness.

Feeling a jolt of excitement, she was wildly amazed at her good fortune, and she hoped that while in Atlanta she would be blessed with the chance to test her private experiment on one of the many out-of-town ministers. She shivered with undisguised ecstasy. There were an astonishing number of black clergymen slated to attend the confab, so this virtually assured her of locating a recruit.

Hotlanta was going to be such fun.

The following day.

Epps was busy doing a crossword puzzle when the phone rang. He picked up the cordless. "Hello."

"Epps, this is Reverend Mayfield."

"Ah yes. How's the saving soul business, my brother."

"I need to see you without delay. You'll want to hear this."

"In that case, I can fly down-------"

"There's no need for that. I'm here."

"Here?"

"On the Northside at Floyd's on Graham Street. Hurry."

When Epps met Reverend Mayfield at the diner, it was almost eleven o'clock, but under the circumstances he had gotten there as quickly as he could. He lived on the other side of town.

"Man," Reverend Mayfield snapped, "it's about time." He threw his hands up in frustration. "You sure took your own sweet time getting here. My grandmother drives faster than that."

Epps laughed. "Slow down, recite a bible verse and let's start over. First, I'm glad you made it here safely, and on behalf of everyone in town, I extend a big, ol' Queen City welcome."

Reverend Mayfield reached out and grabbed Epps' shoulder.

"What is it?" Epps asked, startled.

"I met a maniac."

"A maniac!? Where?"

"In Atlanta."

"And now you're running from that person?"

Reverend Mayfield shook his head vigorously. "Following that person would be more like it."

"You-you followed him here? A maniac? Show him to me."

"She probably hasn't gotten here yet, but she's on the way.'

"She ?!"

Reverend Mayfield nodded slowly. "She."

"Okay, okay, she. But you just said you followed her. I don't understand how you can follow someone, and then beat them somewhere."

"Let me talk, will you," Reverend Mayfield growled.

"But you're not making sense. You start off telling me about this maniac you followed who's now following you." Epps shrugged. "You lost me."

"Can I ask you a personal question?"

"Help yourself."

"That killer Christian preacher you tried to get me to believe was real. Has an arrest been made yet?"

Epps slowly shook his head.

"And you won't either."

"I'm not sure what you mean by that, but do you have a logical reason for that statement or is it something you dug up out of Revelations?"

"Normally, I wouldn't impose my view upon the law of the land, but like I said, there won't be an arrest."

Epps sighed wearily. "And why is that, pray tell?"

"Because the killer is not a minister, and it's not a man." Reverend Mayfield sat up straight in his chair. "Keep your eyes on a woman named Princess Washington."

Epps almost fainted.

It was later that same night and, for once, he believed that everything was beginning to fall into place. Still, he was shy about puffing out his chest too far.

Princess Washington!

The bitch was surely trying to make a point.

Epps tried not to remain pissed off at himself, but found

that it wasn't necessary. He would bring the bitch down. He had no choice. It was as though she was out to be the murder sweepstakes winner. Maybe killing was her way of having a good time.
Epps scoffed at how far-fetched that sounded because it would mean……well, quite honestly, he didn't know what it would mean.

A few moments later, however, he decided to flesh that conclusion out. What exactly would that mean? At first, trying to think his way clear was as painful as slicing open a vein in his arm, but he was just lucky enough to feel justified in saying these killings were opposites of her first three. Opposites like night and day, darkness and daylight. Heaven and hell. God and Satan.

Epps dozed, but at 3:00am, his eyes popped wide open. Every brain cell in his head knew that he was onto something and the more he thought about, the faster he wanted to rush things. Given the way his ego was pumping itself up, he knew he was prone to get carried away and then make a costly error. He needed an apprentice.

The next day.

The person he had in mind, Tolly Evans, occupied a small, cramped office on the top floor of the Craig Building directly around the corner from the Internal Revenue Service. The building had a musty, closed-up smell to it. Epps ignored it, and rapped on the door of Evans Investigations, Inc. with an urgent sense of entitlement and while standing on the outside, he hoped that Tolly hadn't left town or been incarcerated. More importantly, he prayed Tolly was still low-down, and still loved to play dirty.

A few knocks later, a female voice sounded behind the door. "Come in," she intoned.
In a single glance, Epps took in the secretary, the ancient bookshelf with the tattered volumes on law and whatnot, the wall portrait of Sherlock Holmes, and the fresh flowers. He wondered about the flowers. Not what he'd expect from a character like Tolly, so he guessed that the flowers came out of the secretary's pocket.

"Hi, may I help you?"
"I'm looking for Tolly Evans."
"Do you have an appointment?"

"No. Just tell him I'm a walk-in."

"Name?"

"The Big E."

Reaching for her phone, the secretary pushed a combination of buttons, and then spoke melodically into the receiver. At that point, Epps looked off into the distance at the Sherlock Holmes painting. He wasn't deeply moved by it at all, and under more intense scrutiny was compelled to believe there was no justification for it. People despised bad art.

"What's your name again?"

Epps firmly but politely repeated the information to the secretary who dutifully repeated it to whomever was on the other end of the phone. For a moment, he seriously considered asking what, if anything, was the matter because from the mystified expression on her face, it was fairly obvious that something was amiss.

Once the woman realized she wouldn't be able to make any improvements in the information she had already offered, she shifted slightly in her chair for a better look at Epps and then described him over the phone.

"But on the other hand," the secretary retorted, "why don't you just come see for yourself. I'm quite sure I would know a ghost if I saw one."

On his way out of his office, Tolly Evans took a brief moment to compose himself. At 6'2" tall and 215 pounds, he was a big man, but it wasn't often in his career that he'd met anyone larger than life. The Big E was one such person.

"Does he look like a ghost to you?" the secretary asked sassily when her boss entered the reception area.

"Don't be silly, Latifah," Tolly smiled. "I would like for you to meet the legendary E, master investigator." He shook hands, greeting Epps warmly. "Come on back and let's see what brings you here."

"Is there anything I can get you, E" the secretary asked politely. "What about a blunt and some Alize?"

Tolly made a face. "Good help is so hard to find."

"Especially when you're sleeping with the help," the

secretary giggled.

    For a number of reasons, it was hard for Epps not to feel good because from all indications, Tolly Evans was still a maverick, bad company is what they called him, and that's just what was needed. Someone who didn't give a damn, and from what he had been told, Tolly was exactly the man he sought.

    As soon as the pair had retreated to the inner office, the young detective produced a bottle of very fine bourbon and two clean glasses. "Wouldn't be right to let an opportunity like this pass without having a drink with the Big E. Whaddya say?"

    "Why not?"

    From where he sat, Epps had a good view of the office, and he quickly trotted his eyes all over the place, attempting to read what it all said about the owner. "Nice place."

    "I may not be as sharp as some of the others make me out to be," Tolly explained after the ritual drink, "but rumor has it that you had relocated to an Indian reservation up somewhere in the Dakotas, and had gotten mauled to death in a fight with a grizzly bear."

    "Oh that," Epps grinned kiddingly. "I won."

    Tolly laughed. "The great Epps live on."

    Instinctively, Epps recognized that the dark-skinned man had the horse sense and the ability to think on his feet that would be required in this case, but convincing him to take an active role, considering the financial rewards, might not prove easy. If there was dirty work to be done, he was sure that Tolly would not flinch, and to a slightly lesser degree felt Tolly was discreet enough to keep his business too himself.

    "This is my last great adventure." Epps decided to lay it on thick, to play the legend role to the hilt, hoping to make his offer to go along with the Big E on his last hurrah as irresistible as possible. "Yes sir, this is it. I pretty much came out of retirement for this one and if you ask me, it's going to be one for the books. It wouldn't surprise me if this baby doesn't surpass the sensationalism of the Detective Dan case back years ago."

    "But that was---"

    "Shit compared to this." Epps shook his head. "Naw, ain't

none of my cases can touch this." He paused for a moment. "Good ol' Captain Winters up in Richmond thinks highly of you. When we talk about the new kids on the block, your name always the first one to come out of his mouth. Told me one day, in no uncertain terms, that if I ever decided to hook up with anybody to hook up with you, and forget everybody else. So here I am."

Both men, for a while, sat in the silence. Both their hearts went out to the thrill of the chase, and nothing else besides pure adventure made any sense to them.

"So what prompted you to call my old mentor in the first place," Tolly asked, his adrenaline already churning, knowing that the call had been for more than simple conversation. Under any circumstances, having the Big E inquire about you was healthy for your ego, but to have him show up at your office was even more mind-blowing. "Or is that private info?"

Epps cleverly concealed his purpose behind vacant eyes and an empty facial expression. At the time, he understood he had no more and no less of a real chance of hooking Tolly than he had of running a marathon. He mentally toyed with his options, and for the occasion decided to let Tolly invite himself in. To do this, he'd have to strip his approach down to its bare essentials and gloss over the blank spaces.

"As I mentioned a minute ago, I'm on my final mission and even though I'm one of the good guys, my only prerogative right now is to play dirty."

"And our mutual friend told you that I might be interested. I see."

"After all," Epps intoned, "there is some accuracy to the reports that you like to play……..above the rim, shall we say. I did a background check, and found that your methods are highly unconventional."

"A man gotta go what a man gotta do," Tolly offered smugly. "Plus, when you play to win, everything is fair."

"My sentiments exactly." Epps nodded respectfully. "But I feel duty-bound to tell you that this is a life and death mission and at the moment, even I don't know where it will lead or who it will lead to, but I'm not letting go regardless of where it takes me. By the way, I'm not trying to get you interested in the sordid details of where this investigation may lead although I hope not to make you feel threatened by unknown challenges."

Tolly laughed loudly. "Threatened? Me? By whom? I ain't scared of shit."

"What about the devil?"

Hell, no."

God?"

Him neither."

Epps nodded his head towards the door. "Your woman?"

"A whole lot," Tolly grinned. "Do I still qualify?"

"Now, more than ever."

Tolly felt a tingle run down his spine. "I'm thrilled to be along with the Big E on his last caper. What's up?"

Epps' tone changed. "Letting you in on this assignment has everything to do with you, not who you know so keep everyone at a distance, even her." He motioned towards the door. "On this case, everyone, other than the two of us, is an outsider. We don't need any friendly puppies nipping at our heels while we're slipping through the darkness, you dig?"

Tolly didn't respond because he knew he wasn't expected to. Just the same, the point was made and acknowledged.

"We start this investigation at the bottom," Epps explained, "basically because we're forced to. I don't have shit."

"In that case," Tolly cracked. "Let's get some shit."

Epps frowned in distaste, but the point was made nonetheless. It was time to either shit or to get up off the commode.

CHAPTER 28

The next morning, Epps met Tolly at Tanners', a breakfast place on North Tryon Street.

"And this preacher guy?"

"There's nothing to hide. Mayfield is rock solid. All his life, he has rung all the right bells, was squeaky clean even in college. It's just beats the hell out of me why Washington would think she could bounce that first degree bullshit off on Mayfield." Epps paused. "Word was that she carried a pretty mean aura at the convention in Atlanta."

"So she spooked your boy?"

"And then some."

"Wrong kind of swagger for a choir girl."

"Intimidation is a tough cookie under any circumstances, but from everything I've been told, Sista Washington was pretty big on selling wolf tickets. Nothing soft-boiled about her approach either. Very threatening."

"But how smart is she?" Tolly cracked. "Being a Christian bully is one thing, but it's a shame she didn't have sense enough not to go around telling a roomful of preachers that God didn't answer prayers. Was that stupid or what?"

Epps rubbed his chin in thought. "You've got to consider

that she had no way of knowing that her remark would register any more that a shake-of-the-head. If she is our woman, it's a fairly safe bet she had no idea in the whole frigging world that anyone, let alone Reverend Mayfield, would have any knowledge of any of the murders and if they did, what would be the chance that they would know about the whole God-doesn't-exist, prayer-doesn't-work motive? As a matter of fact, she had no reason to believe anyone knew about her prayer-before-dying M.O."

Tolly now agreed. "You're right. The honey would have no cause to believe anyone had reason to connect her remarks to anything other than spiritual stupidity, but isn't it strange how, of all the church conferences in the world, your girl would choose to drop in on one where you had a contact?"

Epps shrugged. "Maybe this is God's way of letting us know that He wants this dame shut down."

"If God wants her that bad," Tolly grinned, "why doesn't He send an angel?"

"Probably because He knows you'll work cheaper."

*****

Tuesday. Sometime after one o'clock.

It annoyed the hell out of the doctor that Epps was back again, but the detective didn't care. A lot was up for grabs, and he wasn't about to waltz around his investigation without speaking to the minister again even though the patient was still in pretty bad shape.

The doctor rubbed his chin disconcertingly as he derided Epps for his complete lack of compassion, but no matter what was said, Epps wasn't in the mood. He'd set the record straight later. Right now, he was on the chase for clues, and nothing was going to stop him.

Bursting into the minister's room, he saw that the man was flopped down on his back, looking besieged by all the monitors and machines he was hooked up to.

When he opened his eyes, the minister looked like he wanted to go instantly back to sleep.

"I'll get back with you," Epps growled at the doctor.

Feeling insulted, the doctor moved closer to the bed, inspecting the minister's vital signs. "Around here, a patient's welfare comes first."

His face trembling with rage, Epps backed down. "Handle your business, doc."

"Thanks a lot for letting me do my job," the doctor said with biting sarcasm. "Maybe the minister's congregation will recommend you for Man-Of-The-Year."

The doctor deliberately took his time recording all his clinical observations on the clipboard hanging at the foot of the bed, and when he was satisfied with his report, sighed wearily and scolded Epps again for the unwelcomed intrusion.

"Have a nice day, doc."

The doctor walked away, stopping momentarily. "If by chance you ever shoot yourself in the foot or find yourself choking on a M&M, try the other guys across town. I don't think this hospital would have any room for you."

Once Epps was alone with the minister, he found he had another genuine worry. What if the minister was unable to reassemble the images from that night? Maybe he had blocked the woman's face out of his memory.

When the polite joke Epps told failed to energize the minister, Epps decided on direct action.

"Do you like Yolanda Adams?"

"Of course."

"What about CeCe Winans?"

"I do."

"Mary Mary?"

"Again, the answer is yes. They are all wonderful, Christian singers."

"So you're into singers. That's good and I should have known that you would be familiar with the ones I mentioned, but do you have any favorite pop singers?"

"I'm tired, detective. I----."

"Okay, okay," Epps pleaded, "I'll get right to the point. "Do you know how Brandy, the singer, looks?"

The minister's head jerked violently as the image of Brandy

keyed into this brain. He shook for a second or two, then laid still.
 "Are-are you okay?" Epps asked softly.
 The minister nodded.
 "Who does Brandy look like?"
 "T-the bitch that shot me."

CHAPTER 29

Just as the Charlotte-Mecklenburg police were dragging the body of a local pastor, Paul Headley out of the Catawba River, an unidentified white male jogger discovered the cold, lifeless corpse of another minister, Charles Notes, sitting behind the wheel of a black Escalade in New York.

The following evening in an exclusive suburb in Union County, Jay Kidd, was found stiff and cold on blood-splattered satin sheets with multiple stabs wounds in his upper torso. He was as dead as the other preachers.

Strangely enough, within the space of seventy-two hours, the list of dead black, "celebrity" preachers had grown to almost a half dozen. Even stranger was that none had died peacefully, but no one suspected the chain of murders were even remotely connected until deputy sheriffs scouring the backwoods of Mecklenburg County for the body of a local televangelist, Joe Blue, declared missing, turned up still alive….though just barely.

On the way to the hospital, the young man cursed the devil, begged the Lord, and then spoke in his signature raspy baritone. "You not gonna believe who did this," he blurted. "Find Brandy. That's who it is."

A week later.
Epps received about as much satisfaction from questioning

the young, light-skinned minister as he would from eating a cold bacon sandwich, but he felt he was a little closer to the truth that he had been forty minutes ago.

"We started out in this church game, me and Joe Blue, with nothing but our spiritual swagger." Saul Jones spoke slowly in a thick southern drawl. "We ain't have jack and ain't nobody give us jack. Everyone thought we were just a pair of thugs from the jailhouse on a new hustle, but that nigga's preaching is what took us to the mountain-top. Now his ass dead. That's bullshit, man."

Within minutes of the interview, Saul Jones, the musical director and sermon writer for Joe Blue, had gone from being contrite to being boastful. Now he was stuck somewhere in between angry and confused.

"You know something else about my boy was that he loved every sermon I wrote for him, and he preached the text like he had come up with the words all by himself."

Epps screwed up his face in dismay. He didn't want to hear this shit. He wanted to hear about who may have killed Joe Blue, not how well he could preach.

Picking up on the detective's bad attitude, Saul Jones switched tracks. "Following the funeral, it was like the blind leading the blind. Everybody knew some cold shit was about to go down, but didn't nobody know where it was going to come from---or why. Everybody and their Mama wanted to take over the church."

Epps sat straight in his chair. "But somehow or another, you got the top job."

"It's like I told you, man, when the going gets tough, the tough get going. We operate a million dollar enterprise here, and some folk are more concerned about trying to fatten their pockets than about staying alive. Who knows, maybe there was a conspiracy but personally I feel this whole shit you talking is a bunch of bullshit. Plus, if you want to know the truth, y'all ain't really trying to solve no case about no preachers getting killed." Saul Jones smiled. "Y'all too damn busy trying to lock us up so how the hell you gonna convince me or anybody else with sense that all of a sudden, y'all got our backs. That shit funny, dawg."

"I take my job seriously."

Saul Jones shrugged. "I can't argue with you about what you like or don't like. All I know is that if I thought there was some sort of conspiracy to murder high-profile preachers, then I'd be off and running to the feds, begging to get up in the Witness Protection Program, but look at me? Do I look shook to you?"

Less than ten minutes later, Epps found himself back out in the picture perfect seventy-two degree Charlotte weather, wishing that his optimism was as high as the city temperature. One after the other, black ministers had met their Maker, and somewhere buried beside these blood-red statistics was a conspiracy, the single worst one yet in the history of the black church, and he was clueless. Epps chuckled. What a way to launch an investigation.

In the stern darkness, the front of Reverend Mayfield's home looked like it was squatting down upon the lawn, waiting to descend into the damp earth.

Pearl took a few steps back into the distance from which she had come, somewhat happy that the house was tucked deep within a deserted stem of the cul-de-sac. She took two more random steps, then stopped, backing up one. This would get crazy, she reminded herself.

Behind her, she could hear the soft rustle of the October wind as it lightly blew through the trees. She grinned fiendishly. Reverend Mayfield, in a short moment or two, would be wishing he had been anywhere else in the world besides at home. Pearl giggled absently. "I guess he doesn't know when to step out for a minute."

As she stepped forward, she had to command that she get a grip on herself, but long seconds later after she had calmed down, she still experienced a tingle that chilled her spine. Initially, she had thought that Reverend Mayfield may have been the one person whom she could trust on her personal mission, feeling that he was ripe for conversion, but now she was not so sure.

Pearl remembered the look in Reverend Mayfield's eyes when she had whispered in his ear that she knew that he knew the truth. It was then that she had come to believe that the young minister would be receptive to her new theology that God didn't exist. She would now see.

She approached the house……cautiously.

From the other side of the door, she sucked in her breath, pushing the excitement deep down into her gut, but it was a tremendous burden holding it there because just as soon as Reverend Mayfield opened the door, the adrenaline burst like a dam.

Pearl could tell that the minister was startled to see her, and though he offered his hand grandly, she felt no warmth as they shook. Pearl detested not feeling welcomed.

"If I had known you were coming," Reverend Mayfield announced calmly, "I would have made dinner arrangements. It's still not too late, you know."

Pearl was afraid the minister might say that or try to drum up an excuse to get them out of the privacy of his home. Already, she knew that Reverend Mayfield was frightened. "I'll only be a second."

"How did you know where I lived?"

"You're very popular."

The reverend spared himself a response. "What may I do for you?"

"There's something I'd like to discuss with you."

"Please, let's sit."

Even though this wasn't the first time Pearl had been called upon to act out a murder without a script, she felt completely enclosed by the falling apart of her original plan. "What's your take on, er, let me think how to say this. Ah well, let's see. On second thought, I guess it might be a little early for such a question. So I'll ask this one instead. Just how large is your congregation?"

"Large enough, I suppose."

Pearl straightened up. "Nice house."

"I enjoy it."

"You know something," Pearl leaned forward. "There has been a lot of controversy lately over gay marriages. It's all over the news. I think-----."

"Don't take this personally, but I hardly believe you came

down here to voice your opinion about gay rights."

Pearl leaned back, smiling. "Just trying to get your conversational juices flowing, but you know something, I like a man who doesn't pull any punches because that frees me up to just be myself." She sat straight. "Yeah, I like that. I'll be me. You be you. That should keep us going all night."

Reverend Mayfield shifted uncomfortably in his chair. "I don't know what's on your mind, Miss Washington, but don't make me regret inviting you into my home."

"Look," Pearl's voice had menace now, "it doesn't seem right that you should get so hostile towards another believer."

"After some of the things I've heard you say the last time, I'm not very sure about your beliefs. You upset a lot of us."

"Is that right?"

"Yes, that's right."

"Then, good." There was anger in Pearl's voice now. "That means that the time has come for all the soldiers to stand up and come forward. You included. Aren't you tired of being a damn spiritual punk?"

Reverend Mayfield stood. "I'm must ask you to leave, Miss Washington."

Pearl pulled out the gun. "See what your southern un-hospitality has unleashed." She sounded genuinely hurt. "I'm surprised at you." She leveled the gun. *"Pray!"*

Pearl had never seen anyone die like that. There had been so much blood, but the thick, plush carpet had absorbed it like an expensive sponge. However now she felt embarrassed, ashamed that she had stayed overnight in Atlanta just so she would have the pleasure of reading about the killing in the morning's paper.

She had already read the grisly article twice, but found herself reaching for the newspaper again, and pushing her plate of buttermilk pancakes away as her eyes involuntarily surged across the bold-faced caption that spelled out the details of her dirty deed.

Whoever had written this was good, Pearl admitted to herself in a congratulatory fashion. Bastard could write his ass off, and her admiration for the reporter was so great at the moment that she wished she could hire him as a private correspondent to write about all her murders and the other shit she liked to do.

Four hours later when she arrived home, she parked her car on the side of her residence where it wasn't visible from the street, and immediately dashed inside to download some CDs.

"I swear to God," Epps groaned, "I don't believe this shit. The bitch!" He groaned again.
"Yeah, but still we better make sure, check a few things out, see how things shape up."

Suddenly, the room was quiet. Epps was awed by the reckless passion of the murder, but from the very moment he had heard about it, he had been sure that Princess Washington had done it. This made Epps uncomfortable because he clearly recognized that the woman was not some primitive murderer. Instead, she was an absolutely clever killer when it came to settling scores as she had so aptly demonstrated when she had disposed of Reverend Mayfield.
With that killing, the operation to bring Princess Washington down moved to a higher level, but the stinging irony was that both Epps and Tolly were distressed by the possibility that they didn't have the evidence they needed to make a case against her. And totally dispirited, both men speculated how long it would be before another Christian minister died.

"What the hell are we supposed to do now?" Tolly whimpered in anguish. "You think I like letting the killings go on."

After a long time studying his reflection in the bottom of his coffee cup, Epps said what always seemed appropriate under the circumstances. "We'll come up with something."

"Yeah." What else could he say? Tolly looked out the window. "I could check out her alibi. That would give me a chance to measure her, you know, to take in her whole attitude. See where her head is at."

Epps shook his head. "Wouldn't do a damn thing but spook her, you get to asking too many questions. She wouldn't dare make an admission about being in Atlanta, anyway." He looked at Tolly without expression. "You thinking she would?"

"I could check out her phone calls."

Epps appeared skeptical, but said nothing.

"Who knows. If she was in Atlanta, which we are sure she was, then it's possible----"

"You really believe she had time for that bullshit. Hell, she was too busy playing executioner. Why should it bother her if no one called her phone? I'm sure she wasn't expecting a message from the Nobel Peace Prize folks."

"Maybe not them," Tolly returned matter-of-factly,"but what about a lover or if she simply called home to check her messages?"

"In that case, check the phone records."

Tolly tapped on the desk all the while smiling, and looking at his drumming fingers.

"Okay, let me see if I can't get a tap for her phone."

"Why waste the time when I can get it done much quicker by breaking into her house?"

"I didn't hear that, but just the same.......whenever you get the phone records, you can come back here and we'll go over them together."

"I know you not paying any attention to what I'm saying, but just in case a lil' bird is listening, I'd like him to know that I'll set the listening post up at my crib."

Epps smiled. "I like birds."

It was still unseasonably warm and Tolly loosened his tie considerably. The damn thing felt like it was choking him. He rounded the corner, and stood momentarily in the building's shadow, scowling in disbelief at the sun before dashing into the entrance of the old, dilapidated apartment complex.

The stairsteps rose out of the floor like dust-encrusted centipede feet, and near the first landing, he remembered to step over the next to last step. He always tripped on the ripped piece of carpet.

Just after inserting the key into the lock and slightly before opening the door, he engaged in some wishful thinking. He hoped the mikes had picked up something. Inside the hushed, cramped bedroom that had become his sanctified listening post, he embraced the unquestioningly real possibility that the tapes held nothing. Zero.

On the surface when Tolly placed the headset over his ears to transcribe what was on the tapes, he seemed far removed from his private passions, but inwardly he was anxious. By the time he started to work the machine, he was beset by the choice of not listening or only half-listening. He decided to half-listen since he was too scared to face Epps without transcript notes.

Lending just half an ear to his duty, Tolly completed the first tape, noting the unimportant chatter of Miss Washington, but by the time he had started the second tape, he picked up a radical shift in her tone. She was clearly agitated. Tolly's interest was ignited, and with a seasoned ear listened intently. He was encouraged by how sharp Princess Washington was, and when he reached the point where she was cursing wildly, he understood he was onto something compelling. He was largely successful in editing out all the incoherent mumbling and woeful lamentations on pages five and six, but quickly realized that the woman was about to verbally lash out at whoever or whatever it was that had so incensed her.

And true enough on page seven, near the bottom, there it came, the opening salvo of her venomous tirade against 'the fraud'. The language was so hot that Tolly was momentarily embarrassed by listening to it, but immediately regained his composure.

The more he listened, the more he understood how Washington's hatred was not merely self-crippling, but how it menaced the lives of black preachers everywhere. And for the first time, Tolly was able to grasp the slow process that had changed the choirgirl's attitude and values.

Besides her unbridled rage against men of the cloth, Miss Washington angrily lashed out at a God she claimed didn't exist, but that had physically deprived her of the greatest gift in her life. Tolly absently wondered what that gift had been, but the woman failed to say.

Once the tapes ended, Tolly was infused with renewed hope. These transcribed notes dramatized what he and Epps had suspected all along: that Princess Washington was the architect of a whole lot of murders.

To be fair, he held his optimism and enthusiasm in check, but still he jumped in his car and drove like never before. Epps was going to like this.

Tolly's "breakthrough" tapes made a powerful impression on Epps. The discovery put them into the fight for the first time, and if they could produce gold out of these audio surveillance tapes, then Princess Washington wouldn't escape justice after all. Still, it would be quite a while before they could look to make a final charge against the former choirgirl, but for right now, Epps was elated with what he was hearing.

Thanks to the expertise of Tolly, the sixty-three minutes of audio had been trimmed and transcribed into a coherent, greatly condensed ear-fest. To his credit, Epps remained theatrically stoic as he listened to the tape the second time, effectively blocking out his unconscious habit of getting too far ahead of himself.

When the tape ended, Epps sullenly clapped his hands with all the drama of a patron of the arts who had just experienced a dazzling tour-de-force performance. "Bravo", he announced flatly. "Bravo!"

Tolly beamed.

Reining in his joy, Epps persuaded himself to speak softly and without emotion. "Now, let's see what the phone records tosses up."

Once more, Tolly crossed his fingers, hoping the phone records did indeed toss up some light on whether or not the choirgirl was anywhere in Atlanta on the night Reverend Mayfield was murdered. He already knew just how much trouble it had taken just to obtain the subpoena to secure these records from the phone company, and at first glance, it appeared doubtful what, if any damn thing, they would disclose.

"Which stack do you want to attack first?" Tolly inquired. "Personally, it looks like one is just as bad as the other."

"Let's do the phone record. We know what night Mayfield was killed, so that's our date. Look for a 404 area code. Find that, and we see how big a window of opportunity we get."

Tolly and Epps both eyed the mountain of pages that contained countless long columns of telephone numbers tolled to the residence belonging to Princess Washington. And it was the deepest hope of both men to tie in a possible call from Atlanta on the night of the killing, and then work from the premise that it was Princess Washington who had made the call.

Both men greedily soaked up the numbers attached to the date of Reverend Mayfield's murder, but what was especially striking about the numerical puzzle was how easily the pieces fell into place.

"Bingo!" Tolly yelled. "There that 404 motherfucka is!"

For his part, Epps sought to make some sense out of what this revelation brought into existence. Now that they had it, he knew it would prove a hard sell unless one of them electrified the assumption that Princess Washington had phoned home from Georgia.

"Two things," Epps enunciated slowly. "First, I need to know precisely where this call was placed from and secondly, I want a list of all the people in the Black Ministers' Alliance."

"You've got it," Tolly said, "but more than likely the number belongs to a public phone."

"Could be, but if we're going to get any juice out of this, we've got to be sure. When we go to court on this, we can best believe the choirgirl won't have a looney tune attorney representing her. Therefore, in the absence of anything else, we have to rely on the truth." Epps smiled. "And that's why I miss the good ol' days."

Epps didn't believe he was too far off the mark by hoping to build a strong case out of the mysterious phone call if he could make it more threateningly efficient. If he could somehow push it out of its rhythm. Otherwise, a phone call was a phone call. And how did they prove it was Miss Washington who placed the call? Anyway, for all he knew at the moment, it could have come from a secret lover or a relative, but he refused to believe that.

"Shit," Epps cursed to himself. If his efforts, primarily to find the smoking gun, were to be anything less that catastrophic, then Tolly was going to have to pull a rabbit out of the hat down in Georgia. He knew Georgia was known for its peaches, its rainy nights, and its midnight trains, but Epps wished Tolly could distort this cozy picture a little bit to include bunny rabbits. They should as hell needed one. Bad.

    The antidote, Epps had informed Tolly before they parted ways, would be to locate the phone booth where the call had been made and then to confine Miss Washington there, but now that he was in Atlanta, Tolly saw how immediately frayed that possibility was. Beyond the fact that the call had not been made from a phone booth destroyed the fundamental illusion that he could dust the area down and retrieve fingerprints that matched their suspect's. Additionally, there was also the bitter betrayal that the place where the call had been actually made was a well-known diner where the phones got wiped down every night prior to closing. General cleaning procedures, they cited, and while that may have scored them an "A" from the sanitation inspectors, it had just given a "F" to his investigation. Tolly cursed angrily. As a result, the limited assets of the facts he had to negotiate with became even more limited and still worse, all the employees were powerless to identify the photo of Princess Washington as someone they had ever seen before.

    Following this defeat, Tolly had no choice but to loot other options, and the more he strayed away from the telephone booth premise, the more he knew he and Epps had overlooked something. But what? Tolly understood how to make clues flow by putting pressure on valid assumptions, but had never learned how to produce gold out of leads that went for broke too soon.

    At 2:15pm, he phoned.

    There has to be more," Epps lamented sadly, resisting the news.

    "That's it, brer," Tolly countered, "and shit ain't going to get any better. They don't remember shit down here."

    Epps' usual practice when confronted with opposition to one of his plans was to fuss and to fume, but this time he recognized the futility of doing so. And having no resources to fall back on, his voice became less melodramatic. "I guess it is possible that employees in the deep south don't start remembering shit until after lunch. Being rational at eight in the morning might be asking too much….." Epps paused, then exploded. *"Dammit, Tolly, that's it!"*

"Wh-what is it, man?"
"What do you think it is?"
"I-I don't know."
"How does this sound? If the bitch was in Atlanta that time of the fucking morning, and Mayfield had gotten iced the night before could only mean one thing. Unless the bitch is a damn owl, she had to sleep somewhere."
"A hotel?"
"Exactly."
"I'm on it."
"Let me know what you come up with."
"Sure thing, boss."

By six o'clock, Tolly had struck paydirt and although it wasn't the cushy place he had imagined it would be, he had finally identified the hotel where Princess Washington had spent the night. Such a realization he knew permanently rigged the deck against the choirgirl because, in its own way, everything else would now fall into place. A solid clue was just that sweet.

CHAPTER 30

The moon was so full that it gave the impression that the night was stuffed down inside the crotch of the darkness. Pearl almost whooped and cheered because this was where she would bury the body.

The site where she would bury the body was deep in the country on a stretch of land that was utterly desolate and bleak, surrounded by tall, dead tress that appeared spooky when daylight was cut off. A perfect resting place.

Turning away from the main road, she gazed at the tombstones. They were all carefully arranged like elaborate, stiff hairdos bound up in concrete grey.

Methodically, she followed the line of trees into the seclusion, and parked directly to the left of the glittering star that shone brightly over her head. Discreetly, she chose the burial site. And instantly, her anxiety was gone, now replaced by a dangerously cool calm.

Pearl smiled. It wouldn't be long now.

She walked swiftly to her car, got in, drove away. Before her, the lights of the city softly beckoned, and though the precise nature of her preparations were snap-of-the-finger quick, she felt she was in a great position to pull it off without any problems. Or so she hoped.

Anyway, just ahead of her, the night was a paler shade of black than at the burial site, but she was not tripping. Instead, she focused on how best to get into the fashionable house of Reverend Bridges. Her mind worked furiously doing the mental math needed to get inside the home, but it was still early so she had time.

Stopping at the fringes of the well-kept lawn, she searched for any signs warning of an alarm system. She saw none. Still, that didn't mean there wasn't one. She now cursed, knowing she would have a problem if there was a silent alarm. She spat nervously, the implications too big to ponder. Well, at least she knew the dangers involved. That, by itself, was a plus.

Abruptly, she wished she could spend more time going over her plan, but she couldn't. And she couldn't withdraw. And since it wasn't her style to put off or to postpone the inevitable, she walked up to the white rail fence, and stood alone on the Reverend's private property. Now, all of a sudden she had to get in the zone. This wasn't going to be perfect, but everything now was clear. Pretty soon, she would get her proof.

Thirty minutes later.
Inside the church, Pearl snapped the door shut with her foot. She wanted to take a look around. She wanted to make a test run.

Brooding and intense as she walked around the front perimeter, she was certain Reverend Bridges would retire to his study tomorrow to work on his sermon, and to that end she wanted access to him there. She could wait another day so she instantly dismissed the idea of testing him at his home. Besides, the church would be more handy and convenient. On the surface, it would give her the sort of control she needed to conduct her experiment properly because if nothing else she understood churches, knowing they were the nerve center of a minister's life.

"Well, well," she mumbled too herself after checking out the church's interior, "somebody better get ready to inherit this pretty place.......unless Reverend Bridges passes the test." She doubted it very seriously, but you never knew. She had never factored in spiritual bigotry. Maybe there was more to white privilege than originally suspected. *Soon, she would know.*

Ambling back to her car, she found she couldn't clear herself of all her guilt which had reached a new level by the time she had spotted the telephone booth. The phone seem to beam at her and the booth glistened like some sparkling command center. She pulled over.

Am I doing the right thing, she wondered as her hand went for the receiver. She remembered that she needed to do herself the favor of keeping this killing as impersonal as possible because if not, her bloodlust could reach the point where it became selfish. And she didn't want that. Staring at the phone, she made up her mind but still paused before punching in the digits.

Not a single muscle seemed to twitch as she listened patiently to the ringing, waiting; hoping that Reverend Bridges was in, that he would pick up, and when he did, Pearl snapped alert. Instinctively, she hunched down in the booth, and kissed the phone as if it was a holy relic. She squeezed the receiver tightly.

"Hello."

Inside the booth, Pearl felt emotionally hot. She clearly recognized the voice, then clicked the phone off without saying a word. She glanced at her watch, and waited an impatient thirty seconds before re-dialing the number. This is a good idea, she convinced herself. Make him sweat. It made good sense, but now it was time to tread into the man's private space.

She listened to the phone ring, and it wasn't much of a worry when the reverend was slower answering this time. Pearl understood so she didn't panic.

"Hello." Reverend Bridges' voice was noticeably louder now.

"Reverend Bridges, this is Sherry Long, you know, the lady in the parking lot. Oh yeah, I'm sorry we got cut off a second ago, but you can't believe how much I have thought about God." Pearl strained to hear the forced change in the direction of the minister's breathing, but it was there. Frustration giving way to relaxation. So she made the decision to remove any feeling of ease the man might experience. It was best to keep him on edge, against the ropes. "Why do so many people not believe in God?'

"The devil."

As great an answer as he thought that should have been, it failed to stifle Pearl's impulse to want to dig deeper. "You mean to tell me that the devil's reach is that great?"

"It would be asking too much, Sister Long, to try to trace the history of spiritual disbelief in one, short telephone conversation, so what I suggest is that you get up the courage to join the church."

"*Courage?!*" Pearl's voice trembled. "Just how much courage do you think it takes, Reverend Bridges, to be like a lamb being led to slaughter? I, personally, call that foolishness."

The jagged edge of Pearl's tone ripped into Reverend Bridges' ear drum, rupturing his calm. "W-what do you know about God?"

Pearl delighted at the trembling in the reverend's voice. "Nothing. *Much.*"

"Do you believe in the existence of God?"

"Who can answer a question like that," Pearl rasped. "Very few people actually know what they believe in."

"And you think God is a good example of that?"

"Why not?"

Reverend Bridges could sense the growing dark presence of the woman's voice branching out, inheriting even more darkness. Suddenly, he felt encouraged to penetrate the veil of evil. "Who are you?"

Pearl grunted. "Is that all you want to know?"

"That's not unreasonable, is it?"

Pearl forced a laugh. "I am who I am, and you can quote me on that." She hung up the phone.

Much to her surprise, Pearl was not as mad with herself as she thought she should be. For all practical purposes, she'd blown it. Killing Reverend Bridges tomorrow was now a moot point. The man was spooked, but what the hell? Tonight was as good a time as any to commit a murder.

Reverend Bridges didn't recall exactly how the startling revelation had come to him, but it had come, and it had reduced him to a bundle of nerves. Automatically, he now knew who Sherry Long was, and in his social circle that wasn't anything to croon about. He called Epps shortly past the hour, but there was no response. He left a message.

The return call came exactly twenty minutes later, and Reverend Bridges sighed in relief. "Good grief, Epps, your killer is on my tail."

"Slow down, old buddy," Epps cautioned, "and let's start all over again." He could hear the panic in the man's voice, and knew it would get stronger unless he calmed him down some. "Trust me, there is no killer on your case."

"You're telling me. I'm telling you," Reverend Bridges shrieked hysterically. "I had her on the line not long ago, and now she's waiting to sink her teeth into me. It's her, Epps."

"And you talked to her on the phone?"

"Not only that. I saw her."

"Yo-you saw Princess Washington?"

"Only she called herself Sherry Long. Want me to describe her? Black and beautiful, with an impossibly nice figure. Want to know something else?"

"What?"

"She's going to kill me."

"Hold on, Walt," Epps pleaded. "Now is not the time to overreact. At any rate, it is my understanding that Miss Washington is still right here in Charlotte."

"And just when was the last time you looked?"

"I mean she's not under surveillance or anything, but my assistant and I do monitor her whereabouts periodically."

"Check."

"Huh?"

"Run a quick check, Epps, and if she's there, I'll eat my hat." Reverend Bridges was upset. "It's your girl. I know it."

"I'll see what Tolly can come up with."

"Okay, fine, but what am I supposed to be doing in the meantime? I'm thinking of notifying the authorities."

"Walt, listen. I know you're upset."

"Wouldn't you be and trust me, I'm a lot more than a little

upset."

"Just the same, you can't demand police protection without a plausible explanation for it. I-----"

"For God's sake, man, I'm being stalked. What more proof than that do I need?"

"Actually, Walt, you observed a woman whom you think may be involved in attacks that I'm working on. Until you have proof that this woman is indeed Princess Washington, please try to remain calm. Did anyone else see her that you know of?"

"Why? What do you need, a second opinion? You think I'm making this up?"

"Who else, if anyone, is there?" Epps said firmly, "that you know of who can give me a description of the person you saw."

"Carmela Simpkins."

"Who?"

"She was there."

"Can you contact her for me?"

"Hold on and I'll three-way her. She's always home at this time. She'll tell you. You'll see."

After the phone at the Simpkins' residence continued to ring, Epps broke in. "Perhaps she stepped out for a minute."

"No," Reverend Bridges commented shakily. "Never."

"Than what are you saying?"

"She's killed her for chrissakes. Epps," Reverend Bridges wailed. "She has killed her so she can kill me. Does someone have to paint you a picture? I'm calling the cops."

"No, Walt," Epps yelled, "please don't misread this."

"I don't believe you, man."

"Look," Epps sighed. "I'm with you on this. Make sure all the windows and doors in your house are locked. Stay put, you hear me. And don't call the cops, I will."

"You will?" There was relief in the minister's voice. "When?"

"As soon as I get off the phone with my assistant. I have a P.I. friend up there that I'll send by the Simpkins' place to see what's doing there. Then I will have my assistant check in on Princess Washington."

"So you still think the killer is there when I'm telling you that she's here, right in my own backyard."

"Just let me check. If she is here and your friend is safe, then I'm going to tease you about this until we're old and gray."

"We're already old and gray, Epps," Reverend Bridges groaned, "but she's here and Carmela is dead."

"Go take a drink or two of the strongest beverage in your house and relax because until my impromptu investigation is over, nothing is gospel, okay?"

"For the last time, man, I repeat, she's here and Carmela is dead."

As usual, Epps didn't want to sound as hard-as-nails when he demanded something extra of Tolly, but he couldn't skirt his obligation to know just where Princess Washington was. If that maniac was in Tennessee.....

"No way," Epps said as he dialed Tolly. "No fucking way that bitch is not in town."

Epps stopped talking to himself when the phone on the other end started ringing, and he momentarily experienced a second pang of guilt about having to ruin Tolly's evening by getting him up and out of his house to keep tabs on Princess Washington, but they did have the duty to ride the hell out of this investigation until it concluded. Tolly was a professional. He'd understand. Plus, Tolly wasn't the kind who enjoyed sitting on the sidelines when there was a clue to be squeezed or a lead to be pursued. That was just how Tolly was, a real trooper. Epps smiled at the image

When the conversation ended, Epps couldn't help smiling some more. He and Tolly had both agreed that there was no conceivable way Princess Washington could have left Charlotte without one of them knowing it, so he pushed aside the notion. Miss Washington was still home. He hoped. He had badly underestimated other suspects before, but it was not because they were too complex or too crafty. It usually was because they had gotten lucky. Even then, he would still nab them because most of them would let their good luck rot like a raisin in the sun.

When the phone rang some minutes later, Epps gave it a stone-cold glare before picking up the receiver. The call was not unexpected.

"And now after our little conversation, do you still feel this out-of-the-blue excursion is necessary?"

"Sure do, Tolly," Epps said lightly. "I need you to check it out for confirmation purposes if nothing else." Epps sighed. "I wish I could offer a more encouraging reason than that, my friend, especially since it seems this came up at a rather bad time. Do tell your lady friend how sorry I am."

Tolly frowned.

"No way that I'm asking for an all night stake-out. I just need an observation. Seeing her car parked in the driveway won't do though, you have got to get her into your sights or at least hear her voice. Play lost. Used to work for me." Getting no response, he added dryly. "The quicker you get your look, the quicker you get back to your fun."

Tolly nodded glumly as he came to grips with the fact that he had to remove himself from the warm audience of a comely bed partner to go trekking through the night to check on something that didn't need checking on.

Princess Washington was not in Chattanooga.

Basically, the initial panic that gripped Tolly's gut didn't seem long-term, and this was due primarily, he guessed, to the idea that he thought his eyes were playing tricks on him, but when he couldn't, for the life of him, make out a car in the perpetual darkness of Princess Washington's driveway, he began to have second thoughts.

He peeked even more intently, but his eyes knew their stuff. The woman's ride was gone! He shook his head. To his right, the entire house was dark, looking almost as if it had been recently abandoned. Not surprisingly, it was that very image that seemed to tear his bowels apart. He took a step forward, but he immediately staggered back. There was no one at home. That much he knew.

"Don't tell me that, dammit," Epps screamed into Tolly's ear once he had been reached by phone. "No one's home is the last fucking thing I want to hear."

Yet it was true.

Tolly took a second to gather his thoughts. "I didn't overlook any possibilities. I saw no car. I knocked on the door. I phoned. I peeped in the windows. Hell, I did everything except put out an APB on her ass."

"I have no intention of letting your ass off the hook that easy," Epps yelled.

"What more do you want, man?" Tolly shouted back angrily, "a picture of the empty house. Better yet, why don't you come out and see for yourself. It's not like I haven't done one or two of these in a long time or that I don't know what to look for. I did my job, but I can't control the results. Take 'em or leave 'em."

While Epps took measure of that, Tolly knew exactly what the man was thinking, could almost hear the internal hum of his thoughts right through the phone. Epps was a boldly brilliant investigator, and spoiling for one last win to cap and crown his already illustrious career so he wanted this one badly. Not for the department. Not for the record books. But for the Big E.

Everyone in the game knew that Epps had complete trust in his skills and that he was a battering ram once he got going, and it was to his everlasting credit that once he did get going, it was always in the right direction. Now, he felt alienated from his own greatness, and like so much else about his life, Epps knew someone was watching, eager to report a blunder. He felt offended and embarrassed that on the battlefield where he had triumphed so often, he now had made a mistake.

"I'm sorry," Epps admitted, "if you feel I've insulted your professional integrity. It's just that I didn't think we'd blow something so simple as keeping better tabs on a suspected killer."

"Do you believe then that it was actually Miss Washington that your friend-------."

"Hell yeah. If the woman is not at home, she sure as hell's not cruising the mall looking for teenage boys. Chances are good that she'll try to make a move on Walt as early as tomorrow so I'd better contact him."

"But why your friend of all people?"

"The book, dammit. Somehow, she must have found out about Walt's book. Anyway, forget the book, will you, and get ready to fly out"

"Where?"

"To Chattanooga. Where the hell else?"

"But----."

"We gotta go, Tolly. We have no choice but to baby-sit Walt until this shit blows over."

"Damn, man," Tolly blurted dejectedly, "what about the locals? They do have cops in his neck of the woods, don't they?"

"Yeah, but just like the cocksuckers here, they ain't worth a shit. Plus, if Walt demanded police protection, he'd have to leak the specifics of our investigation, and what do you think our chances of success would be then? They'd go straight to the media and our girl, Princess Washington, would go straight to Cuba."

"Boy, ol' buddy," Tolly snorted, "you sure know how to put the brakes on a man's sex life."

"Don't worry, I'll take you to a titty bar when we get to 'Nooga. That should hold you until we get back."

"Hmmph. I like flesh, not fantasy."

Epps laughed. "Move into your standby mode. I'll tell you when we're leaving after I brief Walt and have him make our flight arrangements."

"What if we don't make it in time."

"Impossible. No one moves that quick. Not even a loose screw like Princess Washington."

It had been extremely tedious, but, at just before 10:00pm, Pearl was in. She quickly ditched the battered knife. It wouldn't be of much use now. From a downstairs bedroom, she could see directly out into a deserted hallway, and upon closer inspection found that she was next to the dining room. Reeling out her instincts, she grew deathly quiet as she tried to mentally connect with whoever was in the house. After this, all that would remain would be to conduct her experiment-----and then kill the son-of-a-bitch.

Over the next few seconds, Pearl recognized that her

present scenario had invented two major problems for her. First, she resented the fact that she didn't know exactly where in the house Reverend Bridges was, and secondly, she couldn't be sure if there were guns within the Reverend's reach. Yet she was not fooled by these obstacles because neither played that big a role in her plans, and she'd surmount them when she confronted them. Right now, all she had to do was to find the bastard.

And she did just that. Oddly, her only reaction to the sound of a Wagnerian concerto coming from an upstairs study was that it goaded her. The prey was at hand. Now, it became vital that she consider her options and she did just that. With little or no difficulty, she knew she would charge into the room, and simply catch both Reverend Bridges and his God by surprise, but what purpose would it serve without announcing her plans and conducting her experiment? Instantly, she ruled out recklessness no matter how provocative the option was, especially since it might taint the evidence of her experiments. Pearl grinned again. This was big. Reverend Bridges represented the ultimate lab rat.

With that in mind, there was no further justification not to act. The time for hesitation was through, but yet she held back, exercising restraint. It wasn't that she was having second thoughts because she wasn't, and she strongly felt that tonight was a perfect night to end it all, but that's what troubled her. After tonight, there would be no next because with the proof she needed to shut God down, what reason would she have to kill again? Pearl toyed with her conflicting emotions, but still she had to do what she had to do because, more than anything else, she had to win. She had to get the best of God.

She tiptoed down the hallway.

She snuck up to the door.

It was 10:02 and from the sound of it, Reverend Bridges was pulling out all the stops. The brassy music swirled with passion and muscle, its power never dissipating, aurally sweeping the entire room and hallway. Pearl stood still, caught up in the martial rattle and hum as the crashing crescendo marched into a furious, final storm. Growing bigger still, Wagner's musical tempest concluded with a flurry of clashing cymbals that inflamed and enraged her.

Pearl burst into the room.

When Reverend Bridges, a mild-mannered man with a scholarly air, looked up and saw the intruder, he pissed on himself.

This was off to a good start, Pearl thought. A second earlier, she had wondered what the pastor's reaction would be. Now, she knew. The man was scared as hell, and that made her 'blush' with pride.

"I make house calls," Pearl bragged, "but I think that you might have noticed that already." She waved the gun in the air menacingly. "This is my 9mm and that," she pointed, "is your bible. Our representative weapons of choice. Now, it may sound a little foolish, but I think my weapon is more powerful than yours." She chuckled evilly. "What do you say we have us a lil' ol' test to settle the matter once and for all?"

"May God protect me from you," Reverend Bridges blurted.

"Oh," Pearl teased, "I see you're already familiar with my little game." Then she turned serious. "I don't believe in prayer and in a little while, I'm going to challenge your knowledge about it. That shouldn't be asking too much," she smiled timidly, "from the man who wrote the book."

"Why-why are you here?"

"To prove that God doesn't exist, that's why." Pearl's face lit up. "You're my first white vic---"

"You fool!" Reverend Bridges bellowed, "you think I don't know about the others you've already murdered, the black ministers?"

Pearl stumbled backwards, a dazed look on her face. And for good reason. No one was supposed to know about what she had done. No ONE! "How-how do you know this?"

"God told me."

"Liar!"

Reverend Bridges sat up straight, staring Pearl in her eyes. "God told me. He's told me everything about you, Princess Washington!"

Pearl stepped away from Reverend Bridges, startled.

"There is no God."

"Then how do I know who you are, Miss Washington, and how do I know about the other ministers you've killed for the sake of your experiment? Tell me that." Reverend Bridges knew it was a long shot, but he had to play it for all it was worth. According to what Epps had told him, he was only one of a handful of people who knew about Princess Washington and what she was about. If he was to stay alive, he needed to use the "top-secret" information to his benefit. It made sense. He had to convince her that God existed and had spoken to him. He buzzed with anxiety as he struggled to recall everything Epps had conveyed to him about either the woman or the killings. "And guess what," he smirked indignantly, "the last time I spoke with God, I learned how you had displeased Him by killing one of His special servants."

"Who…..which one was that?"

To preserve his dignity, Reverend Bridges pushed back his fear. He slowly stood. "You'd really like to know, wouldn't you?"

"You better tell me, preacher-man." Pearl pointed the gun. "And don't you dare come near me. I'll shoot."

Reverend Bridges laughed wildly. "And you think God will just let you do that?" He was well aware of the woman's mental state, but didn't feel he knew enough to know just how hard to push or how far to go, but he was pretty sure that if he let up and surrendered his control, he would be killed. "Now, I get it," he rasped, "you want to see how smart God is, but who do you think you are to want to poke your nose in God's business?"

"You better tell me something, preacher-man, and you better tell me quick or you better fix your mouth to start praying----"

"Reverend Mayfield!" Reverend Bridges yelled. "Does that name ring a bell? What? You think that God didn't see what you did to His poor, righteous servant down in Atlanta. God is everywhere we look, Miss Washington, and that's how I know you murdered Reverend Mayfield in cold blood. He told me."

A frightened look crossed Pearl's face. She slammed back against the wall. "C'mon, man" she begged, "di-did God really tell you that?"

It didn't take Reverend Bridges long to decide what to say next. "Damn right He did and do you know what else He told me? He told me---and He knew you were coming---to tell you to fall down on your knees....*and pray!*"

"W-what?!" And for the first time, Pearl's voice sounded curiously shrill and childish. "And what if I don't?"

Reverend Bridges drew to his full height. He took a gamble. "Then He will do something to you that was a million times worse than what He did to turn you against Him."

"No!"

"*Pray!*" Reverend Bridges shouted. *"Bow down!"*

When Pearl got around to moving, she was backing up, trying to get out of the room, but at the door, stumbled, losing her balance, falling. The gun went off.

A bullet caught Reverend Bridges between his eyes.

"Oh my God!" Pearl wailed hysterically. "It was an accident!"

It was in the interlude between the fourth and fifth call that Epps felt like a loser. He was by no means superstitious, but when he picked the phone up, he got the eerie premonition that Reverend Bridges wouldn't be answering the phone this time either. For some reason, he was convinced that his old friend, Walt, was finished answering phones. But he stubbornly punched out the number. Anyway, he could always hope to be surprised, but he didn't expect that either.

While he was putting the receiver back, he prayed matter-of-factly that his friend had died quickly, but he knew that it was anybody's guess just how gruesome the death had been. Epps had no cause to believe that Princess Washington had made it easy on the white pastor. The way it stood, it was probably just the opposite. Princess Washington, more than likely, had viewed Walt as a trophy, and had put him through his paces just for the hell of it. Then, she had destroyed him. No doubt that was how it had gone down. Epps felt it in his bones.

With a brooding otherworldliness, Epps picked up the phone again, dialed a number, and spoke in a pained, disembodied voice. He explained what he wanted and hung up to await the return call.

One hour and twenty minutes later, the phone next to Epps' right elbow rang. It was snatched up after only a single ring. "Yeah."

The man talked in a clear, disengaged tone.

Epps' knuckles turned white as he gripped the receiver tightly, listening. He fixed his eyes on a spot on a far wall and grimaced. It wasn't easy hearing what he was hearing, but it did help his spirits some when he learned that Reverend Bridges didn't take a lot of heat before he died. A single bullet between the eyes had ended it. The bitch Washington had displayed an act of uncommon mercy. And Epps was glad though he didn't quite understand why.

In a way, he wanted to let the private investigator on the other end know what he was thinking, but the way things were shaping up, what good would it do?

And all this time, he had thought that he had a grip on this investigation, but now with this latest development, the stakes had just zoomed higher, and the case had become even more alarming. And, of course, it could get worse. That was always the possibility when too much was riding on too damn little that didn't add up.

"Yeah, yeah, that's it, Johnny. Thanks. I have another call trying to come through. Probably Danson. Let me see what he has for me. Bye."

When Epps heard the news, he turned philosophical. The untimely, brutal death of Carmela Simpkins was no more his ultimate responsibility than Walt's had been. Sure, he was distressed, but that was just about it. His misgivings wouldn't provide him any lee-way with this investigation so there was no need for him to become infuriatingly coy, and allow himself the intoxication of either pity or sorrow. Maybe later. Meanwhile, he had to pour all his energy into bringing the monster----Princess Washington----down.

In an almost stumbling voice, Epps informed Larry Danson that there were no final thoughts about the murder, and that he should just go on the record as saying that he was tipped off by an anonymous caller who was concerned about Miss Simpkins. Off the record, he could be as specific as necessary, but there would never be any authorization to throw out his name as a source, resource, or contact. Epps went to great lengths to inform Danson that anything more would jeopardize the investigation.

"Yeah, yeah, Danny, that's it. Thanks," Epps muttered. "I have another call coming in. I better see who it is. Bye."

CHAPTER 31

God was real!

Pearl prayed up a storm early Sunday morning. It had been a while since she had fallen down on her knees and prayed with such fervor. It was as marvelous this time as it had been before when she had prayed like a woman on fire.

Now with her experiment completed, she felt more like she could deal with God. She was absolutely certain that if she broke it all down in her prayers, and presented God with a balanced account of her flawed adventure outside the church that she could privately strike a deal for total forgiveness.

She sighed, knowing that a lot of her activities were highly questionable, but she could always point out how it was Ennis who had misled her, and if there was any spiritual criticism about her killing him, she figured she would get her best deal if she pretended she was honoring the biblical command of an eye for an eye. Ennis had killed her innocence so that gave her the spiritual license to take his ass out. As for LaNisa and Angie. Well, they were collateral damage. Pearl smiled at the merits of that assumption. Surely, collateral damage could be absolved.

She started playing around with the mystery and history of God, attempting to strip away all of the mystique, hoping to get to the core of her personal, turbulent relationship with Him. She was still shaken, but at least now, she was certain that God existed and that He did indeed answer prayers. All of her trash-talking had been magically counterfeited by Reverend Bridges' startling revelations. God had spoken to him, and it wasn't merely water cooler gossip. God had put her business in the streets, had informed Reverend Bridges about all the dirt she had done.

Pearl laughed aloud. In what was to be her coup de grace against God had ironically turned out to be her biggest, most spectacular failure. However despite her glaring loss, what it did leave her with was the ultimate opportunity to cleanse her soul.

Falling back to her knees, Pearl prayed.

"Sorry it took so long," she mumbled cheerfully in her supplications, "but more or less I have been kinda busy, and I'm the first one to admit that I got off track a little bit. I was wrong, what more can I say? I was wrong....dead wrong." She paused. "I know my words might not carry a lot of weight right now, but if I could just put my two cents in, I pray that all those preachers I sent home will find a place in heaven." Before she could say anything more, she thought about what she had already said. Then she continued. "Amen.

After bitter, internal wrangling dating back to the night she had accidentally killed Reverend Bridges, Pearl understood, in very clear terms, that she was changing. Again.
Suddenly, her sins meant nothing. Instead, she found herself inspired by the adventure of a game where the stakes were staggering. She felt dizzy. What had her prayers done? In a way that couldn't be explained, she felt giddy that God trusted her enough to give her another chance, but at the same time, she had every reason to want to stay out of the way of her own brilliance. This was for God.

At eight o'clock, she fell into a fitful snooze, but after two and a half hours, sleep ended. She awoke and fifteen minutes later made the first of many phone calls she would make that evening. Then she went back to sleep.

It was two in the morning when she finally arose from bed

and marched, butt-naked, into the bathroom. She didn't want to sleep any more, and for the longest time had been occupied with the morbid thoughts of the needless murders she had committed.

She grieved.

For the tiniest of seconds, she stood still with her dainty hands covering her face. This gesture seemed to soothe her, and instantly she began to feel better. Then on impulse, she shaved her head! She was going to change, to start anew. She was going to be a soldier of God, so she had better look the part.

She had just kissed her life as an unbeliever goodbye.

CHAPTER 32

The argument could be made that Princess Washington was so smart that she had willed herself to be born when the disposable income of African-Americans represented the greatest concentration of minority wealth the country had ever seen. No doubt growing up in a family flush with cash had helped fashion her universal attraction for material things.

At a very young age, she had found herself thrust into the royal world of upper-crust Niggerdom, and while it may have been true that she seemingly caught the virus of believing her shit didn't stink, riding high on the hog ultimately failed to blind her to what was actually going on in this country. In time, she began to represent what her family felt was a weakened confidence in the sporting power of the almighty dollar. This 'illness' terrified her family.

The patriarch of the Washington household, Joe Willie, had been thoroughly mystified and had tried to patiently explain to his well-heeled black friends that his daughter was introspective and given time would be throwing money around like she was crazy. Princess never did. She would rather give it away to the less fortunate.

"It's certainly not my fault," her mother, Linda, would always point out when questioned about her daughter's obsessive compulsion to look out for the poor. "That shit does not come from my side of the family. We detest poor niggers."

When Princess disgraced her family by not wholeheartedly participating in the spending mania that accompanied the biggest money boom in the history of black capitalism, the Washingtons saw their community status dropping, dropping...dropping until Princess went off to college and amazed all her professors with her brilliance.

After college, she had moved to Charlotte and had joined the church where she had embraced the unlimited potential of being a good, God-fearing woman.

And this is where the road ended for Epps. This was basically all he knew about Princess Washington other than the fact that she was a cold-bloodied serial killer. Epps was deeply puzzled. The woman was a true Black American Princess who should be living one of those success stories that would be rare even by Hollywood standards. Instead, she was a murderer; a damned good one, at that.

Go figure.

At the end of the week, Pearl read in the newspaper that the police department still had no leads in the gruesome "men of the cloth" murders. Everyone, including the illustrious Big E. was silent on what clues he had. So far, the most he would say was "no comment".

This lack provoked Pearl to joyous heights because she would have expected some break in the cases by now. Damn, she must have really done a truly good job. She had stumped the well-respected Detective Epps, and that suited her just fine.

By that following week, Epps was mesmerized by how cold and numbed he felt. It was a pain that grew and grew, twisting itself around his existence like industrial strength coil. Eventually, it would stop, he hoped.

But today, he was going to interview Princess Washington!

Although it was uncommon for him to feel so happy about conducting a routine interview, he struggled to contain his enthusiasm and emotions. He was eager.

Why?

What fantastic revelations did he expect from her? He didn't know, but he was still tempted by the budding impression that he would at least be able to gain some insight into her tortured psyche.

He had called ahead to let Miss Washington know he wanted to visit. The permission was granted reluctantly. He wouldn't be long, he had told her. It's just routine was another line he had given her. He knew that she didn't believe that any more than he did.

As soon as he turned off the main highway, the place where Princess Washington was staying immediately came into view. It was really nice, and had to be reached by riding down an immaculately-landscaped driveway. Impressive.

He parked as far away from the house as possible. He would use the extra time to mentally rehearse his lines which he thought was a good idea. He also knew she would be watching, and that would give her a few extra seconds to size him up, to make the decision whether to lie or to confess. Either way, that wouldn't stop him from asking any questions that might help him sketch out her ambitions as a serial killer.

She met him at the door, sweeping away his chance to make her teeth rattle with his trademark police knocking. Standing in the doorway, he tried not to look past her into the living room, but trained instincts took over, and his gaze went every which way at once.

"Miss Washington, no doubt," he said with a firm, detached professionalism. The bald head caught him by surprise.

"Yes, I'm Princess Washington. I've been expecting you," she admitted, leading him into the house, "although I don't see how I could possibly be of any help." She smiled saintly. "Yet, I will try my best." She indicated a plush chair with a grand gesture of the hand. "Be seated."

The closeness of her presence instantly riveted Epps to every facet, each detail of her starkly, beautiful face. He sat down, visibly dazed. Her shaved head squeezed his attention to her delicate, bright eyes. They blazed a quiet fire, but also twinkled with intellect and refinement, exuding a healthy glow that suffused her whole face.

The blushingly pink lipstick she wore only sharpened the juicy lines that cut into the left and right of her perfect mouth when she smiled at him.

"Where do we start?" she shrugged. "If it would help, I could go sit under the bright light in the basement."

This caught Epps off-guard. "Huh?"

She blazed him a playful smile. "In the movies and on TV, interrogations always seemed to go so much better when they made the subject sit under a hot spotlight. It must be hard to lie when you're sweating."

Epps almost chuckled, but didn't. This was not a social visit. Still, he devoured her long, shapely legs before gazing over the top of her head out of a squeaky clean window. Weak, failing sunlight splattered outside on the trees. The view was pretty.

"What you may not know," Epps commented blandly, "is that I'm investigating the murders of several ministers here in Charlotte."

"I do read the papers, Mr. Epps, and if we are going to get anywhere, I suggest you hop right to the meaty questions."

"Did you know Reverend Baker?"

Pearl shrugged. "No." Nothing more. Stillness enveloped her.

"What about a Reverend Mayfield?"

Pearl screwed up her face in concentration. "No." Again.

Epps half-rose from the soft chair, and pushed his butt back further into its interior, fidgeting, having trouble working his way up to his next question.

Pearl had seen this before----on TV, but still she was at a loss for what he might ask next. Whatever it was, he was intending not to force it. In addition, she knew that he knew that she knew the answer to the question. Pearl found herself holding her breath.

Epps was watching her. The muscles around his mouth loosened, giving way to a half-hearted cross between a smile and a frown. "Do you believe in God?"

Pearl bolted upright in her chair. She sputtered. "I beg your pardon." Her shock seemed real. "What kind of question is that?"

"Hopefully, a good one," Epps responded, showing no trace of regret.

"Just how do you even remotely believe that my religious beliefs will help you find a killer?"

"Do you believe in the power of prayer?"

"I think I'm ready for you to leave now, Mr. Epps."

"But you haven't answered my question, Miss Washington. Do I take your silence as an attempt to hide something?"

"Get out!"

Epps stood. "I'd like to know. Do you even believe there is a God? I think you may know something about why I asked that question."

Pearl frowned at him, then wheeled around. "I think I need a drink."

"Nothing for me," Epps said pleasantly.

"I don't recall making the offer," Pearl snapped.

Epps sat back down. "But I detected your graciousness." He let his gaze linger on the back of Pearl's shapely calves. "I didn't mean to anger you a second ago. It's just what I do for a living."

"Forget it," Pearl snapped. She returned to her chair, nursing the drink she had made. "No offense, but you're very despicable."

"Sorry, all of us crime-busters can't be Batman." Epps grinned." Someone had to be me and I guess I got stuck with the job."

"And I had the gall to let you upset me a moment ago." Pearl stood up dismissively. "Come back when hell freezes over."

Epps stood, bowed slightly. "Go talk to a lawyer, Miss Washington, because I look forward to seeing you in court."

When most of the night was finished, Pearl started her cycle. The painful stiffening of her nipples always came first. They instantly became the objects of her attack, and just by squeezing them, she could awake an orgasm. Which she did. After all the necessary interest in her large titties was suspended, her hands slowly slid down her body to a horizon of more immediate, much greater joy. *Her pussy.*

The more she became absorbed in the general process of transforming her craving into the natural expression that her very disciplined fingers could produce, the more pleasure her thumb and forefinger gave her. She virtually foamed at the mouth, and after a second or two had to physically twist herself into a pretzel-like contortion to bear the pleasant stimulation. Now, she began to hump her hand. Her breasts slapped against her chest.

The phone rang.

Who the fuck was that?!

"Hello."

"Miss Washington, this is Detective Epps. I hate to disturb you-----."

"Well, you have." Pearl's voice was angry. "What is this all about, detective. I really hope this is important."

A lewd image of Princess Washington popped up in Epps' mind. *"She was naked and undressed, her naked body a sensual palette of places he could touch and kiss.* "I'm not really good at lying, so I must be honest."

"Please hurry up and state your business. I have more important things to do."

"You know something," Epps began, "it was mindless of me to call you. I apologize."

Pearl sighed. "But since you did call, you might as well tell me what's on your mind."

Epps felt like patting himself on the back. The woman didn't seem mad any more. "You got a few minutes."

"I haven't hung up yet, have I? You've already ruined what I was doing, so go right ahead and talk."

Epps hurriedly tugged and snatched off his pajama bottoms. He had no trouble getting his dick hard as he stroked his penis a few, quick times. Slow down, he warned himself. He'd be a fool to rush this. He carefully made small talk, easily making her talk back as he set her photo in front of him. He recalled those naked images of her in his head, and he groaned while applying Vaseline up and down the length of his dick.

"You know what I think, Miss Washington?"

"No. Why don't you tell me and then be done with it. I don't play guessing games."

The more Epps talked, the more strained his voice became.

"What in the world are you doing, detective, push-ups?" Then she knew. Or thought she knew. All the signs were there, all right. The rasping, ragged breathing. The nonsense talking. How well she knew. She wanted to curse him out, and to give him a piece of her mind, but decided not to. The night might not be wasted. She touched her pussy. After all, two could play this game.

"If I remember correctly, detective, you said there was something you wanted me to know. I'd like to know what it is."

"I'll get to it."

"And I'm supposed to wait?" Pearl whispered huskily.

"Yes," Epps groaned. "Please wait. Don't hang up."

Pearl shoved a finger deep within her pussy. In a dazed, foreign way, she was unnerved at what Epps was doing, masturbating off her, but as she came closer, drawing near to the approach of her own orgasm, it disturbed her less and less until she felt empowered by her sexual power. "I'm listening." Pearl could sense that Epps was almost ready to cum. She had to catch up because she wanted to skeet when he did.

Neither spoke as they climaxed.

"Good night, detective."

"Pleasant dreams, Miss Washington."

CHAPTER 33

They weren't exactly dimples. Instead, they were more like inverted air pockets knocked into both his cheeks. Anyway, his face always looked like that whenever he was in the zone. Today, doing it had him humming right along. The pace was particularly uptempo, quick even for him, but when something----or someone turned him on, Epps didn't let it chew or claw at him for too long. He simply got it on----with himself.

Not like in the old days. Back then, he had fucked a lot of bitches. All kinds. Black. White. Latina. You name them and chances were that he had made love to dozens of them. Fucking bitches had been the best part of his life, almost all that his life had been. Not like now.

Maybe one day, he would be able to get it up for a woman. But right now, he couldn't. No matter how hard he tried, he just couldn't get his dick hard enough to fuck a woman, so he masturbated off them.

No one knew.

His breath was trapped in his throat again, and he was still astonished at his frantic pace, the way he was pushing himself. When it came to jacking his dick, Epps didn't have a vain bone in his body. He knew how to please himself, but this was something else.

His dick felt crudely magical. Perfectly straight, it gleamed with glistening sweat, a one-eyed beast that grew out of a patch of coarse, black pubic hair.

Although he couldn't actually bring himself to admit it, he knew, without doubt, that it was Princess Washington who drove him so damn wild. He enjoyed being turned on by her.

He suddenly loosened the grip on his dick. It still remained rigid. Then he switched OFF the recorder, leaving Princess Washington's voice to fade into nothingness. His dick dropped. This was no game he was playing. This was his life, and here he was jerking it off. *Just like a jerk.*

Just thinking about it, Epps was barely able to recall what sex with a woman was like, but he did understand that his wife had psychologically castrated him, emotionally stripping him of his balls. Mentally, the divorce had turned him into a pussy.

Then it happened. Just like that, he admitted it openly for the first time that it was time for him to overcome and triumph over his past tragedy. He found that admission both sensible and reasonable. It was time for him to get some pussy, and Princess Washington was going to give it to him-----or else!

Oh shit!

Epps got out of bed and paced the bedroom floor, gripped by severe anxiety, however the urge to lay down with Princess Washington was still very powerful. Leaning against the wall, he took turns accepting and then rejecting the notion of whether he would rape the bitch or not. He couldn't decide so he left the question open. Maybe he would bribe her. If she gave up the ass, he would let off her the hook about the killings.

Now, he tuned to more positive thoughts. How long would he make her suck his dick? Would he fuck her in the butt? Did he want to shoot off in her ears?

Those kinds of thoughts made him feel a lot better until he remembered.

His limp dick problems had started with Elsa, his second wife.

Elsa! A colossal slut. A woman whose chief interest in life was money. She had no secondary concerns. She had encouraged him to give her everything and he had done just that. And more. Whatever else he may have lacked as a husband, giving to Elsa surely had not been one of his shortcomings. He possessed what his therapist had told him was a clinical desire to be used. If this was true, he still wondered who the hell had clued Elsa in.

The woman had measured him well. She weighed her success in draining his resources by how fancy her car got each year, and by how much she could cheat on him. She did well in both, but the day he had caught his father, Greg, in bed with her had been the worst day of his married life.

That sordid episode had wrecked him. Not so much because he had developed a mistrust of his father, but that they had come to blows over Elsa. And that wasn't supposed to have happened.

After he had caught them fucking the first time, it had been decided by the three of them to simply sweep the matter under the rug. Truthfully, that had been Greg's and Elsa's idea because he had wanted to throw the slut out, but later on went along with the original plan. Why start a stink. After all, it was only his dear old dad and his wife.

Needless the say, the night had ended on a somewhat sour note. Things, however, would get worse. Some two hours later, after he and Elsa had retired for the night; he to the sofa, she to the master bedroom, there came a thunderous banging upon the front door.

Guess who?

Dad!

Greg Epps had stormed into the house, full of gin and juice, and had informed his son to kiss his black ass, that he was talking back all the shit he had said earlier. In essence, he made it clear that he had every intention to keep right on 'putting dick to Elsa', and just to show that he wasn't bullshiting had been determined to get some more that very night.

That had been when they had started fighting. The thing that surprised him most was that Elsa had jumped on his back, and had held his arms while his father had punched him in the belly just to teach him a lesson.

Then Elsa and his dad had fucked again.

If he had owned a gun and had shot both of them at that moment, he probably would gotten off the hook, but he hadn't. As a promising young attorney, he knew that anything that came afterwards would be premeditated, and the penalty for that would have landed him in prison.

It had taken two years for that bitch to get run over. Now, that had been a happy day and would have been even more joyful except that it had been the day he had learned his dick wouldn't get hard for a woman.

Some celebration he had.

Shortly thereafter, he had quit the legal profession, left Connecticut, and somehow ended up in Charlotte.

Epps was preparing to blow his load and it was going to be special; utterly fantastic. He didn't get many like this and he wasn't about to lose it, so he kept hammering away, pounding his dick like he was possessed.

"Yes, Miss Washington…oh yes….that sounds….so stunning."

"And if I remember correctly, you never finished telling me about the time you went skinny-dipping. Oh yes, I must learn all about that." Pearl gasped. "It would thrill me endlessly to hear….. everything."

Pearl's eyes were heavy-lidded, practically hooded and had turned an almost muddy color. Her skin was flushed as bulging veins popped out in her neck. She sat brazenly on the edge of a footstool, her chocolate thighs spread wide open with a please-touch-me-there appeal oozing from her juicy pussy lips.

"Mmm hmmm," Pearl moaned. "How did the cold water feel on your----skin?" Pearl shamelessly swung one of her legs further open and stretched the other one straight out. The insides of her greedy pussy could feed more easily on her fingers this way.

Epps knew what the woman was doing. He congratulated himself.

By the end of the half-hour, they both had fallen into the

abyss of sexual completion with a most satisfying climax. As usual, they thanked each other politely and hung up.

CHAPTER 34

The atmosphere crackled with electricity.

No courtroom in Mecklenburg County was more packed or breathed such burning intensity. Emotions ran high on either side. The battle lines had been drawn early, and the name-calling had gotten particularly nasty as it seemed that everyone in Charlotte had come out to witness the courtroom spectacle of the great detective versus the pretty woman.

A cold wind blew.

Epps had come mentally prepared for a media circus. He knew that he had been cast as the villain in this sordid mess because over the last few days, every bit and scrap of information, even the most trivial ones, about how he had sexually harassed Princess Washington, were either written of or spoken about in one media format or another. In the end, he had come to feel as if he had been raped.

Outside the courthouse, people still chose sides, clotting the main artery of streets near the old building. The air was combustible. And it got even hotter when Pearl daintily stepped out of a Mercedes-Benz, and pushed through the crowd with her lawyers.

While a great number of the crowd marveled at her terrific beauty, many others booed and hissed at her. How dare she slander the name of the Big E.

Inside the courtroom, the Judge was prompt and in due time, everyone's attention zeroed in on the two main players in the soon-to-unfold drama of telephone sex and verbal intimidation. The pair, Epps and Pearl, quite naturally looked reserved, sitting uncomfortably at counsel tables opposite each other. Both politely stared at their hands.

The sense of anticipation was rabid. Ever since Miss Washington had gone public with her accusations, the District Attorney had promised to rain fire and brimstone down upon the head of Epps. The detective, in return, had vowed to fight back so this had all the makings of a good, legal soap opera; however even before things could get hot and popping, the spectators were treated to an unforeseen shock.

Thomas Slater, Pearl's attorney, stood to face the Judge. "Your Honor, if it would please the Court, I'd like to request a postponement of today's proceedings. My client, Miss Washington, is too sick this morning."

Judge Crenshaw glared at Pearl. "Is this true, Miss Washington?"

"Yes, Your Honor," Pearl rasped. "I do not feel well this morning."

A collective moan filled the courtroom. The people hoped the Judge wouldn't let her off that easily and screw up their morning. As long as she was not festering with open, pus-filled sores or infected with some unspeakable contagious disease, most believed the trial should get underway today.

Judge Crenshaw addressed Slater. "Why wasn't this brought to the attention of the Court earlier? Every resource has been used to get the proceedings started this morning."

"It, my client's illness, was only made known to me this morning, Your Honor. I beg the Court's indulgence for any inconvenience that might be caused by this requested delay."

The Judge looked at Epps's attorney who took a second to confer with his client. Standing, he said. "As ready as we are to commence this trial this morning, I'll tender no objection to the Motion For Continuance."

With the bang of the gavel, Court was adjourned.

Epps decided to park. He had driven around the cemetery at least a half-dozen times, making circles, wasting time. He had already spent most of the morning feeling sorry for himself.

His empty stomach growled, and the muscles in his neck throbbed. He knew it was stress. The last few days had robbed him of all his power, both physically and emotionally, but he also knew that he couldn't just sit around waiting for his mental wounds to heal. He had fucked up!

He no longer debated what had gone wrong in this case, and he recognized that he could not blame his present state of affairs on either God or man. He, himself, had fucked up because, for once, he had underestimated how vulnerable he was.

Given this notion to deal with, he was compelled to admit that Princess Washington was the perfect woman, so much so that she had toyed with his imperfections until he felt weak. Suddenly, he noticed the cold. A bitter wind with a wolf's whistle howled through the graveyard, smacking head-on into the tombstone of Elizabeth Reed before bouncing off a rotting oak tree.

Once it became clear that he should move on to whatever came next---he did. Discovering that it had gotten colder, he turned up the collar of his coat and dashed to his car. He would grab a bite to eat later.

After being home only three minutes, Epps made up his mind. He speed-dialed the number.

"Hello."

"Hello, Miss Washington, this is Detective Epps."

"I was wondering when I would hear from you again."

Epps tried to keep his face impassive. "I mainly called to commend you on your sick routine this morning in Court."

"And that's all you called for?" Pearl's voice was teasing. "Are you sure?"

Epps' pulse quickened. "We can always just chat." Already he was unbuckling his belt and removing his pants. "I know I shouldn't be talking to you after that shit you pulled, but I-I do enjoy talking to you."

"Do you think I have a nice voice, detective?"

"Yes."

"Is it…..sexy?"

"My God, yes."

"Does my voice----excite you, Detective Epps?" Pearl purred.

"Hell yeaah," Epps blurted, stroking himself. "I-I go crazy."

"Not tonight, detective," Pearl rasped coldly. "I'm supposed to be sick, you know."

The phone went dead.

At first, Epps was too busy trying to keep his dick hard that he didn't have time to be mad at Pearl for hanging up on him, but once his dick shriveled up, he experienced earth-shaking rage.

"*Bitch!*" he screamed, his voice choked with frustration. She knew he needed her as a sexual prop and right now he wanted----needed----to shoot off. His cheeks were flushed. His eyes blazed, bulging out of their sockets like two hot potatoes. After a few seconds, the numbness in his brain was gone, but nothing could reduce his tremendous need to cum. Then it dawned on him. One way or the other, the bitch would help him get off.

He grabbed his hat and coat and dashed out of the front door.

He raced across town.

Out on the lawn of Pearl's house, he stood in the shadows of a huge elm tree. Being dragged along powerlessly in the brutal tug of his sexual excitement, he felt like a strange, mythical beast. He yanked his dick out, letting it flop down the front of his pants like a limp noodle.

He crept closer to the house.

Moving away from the large picture window at the front, he went to the kitchen window, and peeked in. His soft dick stirred, but the room was empty.

He peeped into another window, his breath coming in jagged spurts. His dick tingled, stiffening. He studied the interior of the den closely, remembering that she had told him that it was her favorite place in the house. The room was slightly dark, but

Epps could see easily enough. He could see the books. He saw the drapes. Then he saw something else! His head swam. His knees buckled. His vision blurred. There---on the floor---were Pearl's panties.

"Oh shit!" Epps croaked excitedly, almost too loudly. "Damn." The satiny, peach-colored panties lie there in a heap, only a short distance away from a matching bra. She must be in the shower, Epps thought. That meant she would probably return to the den---naked. "Oh Jesus," he moaned in delight at the possibility of seeing her pussy, but already he was whacking away. *The panties*. They were too much of a turn-on.

His dick had never been this hard before, and he pounded himself with big strokes. No part of his body or mind was uncooperative in his mad dash to make himself shoot off. He had to get a nut.

He was getting there quickly, the vast machinery of his entire being tied up in his right hand. He, for the moment, was sadly incapable of doing anything else other than running his fingers up and down his dick. And slowly, surely, the murmur in his gut became a stereophonic roar. He had done it.

He had come.

He had cum.

He went home.

A minute later, Pearl sashayed back into the den. Tonight, she wanted to see how far she had progressed in her yoga classes. She hoped that she was now limber enough to suck her own pussy.

Chapter 35

Pearl felt magnetic. She felt lucky to be a vital part of all that was going on in the city. This was unique, and there was something darkly gratifying about knowing she was the one that had started all this shit. In a zany sort of way, she felt grateful to all the ministers she had killed because it pleased her that she could cause such hysteria.

There was a lot of news now about the preacher killings. There were still no clues. Pearl smiled. During quiet moments, she felt almost compelled to commit another murder but at other times, she was intent on restraint. She wondered how Epps was taking all this? She was not surprised when she started scheming. Maybe she would give Epps some pussy.

She got up from her settee and slowly began to pace the floor, her eyes glued to her cell phone which rested on the table. Standing over it, she raised her eyebrows as if she was shocked that she wanted to call. Still, she didn't want to do anything rash, yet was far from willing to wait on nature to take its course. Sometimes, nature let shit go on longer than necessary, and as far as she was concerned, the sooner she sucked Epps' dick, the better.

She took a cold shower. After drying off, it occurred to her that Epps was like a wounded beast so therefore she still had to be careful. She relaxed, feeling she distantly understood him. He was a man. He was competitive. He liked good pussy.

Falling back upon the bed, she relaxed even more. So far,

she had only shown a polite interest in playing with her pussy, but when she felt the sensual tug of the silk sheets on her naked ass, the temptation gained momentum on its own, and she became very nice to herself.
No sooner had she went inside of herself, allowing her fingers to wallow in the wetness of her pussy than she started to breathe heavily.

Pearl got a nut. A really, really wet one.

The dream intrigued Epps, but upon awakening he declined to focus on it. It was practically a waste of sleep so he gritted his teeth as he contended with how badly he had misbehaved in his dream.

He had fucked Princess Washington!

In the dream, the woman had violently excited him, and he had made love to her in a way far more brutal than anything he had ever attempted with any other female.
He wanted to slap himself. He couldn't afford to let the dream take advantage of him because all things considered, no pussy could be that good. At least, that's what he told himself.

The weather had started acting up on Saturday, and here it was early Monday morning and the wind still lashed out cruelly like a whip with a ball-and-chain attached to its brutal end. Yesterday there had been the threat of a severe thunderstorm but nothing had come of it except a handful of dirty, pot-bellied clouds that hovered over the whole county. Maybe, today would be the day that the weather did what it was supposed to have done yesterday. Who the fuck knew?"

Later the night.
8:00pm

The prostitute snatched the one hundred bill out of Epps' hand incredibly quick. "What do you want me to do?" She stuffed the bill in her bra. "Name it."

For a response, Epps slapped her across the face. "Bitch!"

The prostitute was stunned. She involuntarily stepped back in fear, tempted to turn and run the hell out of the hotel room, but before she could, Epps quickly handed her two more hundred dollar bills. It was then obvious to her that he wanted to play some game. She just didn't know how violent it could become. Still, she tucked the bills into her bra where the other one rested.

Epps instantly bared his teeth in defiance. "Princess Washington, you slut," he shrieked at the woman, slapping her face once more. "I'm going to feed you some dick." He reached out for the prostitute, but she knocked his hands out of the way. Epps' eyes glowed fiendishly. "So, bitch, you want to play rough, huh? You want me to take your pussy, eh?"

The prostitute knew that to resist would only set him off further, but he was not that scary now that she realized he was role-playing. She wanted to see just how far he would go. Plus, she had always fantasized about being taken by force.

"You want this pussy," she snarled, "take it." She ripped open her blouse, her huge, brown tittties falling out.

Epps lunged at the woman, knocking her backwards onto the bed. He fell on top of her, trying to pin her down but the girl was cat-like quick. She wrestled her way from under him. "That's it, bitch," he bellowed. "Fighting will make me fuck you better." Epps threw himself atop her and snatched up her short dress. He buried his face into her crotch, and licked through the sheer fabric of her panties.

"No," the prostitute pleaded mockingly, "please don't lick my pussy. Don't do it, please."

Encouraged by her begging, Epps yanked aside the woman's panties and stuffed his tongue inside her pussy. "Don't move, slut. Don't make a sound."

The woman lay flat on the bed. "What are you going to do to me?" she whimpered, trying to sound afraid. "Don't hurt me, please. I'll do whatever you say. See. I'm opening my legs wider."

Epps slapped her. "I don't need your fucking help. I know what I'm doing." He resumed his licking between her legs, grunting like a pig.

The woman didn't want to rush him, but after a few minutes was ready to fuck, but every time she had tried to undress him, he had stopped her. *What was he waiting on?!* She kept glancing down at him expecting him to do something different, but his grunting only grew louder. The ho shuddered. She would never get off like this.

At last the grunting stopped.

"Get out," Epps spat at the prostitute. "Vanish."

The woman made no move to leave.

"You got ears, bitch. You heard me. Get the fuck out."

Without warning, the woman slapped the shit out of Epps. "You the bitch." She slapped Epps again.

Epps was taken completely by surprise. "What's your problem?"

Before he could barely finish the sentence, the woman was all over him. Epps wiggled and pushed, hoping to get away, but the prostitute seemed to have gotten stronger. They wrestled for a while longer, the woman getting the best of it as Epps collapsed, winded and submissive.

"I want that dick," the prostitute shrieked, "or else I got a big, damn surprise for you."

Epps said nothing.

She stood up. "Pull those pants off."

Epps meekly complied.

"Damn underwear too."

Again, compliance.

She knelt between Epps' legs and fondled his dick. Nothing. She took it in her mouth, but it remained limp and soft. She nodded knowingly as if she understood the problem. Or perhaps the solution. "Stay the fuck right there," she ordered harshly. "And turn over."

A moment later after the prostitute had taken off the rest of her clothes, and had finished looking through her purse, she returned to the bed, holding a large, plastic dildo. She ran it in and out of her mouth suggestively, her spit making it glisten. She looked at Epps' lewdly. He thought he understood. She wanted him to fuck her with the dildo since his own dick wouldn't get hard. He grinned, but the smile instantly faded when instead of giving him the sex toy, she strapped it on, fastening it around her waist. He now understood clearly.

"No," he yelled. "No, the hell you're not."

The woman said nothing. She merely ignored him as she greased the plastic penis up with KY Jelly. Then she walked defiantly over to the bed in a wide-legged stance with the artificial dick jutting out in a pose that Epps found insulting---yet exciting.

"No," he repeated weakly.

The prostitute put one knee on the bed and when she next spoke, her voice was filled with power and authority. She pointed at the dildo. *"Touch it!"*

Epps said no.

"Touch it!"

She thrust it towards Epps but he shoved her hands away from him. She slapped him with the back of her hand, and a small trickle of blood stained Epps' lips. "Don't make me hurt you," she hissed. "If you do what I tell you, everything will be okay, but if you don't, I will tear your guts out when I fuck you." She raised her hand as if to strike him again. Epps bitched up. She pushed him over, and he fell back gently upon the soft bed. The prostitute lay full upon him, showering his face with soft, tender kisses. Epps reached out for her.

When she stuck a greased finger into his butt, he held up his hand for her to wait. "Let me turn over on my stomach," he requested.

She entered him with elaborate tenderness, but Epps still went through the fear that he was being split in half. Abruptly, after a few seconds, this feeling gave way to pleasurable sensations that shot through his inflamed bowels, rocking his world. He moaned.

"Do it harder."

The prostitute did as she was told, and when it felt as if she had very little energy left, something strange happened that gave Epps electric jolts of hope. Surprisingly, his own dick stirred, growing, getting hard….bigger. It kept on stiffening until it pressed so deeply into the mattress that it hurt.

"Fuck me harder," he howled. "Don't stop!"

Epps backed it up. He pushed his ass back with so much force that the woman could barely hold on, and just when she had given up all hope of keeping up with him, he moved out from under her, stripped off the dildo, tossed her over onto her back, and stuck his rock-hard dick into her all way up to his balls.

He fucked the bitch as if his life depended on it. He rammed his dick into her hard and furious until she started screaming, but he didn't stop. He kept right on fucking her until he cummed.

Then Epps and the woman slept. Peacefully.

Days after the incident, Epps was determined not to let it get him down. Plus, he didn't give a shit. Maybe, it would only be a phase he had to go through, but nonetheless he was sure that if he hadn't got fucked that he wouldn't be able to fuck. At the very least, that was a sexual innovation he was prepared to live with.

But it also made him face other, totally different facts. Trying to get inside the head of Princess Washington had pushed him out into some dangerous and treacherous waters. He had been forced to learn how to play out of a new bag of tricks. And guess what, it had been worth it. Being able to fuck bitches again illuminated his life; meant everything. It also meant that this new development sped things up because he could now actually fuck Princess Washington. Why wait?

As always, Pearl displayed an immense knowledge about how to bend her knee at just the right angle when she stuck her fingers in her pussy. It felt so much more gorgeous when she did it right.

Still.......

Something was missing and the more she played with herself, she understood that the small contributions her wet, sticky fingers were making only inflamed her growing need for dick. She shoved her fist inside her pussy in frustration, and then cursed her inability to fix her predicament. She was spoiled. She wanted---needed---*dick*.

So, off she went.

The night was outfitted with the maximum blackness possible which suited Pearl just fine. It encouraged her. Everything roared with raw sensuality and the night, being as sexually dark as she was, was tailor-made for sex. It gave a bitch the permission to unleash her inner freak, and to fuck and suck like there were no more tomorrows waiting on the other side of the rainbow.

She brazenly drove across town, and parked in front of a modest, brick house, and then made a phone call.

"Hello."

"Epps, this is me. I'm outside. Can I come in?"

The next time.

"Bitch!" Epps yelled. "Shut the fuck up."

Pearl pulled the robe tight, sat up. "Please, Epps, put the damn gun down."

Epps crossed the bedroom, and stood in front of the bed. He was still naked, his eyes blazing. "Is it you," he asked gruffly, the gun gripped stiffly in his hand, "or is it me?" He continued the confession. "One of us has changed."

Pearl sighed wearily. "It's called growth."

"Growth?!" Epps shouted loudly. "What kind of growth is it that makes me forget about my sworn duty to uphold the damn law? That's not growth, it-it's insanity. Ever since I began this investigation and you popped up, I've let you change me." Epps shook his head sadly. "Chasing a monster like you has turned me into an even bigger monster, so don't try to tell me that bullshit about this being growth."

Pearl laughed harshly. "You the bastard who thinks he just has to solve every crime. Plus, I didn't ask for you any more than you asked for me. We, we just happened."

"I'm the law, dammit," Epps yelled, punching the air with the gun. "Nothing comes between me and my job." He pointed the weapon at Pearl. "Crazy bitch. I should kill you."

"Try it then, nigga." Pearl stood, shoving Epps back.

Stunned by her attack, Epps softened. "I-I can't hurt you, woman."

"Do you want me to take my robe off?" Pearl purred.

"Yes."

"Come take it off."

The offer was so sinfully tempting that Epps was instantly

upon her with a lightness and grace that amused Pearl. She met him at the front bedpost, pushing her body sideways towards him, rubbing her pussy into his thigh.

Epps wondered why he was so turned on, so excited, but the puzzling effect only added to the thrill. He lowered his voice to a partial groan. "Oh, Pearl." He rubbed the gun across her pussy lips.

Slipping behind her, Epps yanked the skimpy robe up with one hand while using the other hand to tilt her over gently, bending her at the waist until her nose was pointed at the floor. He softly massaged the cheeks of her ass with the gun.

"Do me, Epps," Pearl begged. "Fuck me."

Epps felt anxious, but, just the same, he kicked Pearl's legs apart roughly. He stroked his dick, raised himself up on his tiptoes, pointing, then pushing his hard dick in. He rammed into her flesh, cold and unforgiving. His first strokes were wasteful, cruel. He didn't care.

Neither did Pearl. She bucked back, gazing at the floor, not wanting Epps to see the expression on her face. She was going to kill him.

During the short time it took Epps to yank his dick out of her pussy and to shove it up her ass, she decided that it wouldn't be too much longer before he got the last nut of his life. Even when Epps started to fuck her with tremendous power, she kept it all in her head. For once, she was not going to get blown away by how good the dick was. Anyway, it wasn't the dick she wanted to get rid of. It was the motherfucka attached to it that had to go. And she would soon solve that problem.

Epps pushed her face down onto the bed, and straddled her. Hesitant over the choices of holes to stick his dick in, he flipped her over, and thrust his dick between her titties, but by now Pearl had very little interest in what he was doing. She was too busy planning a murder.

With a defiant arrogance, she dismissed what Epps was doing when he started sucking her pussy because she was going to fix his ass once and for all. She hardly thought of helping him get a nut as he poked in and out of her pussy, sweating on top of her. Her mind was somewhere else.

"Throw it back, bitch," Epps commanded. "Pop that pussy."

In a fit of inspiration, Pearl used her pussy muscles to suck Epps' dick deeper within her insides. She squeezed. And squeezed. Hard. Harder. The notion of chopping his dick off pleased her a lot. She squeezed some more.

Epps gasped, the painful pleasure unmistakable.

Pearl wanted to laugh at him. Instead, she gently released her vicious grip, and adjusted her hips so that as she slowly turned, his penis curled up inside the velvety warmth of her pussy.

Epps almost stopped breathing. He had to force himself not to scream aloud. He wished to withdraw his dick and to put it up, hiding it, shielding it from the immeasurable pleasure, but Pearl would not let him go. She was not finished with him yet. She was fascinated by the way she had changed him from a headstrong bully into a trembling lil' boy.

When she sensed the tension race through his quivering body, she whipped her long legs behind his back and locked him into her. And that's how he nutted.

CHAPTER 36

Tolly did not fully understand the ugly recklessness of Epps' death. It was so unnatural and so very unexpected. Had this been where the Big E's head was really at? Tolly didn't know, and he refused to get caught up in it, but he just couldn't believe what was reported in the newspaper that Epps had been fucked to death.

Apparently, some lover had ruptured Epps' insides with a dildo a few sizes too damn big which had caused severe hemorrhaging which had further resulted in trauma, and ultimately, death to Epps. The dildo was found on the bed, next to the body although there were no published photos of it.

At the police headquarters, he had a brief meeting with the Chief of Detectives to fill him in on what progress he and the Big E had made in the preacher murders. Once finished, he immediately left.

He had been gone only thirty minutes when his cell phone rang. Tolly answered it.

"You gonna wanna hear this. Just came in."

Back at Headquarters, Tolly dashed back to the office.

"Get a load of this. Talk about some wacko phone sex."

Following the first minute of the taped conversation, Tolly understood that the polite chit-chat was simply symbolic, a plain-brown wrapper for the highly sexual nature of the phone call. It was not the strongly suggestive phone intercourse one would expect because there were none of the sexual graphics. This was more subtle, less nasty. What was there though was the openly, unrestrained heavy breathing that made it clear that both parties were engaged in masturbation.

"Phone sex?"

"Voice sex," Tolly corrected. "More or less they're into each other's voices. Listen to them. Nothing really stimulating is being said, but damn, just listen to their reactions. If you didn't know any better, you'd think they were in bed together."

The Chief of Detectives quizzed Tolly. "Any idea who the dame is?"

Tolly nodded once. Twice.

"You recognize the voice?"

Another nod.

"Who is she?"

"Princess Washington."

THE FINAL CHAPTER

    All the while Tolly was driving up the long and winding road, he could see the rose-colored building sitting on top of a thickly-cushioned mountain peak. Even though the spring foliage was lush and green, the highest floors of the Salisbury Institute for the Mentally Ill was clearly visible through the pock-marked opening between a dozen or so tall, oak trees.

    He had been driving nonstop all morning, and it had been hours since breakfast, but he didn't focus on the growl in the pit of his stomach. He was more interested about the contents inside the maroon folder. He wanted to know more about the work of Enoch Abernathy. Maybe then he would be able to better explain, if not understand, Princess Washington.

    Tolly knew that when it came time to really dig up the dirt on Princess Washington, he understood that all the psychiatric data that might exist on her might be kept under wrap. That was what made this trip so risky because a lot of the info he sought would be officially classified as confidential. He also knew that if he rubbed the wrong person the wrong way, it was certain that his efforts would be blocked by the mental health community who would band together to seal off his attempts to acquire access to relevant documents.

    What had reduced the risks for Tolly was that he knew

somebody who knew somebody who knew somebody at the Community Health Center, and after patiently raising a little bit of hell, had ended up speaking to Albert Davis. The man, a self-described bleeding heart liberal, had made a copy of Enoch Abernathy's file, and had dramatically presented it to Tolly.

That was how it had all started, but now he had to complete the picture, and that was why he wanted to catch the crew at The Institute off-guard. While surprise may not have offered the best chance of getting him what he wanted, it sure as hell eliminated the chances of any file material being shredded.

"Sneak up on the bastards," Davis had warned, "because there is always the chance that this will cut deeper than you think. Always does," he had chuckled. "Ask for Katie."

By the time he had turned onto the windswept, rain-washed driveway, what Davis had told him weighed so heavily on his mind that he got the feeling he was closing in on a prey that was even more dangerous than Princess Washington.

For a while, on his way to the front entrance, Tolly wondered if he should deal with Katie right off since he had no way of knowing exactly where she stood in the chain of command. Already, he was in his 'kick-ass-and take names later' mode ,and therefore didn't feel the need to waste precious time dealing with some prissy gofer girl. He wanted to look into the eyes of someone with juice.

He pulled up to a security post and being that he was black, watched anxiously as the guard carefully looked at his I.D. over and over again before finally granting him permission to enter the sprawling compound.

He parked his car next to a semi-circular rock garden, and carefully logged in the time of his arrival in his personal organizer. It took him only another second to decide that he shouldn't lug in the maroon folder. He had memorized most of the 'good stuff' any way. Plus, he wanted to have both hands free at all times. This was, after all, a mad house.

Predictably, he locked the car doors, and equally as predictable he saw a man watching him through the glass doors. He wondered if the man had been sent to welcome him or to intercept him. He intentionally stalled to see what the man's reaction would be and as on cue, the man pushed through the glass doors. As an accomplished observer, Tolly saw the move carried no hint of either frustration or threat. He also noticed the lack of tension in the man's bulky frame as he slid through the doors, and headed casually in his direction.

Once they were close enough to speak, the man gestured at the building. "Katie is expecting you." He stuck out his hand. "I'm a friend of Katie's."

"And I'm a friend of Katie's friend." Tolly made eye contact with the man. It was no concern of his if the man didn't want to reveal his name, and it was even less of a concern that the man had seen fit to carefully remove his name tag. Tolly could still see where it had been attached.

"We hardly ever get official company up here," the man said in a hushed tone. "Most people avoid us like we have the plague."

In the back of his mind, Tolly was picking up a combination of things from his escort. The guy was obviously a lot more than a meet-and-greet, drop-off stoogie, but he wasn't the kind of person you would appoint to keep a lid on things. He lacked the swagger for that which made Tolly believe the man had either one of two things: something to hide or something to give.

Behind them, the door clicked locked. As they stepped inside the building, Tolly squinted at the dazzling icy-whiteness of everything, and was glad to see that the penetrating brightness dimmed some seventy-five feet beyond where they now were.

As they walked, the man pulled up the back of his white jacket, and Tolly noticed the huge ring of keys attached to a utility belt strapped around his waist. Tolly also noticed the walkie-talkie for the first time.

Looking sheepishly at Tolly, the man slowed down while he relayed information into the black box. "Control, give me a crack on the red door," he commanded. "Coming through."

"That's a negative."

"Wh-what?"

"That's a negative," the control booth repeated.

"Are you kidding me? I just spoke with-----."

"Apparently, there has been a change in plans. I have been instructed to tell you to escort Mr. Evans to the administrative conference room," the control booth reported flatly. "You will be joined there shortly by Miss Abernathy. Copy?"

"10-4," the man mumbled, stuffing the walkie-talkie back into his belt. "Fucking nincompoops," he cursed. He stared at Tolly out of the corner of his eye. "Evidently, there seems to be a change of plans. I'm to escort you to----."

"I heard," Tolly coldly. "Let's go because I'm not in much of a mood for any more cat and mouse bullshit this morning, so the first chance you get, let Katie or whoever else need to know, be warned."

Ten minutes later.

"Wait 'til you hear this," Katie said grimly. "It's heart-breaking."

"It always is when fools start taking orders from even bigger fools, but who listens to reason nowadays." The old man grunted miserably. "Anyway, the project was code-named Job."

"Job," Tolly asked. "Like in the bible, Job?"

"Yeah, that was what the fools nicknamed the experiment."

"And this is the one involving Princess Washington?"

The solemn nod of the old man's head said a great deal about the inner turmoil he was going through. "When Princess was admitted to us, there was no explainable mental illness. Basically, the girl suffered from spiritual anxiety if anything. She really wanted to go to heaven. Hell scared the hell out of her, but that alone didn't warrant the treatment prescribed."

"So even back then," Tolly smirked "Miss Washington was looked upon as weird?"

"Oh no," the old man quipped, "it was just the opposite. She was viewed as spiritually brilliant. Lil' Princess loved God, felt that God was her everything. One could hardly find a more devoted servant of God than ten year old Princess Washington."

"So what was the problem?"

"Those jerks, that's what. Just as some sort of game, they

wanted to see if they could turn Princess against God. Now, does the codename make sense?"

Katie smiled at Tolly's confusion. "I know what you're thinking. Princess should have been a picture perfect candidate for The Institute to indoctrinate, and send out on a goodwill mission to change the world, especially since she had dropped into their hands like a blessing from heaven."

"That thought did cross my mind," Tolly confessed, "but you just said that the project to sterilize black, urban youth with tainted street drugs was top priority."

The old man, Enoch Abernathy, laughed bitterly. "This experiment just took off, causing a big internal battle. Oh my goodness, the bickering was ugly. More than a few blows were exchanged, but in the end the group in favor of Codename Job won out."

"And Princess Washington became a guinea pig?" Tolly shook his head.

"What the jokers behind Codename Job desired was to find the common thread that could be used to induce mental illness. They wanted Princess to be crazy," the old man stated, but it would be iatrogenic."

"Meaning?"

"Caused by the doctor," Katie explained.

"You see," the old man lectured, "any person suffering from a man-induced reaction can be paced, meaning he or she will appear quite normal until such time as it has been clocked into their brain to act out the illness."

"Oh shit!" Tolly cursed, "I'm beginning to get it now."

Katie smiled. "You would have to be very slow not to. This is the kind of control those jackasses wanted. They fixed Princess so that she would remain docile and sweet, a devout servant of God until her mental clock ticked to the moment where it was set for her to self-destruct."

"But how?"

"Electrode implants in the brain."

Tolly was stunned. "So you mean to tell me that Miss Washington was somehow pre-set to murder?"

"Murder, no." The old man shook his head slowly. "That was something Princess managed on her own. The goal was to totally reverse her thinking about God, to make her detest God. My colleagues were not concerned about the methods she used to display her rage, but I imagine that right now, they're tracking events waiting on her to show up on their radar. They know it's that time." The old man waved away the question he knew was coming.

Tolly could only nod. "Okay, so everything was arranged to happen this year. You mean to tell me there were no wild guesses?"

"None. It happened just when it was due to happen. The people at The Institute were very much against trial and error, and they knew precisely what they wanted, when they wanted it, and how to go about getting the job done so almost from the start, they knew that it was going to work."

"But they didn't know she was going to kill?"

"And couldn't have cared less. After all," the old man snorted, "murder was no betrayal to their overall scheme. If anything, it proved just how powerful the process was, and knowing that pack of foxes like I do, anything less would have not have been suitable. The murders probably will elate the bastards. Generally speaking, if Princess would have simply climbed to the top of The Empire State Building ,and declared that God no longer existed, my colleagues still would have had ample reason to celebrate. Their point would have been made. Lil' Princess no longer believed in God."

"The fact that she acted a little more dramatically than that will really have them jumping for joy." Katie frowned in disgust. "And I bet that right now, all of them are sitting around waiting on news of her to surface."

"Of course, they're waiting," the old man rasped. "They set the clock. They know the time is at hand."

"Despite that," Tolly said, "am I to see Miss Washington as innocent of all she has done?"

"Hell no," the old man spat, "she is a murderer."

"But the others, your partners, are more guilty than she is." Katie spoke firmly. "Princess Washington is a victim if there ever was one." Katie defended Princess Washington boldly. "As you can see," she informed Tolly, "we're divided on this issue."

"I'm no crackpot," the old man groaned, "and I'd argue with all my heart for compassion when it came to Princess even though it remains unknown to me just how deeply influenced or compelled she might have been to murder to fulfill the requirements of the experiment. But, by God, there were other options besides killing to make her point." The old man grew misty-eyed. "I was very attached to Princess. We all were at first. Believe me, I loved that little girl, but she is guilty of killing others. I can't accept that. Denying God is one thing. Murder is another."

It was then that a most troubling thought stuck Tolly. "Are there any more people out there like Miss Washington, waiting to explode this year?" There was alarm in Tolly's voice.

"How many I can't answer," the old man whispered, "but, yeah, they are out there…… somewhere. Princess was only the beginning of it."

Black Pearl | Gibran Tariq

BIO

For most of my life, I was the guy most wannabe thugs wished they could be. Officially declared a "menace to society", I was sentenced to 30 years in federal prison for my role as mastermind of a series of daring bank robberies in the 70s. Two involved shootouts. One with the police. The other with a citizen in a bank parking lot where I narrowly missed being killed. While confined, I took part in an even more daring prison escape.

Despite this seeming penchant for violence, I consoled myself with the notion that I was merely a poet trapped in a gangsta's body and oddly enough, this wasn't far from the truth as I had evolved from a family of teachers, four of whom taught English. As such, I learned, early on, to respect and to appreciate language since my grandmother was very strict and would not tolerate improper grammar under her roof.

From the start, there appeared to be a household conspiracy to convert me into a writer. By the time I was ten, I possessed a private library fit for a scholar, had a new typewriter, a big desk, and plenty of blank paper. By 11, I had mastered the dictionary, was a whiz at Scrabble, and was a honor roll student in school. At twelve, I had completed my first novel.

By my 13th birthday, I had discovered hustling and I immediately dropped out of school and adopted "the streets" as my home. By 14, I was in reform school for assaulting a police officer. While there, I was a star journalist, the first black deemed smart enough to work in the print shop. I served one year and a day.

Black Pearl | Gibran Tariq

Upon my release, with hardly any delays, I embarked on a personal crime spree, and at the age of 15 years-old, I was sent to prison where I was the youngest convict there.

While in the Youth Center, I acquired my high school diploma at 16 years-old, wrote my first play, turned militant, and when released at 19, went to New York to join the Black Panthers.

In New York, I discovered heroin. Writing and the revolution would both have to wait as a drug habit left little room for anything else. When I tired of being a junkie, I kicked my fascination with getting high, but years later would emerge as the "alleged" kingpin of a notorious heroin distribution ring.

Finally brought down by the FBI and DEA in 1997, I again was sent to federal prison. This time I would be gone for another decade, but once more I turned back to what I had turned my back on: writing. I studied journalism, started a writer's colony, mentored other aspiring prison writers. I edited and founded various newsletters, performed freelance editorial services for outside writers while quietly perfecting my craft.

Hailed by some as one of the greatest prison writers ever, I was interviewed by numerous TV and print outlets. My writings have even been studied in an English class at a university where I was invited to lecture.

While in the Atlanta Federal Penitentiary, I published two novels, but soured on traditional publishing after a deal gone bad with a well-known publisher. I also developed two programs. One, PROJECT UPLIFT, which deals with drug-dealer addiction. The second, GIRLSMART, a community service program concerned with at-risk, teenaged, black girls. This program is a counter to the video vixen syndrome where sistas opt to employ their booties rather than their brains.

Lastly, I have finally gone from wrong to "write!"

CPSIA information can be obtained
at www.ICGtesting.com
Printed in the USA
LVHW011627270921
698838LV00012B/1618